The Book Store Rule

The Book Store Rule

Janice Jones

www.urbanchristianonline.com

Urban Books, LLC
78 East Industry Court
Deer Park, NY 11729

The Book Store Rule Copyright © 2013 Janice Jones

ISBN 13: 978-1-60162-752-0
ISBN 10: 1-60162-752-1

First Printing February 2013
Printed in the United States of America

10 9 8 7 6 5 4 3 2 1

Distributed by Kensington Corp.
Submit Wholesale Orders to:
Kensington Publishing Corp.
C/O Penguin Group (USA) Inc.
Attention: Order Processing
405 Murray Hill Parkway
East Rutherford, NJ 07073-2316
Phone: 1-800-526-0275
Fax: 1-800-227-9604

DEDICATION

I dedicate *The Book Store Rule* to the two people who helped me to shape the concept: my big brother and my little sister in Christ, The Reverend Cheval Breggins and Erika Alexander. That simple yet complex conversation in Ms. Jessie's Place will hopefully help others, as it did us that day, to truly understand God's purpose for marriage. Thank you for then, and thank you for continuing to love me now.

ACKNOWLEDGMENTS

As always I have to first acknowledge God as my Father, Jesus Christ as my Savior, and the Holy Spirit as my ever present help. Without You none of this would be possible. Without You there would be no real purpose even to my life. I will bless and praise Your Holy Name forever.

Next, to my sons, Jerrick and Derrick Parker: During the creative process of this novel, our entire family was rocked with a horrendous tragedy that has changed our lives forever. But with God, we are continuing to weather the storm, and as stated in Philippians 3:13, "Brothers and sisters, I do not consider myself yet to have taken hold of it. But one thing I do: Forgetting what is behind and straining toward what is ahead." We shall press forward. Also, to my sons' father, Derek Parker: Thank you for rearranging your life to stand with us as a family, lending your love and support to our healing process.

To my grandson Jevon Parker: You own Granny's heart.

To Daddy: Thank you for always being my daddy, no matter what. I love you.

To my siblings, Sherrie Roberts, Darrius Bumpers, Ronald Binns, Linda Gardner, Darrin and Darnella Bumpers: I have so much love for each of you and each of your children and each of their children. That should cover everyone.

Acknowledgments

To Denise Franklin: We did not go through this one together as we have all others in the past, but I felt your love through the miles and through the internet lines. This one will be as much a surprise for you as it will be for everyone else. Bunches of love to my godchildren/ nieces and nephew.

To Pastor Warren H. Stewart Senior, The Reverend Karen E. Stewart, and my entire FIBC church family: If I could put a dollar value on your support, the tithe from that alone could fund the church for a year. I love you all.

To all of you I truly call friend, which in my heart equates to family: Thank you for your support. Each and every year God blesses me with additions to this group, which makes it impossible to name them all without missing someone, but you truly know who you are. I will mention three, however. Claudia Phelps Wade, Sonya Kelly, and Cesiley Hudson, you ladies were Johnny on the spot when I most needed a friend. And you all cook for me. That is really important.

To my editor, Joylynn Jossel and my agent Janell Walden-Agyeman: Thank you for all of your efforts on my behalf. I believe the best is yet to come.

And last but certainly not least, to my READERS: Thank you for your support, your emails, your Facebook posts, and your text messages even, thanking me for doing what I do and encouraging me to continue. Without you there would be no reason for me to do this. I. LOVE. YOU. ALL.

PREFACE

Let me explain *The Book Store Rule* to you. The Book Store Rule is an ideology that two of my friends and I were discussing in detail while standing inside a bookstore—thus, its name.

The ideology is this: If a person is not married or officially engaged to be married, <u>they are single</u>. Therefore, they are free to date and/or hang out with other consenting single people at their leisure.

Now, there are some sub-rules to *The Book Store Rule*. Rule number one is there must be honesty. You cannot deceive a person by giving them the implication you are in a monogamous relationship with them while "secretly" seeing other people. If you have made someone believe they are the only person you are dating and you then decide to date someone else in addition, you must make the first person aware of your change of mind. It is then up to the first person to either stay and roll with the new conditions of the relationship or opt to leave the situation altogether. The person who has decided to see other people has done nothing wrong as long as he/she is honest about their change of mind.

Rule number two is *The Book Store Rule* cannot be forced on anyone. If a person you are interested in dating tells you they are in an exclusive relationship with someone, even though they are technically single, you must respect that person's decision to remain monogamous. This person has made a decision to walk their relationship through, which is probably on the road to marriage.

The ideology of *The Book Store Rule* is actually based on theology. You see, the Bible, the true Book of Life, offers no instances of a boyfriend/girlfriend, significant other type of relationships. Nobody in the Bible has a boo, with the exception of maybe Solomon, who had over one-thousand boos. But Solomon, I believe, was open and honest about the number of relationships he had. And check out the whole story to see how that turned out.

Single means single; married or engaged means monogamous. He is only your man or she is only your woman if he or she is your husband or wife. Therefore, a person you are not married or engaged to cannot cheat on you if they make the decision to see someone else. They may be a liar, a schemer, or a duplicitous person, but the term cheater should be subjected only to those who are married or engaged.

The Book Store Rule is essentially designed to protect the person who is interested in dating a person who is unmarried or unengaged but may be dating someone else. The interested person in this case has done nothing wrong.

The Book Store Rule is also designed to restore the rapidly deteriorating value of the God-created institution of marriage. "Couples" who are living together, or have decided to pro-create without the benefit of marriage have totally devalued the family as God intended it to be. The Book Store Rule is not intended to be a license to become a player. It is created to give people a reason to put true stock in what God wants from us, not to belittle it or cheapen it with frivolous, unconsecrated relationships.

Hopefully the stories of a married couple, an engaged couple, a couple in a long distance relationship, and a few folks who care and don't care about these couples' relationship status will help you rediscover where a true relationship begins. It starts with a proposal of a lifelong commitment for better or worse, for richer or poorer, in sickness and health, till death do you part.

Chapter One

"I too enjoyed church today. Pastor Abraham took it to a whole other level today. It's been a long time since I have heard him preach about marriages, but today he just got into the down and dirty of it. Makes me think I may need to reconsider this whole engagement thing," Maleeka joked as she and her cousin Tammy, who had driven them both to church, came into her apartment.

"Reconsider it for what? It ain't like that man is ever really going to marry you. How long has it been since Darrin gave you that ring anyway?" Tammy asked irritably.

"That is so mean of you to say, Tammy. Darrin is just trying to straighten some things out before we say 'I do.'"

Maleeka's response sounded weak even to herself. She and her fiancé, Darrin, had been engaged for four years. They were no closer to setting a wedding date than they were on the Valentine's Day he initially proposed to her. However, every year on the anniversary of their engagement, Darrin would give Maleeka a new engagement ring, which would be at least a quarter-carat to one-half carat bigger than the previous ring. Her beautiful ring was now three carats total weight, up from the original one and one-half carat first ring.

"At least he gives me a new ring each year on our anniversary. That shows he is still committed to me," Maleeka added confidently, trying to redeem her fiancé in the eyes of her cousin.

"Anniversary? Yeah right. Unless it's a wedding anniversary it doesn't count. I thought you said you enjoyed Pastor Abraham's sermon today. That can't be true because you obviously were not listening. If I were you, I would get rid of Darrin and his games and give Gerald a chance. That sweet man has been none too subtly flirting with you for months now."

"Tammy, please stop talking badly about my fiancé. He is not playing games. He just wants to be one-hundred percent ready when we get married so that our future will be secure."

"He should have been sure of that when he asked you to marry him. If you count the two years you dated him before he proposed, you have been with him for six years. It shouldn't take nobody that long to get themselves together once they decide to get married, especially once they get past thirty. Maleeka, you are thirty-five years old; too old to have a daggone boyfriend."

"He is my fiancé, not my boyfriend," Maleeka responded in a huff.

"Whatever! Now, Mr. Gerald Miller seems to be a man who knows how to treat a woman. I bet he wouldn't string you along for no six dang years." Tammy knew she was hurting Maleeka's feelings, but she felt her cousin deserved better than the man-child she called her fiancé. Gerald Miller was definitely better in Tammy's opinion.

"Well, I think Gerald is disrespectful. He openly flirts with me knowing I am spoken for." Maleeka retorted what she felt was vindication for Tammy's piety.

"Maleeka, please. With no wedding date in sight after being engaged for more than four years, you are as single as I am. And it ain't no harm in chasing a single woman." Tammy laughed at her own statement.

"You know, Tammy, I'm glad you brought that up. You are always ragging on me about getting married. At least I got a man. When are you going to get one of your own? We are the same age, so if my time is short, so is yours." Maleeka wanted to hit below the belt since Tammy was always putting down her and Darrin's relationship.

"Cousin, there is a huge difference between you and me. I am single by choice. I am cool with it. If God desires that I get married, He will send me my soul mate. And you best believe that I will not be anyone's boo for no six years." Tammy returned Maleeka's low blow.

Finally defeated, Maleeka responded, "I'm sorry, Tammy. You're right and I know it. But instead of admitting I am in an unsatisfactory situation, I take my mess out on you—even though you are the one who started it." Maleeka smiled.

Tammy sat silently on the loveseat at her cousin's home, staring strangely at her cousin, who sat across from her on the sofa. Maleeka's admission about her and Darrin's long engagement being dissatisfying was a first. She was usually prepared to argue the issue until Tammy would finally throw her hands up in surrender. Maybe she was finally letting it sink in that she needed to be rid of that immature man of hers.

"I'm considering forcing Darrin's hand a little with this commitment."

Tammy lifted a brow, indicating that she was waiting for her cousin to explain.

"I'm going to ask him to move in with me. That way we will be living together every day, which should make him realize how great we are when we are always together. He will then see that we may as well go ahead and get married."

The one raised eyebrow quickly changed into two bucked eyes and a wide open, speechless mouth.

"Tammy, why do you look like you're about to have a heart attack?"

Tammy pulled herself together. "I am not going to justify that with an answer. Instead I am going to ask you two questions. First, have you discussed your decision with God?" Maleeka opened her mouth to respond, but Tammy stopped her. "Nope! Okay. Let me ask my other question, because that one was actually rhetorical. I know there is no way you seriously discussed this with God and came to that crazy conclusion. So question number two is, have you considered talking to our pastor about this? I won't even ask you about Aunt Tracey, because I know the answer to that one too."

"I think it was you who pointed out earlier in this conversation that I was thirty-five years old. That makes me a grown woman, who doesn't need her mother's or her pastor's permission to make a decision about my life."

Maleeka's earlier humbleness seemed to completely vanish to be replaced with a neck-rolling sister who was prepared to defend her man, her relationship, and her decision at all costs. As the old Maleeka returned, so did the old Tammy. She again gave up and made ready to leave for home.

"All right. As usual you're determined to do what you want to do, and I am resigned to let you, with no further input from me. I'm going home. I love you. I will talk to you soon." Tammy got up from the love seat, grabbed her purse from the coffee table, and left.

Maleeka stayed glued in her seat, immobilized by her emotions. She knew her cousin was only trying to look out for her. If she were completely honest with herself, she would admit that what Tammy said was correct. Yet, she loved Darrin. She had invested too many years to just give up on him now. Maleeka felt she had to believe they would get married and do it soon. She rationalized, convincing herself that moving in together would give Darrin the push he needed to take the final step.

April Colston threw off her hat, which landed behind her expensive sofa. She kicked off her shoes, one landing on the sofa and the other in her beautiful flower planter with her rubber tree plant, and she tossed her purse, which bounced off the elegant mirror on the far wall. Being that April was very materialistic, always insisting that only the best—which equated to only the most expensive—was good enough for her, she had to be pretty upset when she walked in, throwing a tantrum with no regard for her precious possessions.

April had fumed silently on the seventeen-minute ride home from church, unable to believe how disrespectfully she had been treated in the house of the Lord. Once she crossed the threshold to her luxury apartment, she let the venting begin. She stood in the spot at her front door with her fists clenched at her sides, stomping her feet, swearing, and using words that no woman as classy as she believed she was were even supposed to know, let alone use.

April Colston had been having a sexual affair with William Rucker for fourteen months. She met William while shopping at the Scottsdale Fashion Square. He sat eating lunch alone at Five Guys Burgers and Fries in the Palm Court area, looking as if he had lost his very best friend. Seeing a man who looked the spitting image of a young Christopher Williams was far too much of a temptation for April to walk past and ignore. She back tracked the twenty or so steps she had taken past William, stood and stared for several seconds.

William looked up from his double cheeseburger and found himself captivated by one of the most beautiful women he had seen since moving from Detroit to Phoenix three years ago. As a matter of fact, her outfit, hairdo and aura screamed *Midwestern girl*.

Just as April knew he would, William was the first to break the silence. "Hello. Can I help you with something?"

"Maybe," was April's one-word response.

"Well . . . how long will it take you to figure it out?" William asked the question with humor and a wonderful smile.

April sat down slowly in the empty chair across from William and waited a few seconds before finally deciding to respond to his question. Just as she opened her mouth to speak, she spied the platinum band on his left ring finger. April quickly snapped her lips shut and reformulated her thoughts.

William was definitely not the first married man she had run across and decided to date despite the fact, but he was the cutest. So April decided to throw the bait and see if this fine fish would bite.

"I think I've just about figured out what you can do for me. You can start by taking my phone number, then checking your schedule, and finally calling me later to tell me when you are free to take me to dinner."

That was the beginning of a great time that turned into a nightmare at church today. April joined the church a month ago to be close to William and finally get an up close and personal look at her competition— his wife, Aujanae. How dare that ugly usher get in her face and accuse her of being overly aggressive toward a married man?

"Listen here, Miss Thang," the usher began when she cornered April as she was on her way out of the church. "I am not the only usher in here who has noticed how you go out of your way to get nearer to Brother Rucker each and every Sunday morning. He is one of the few members here at King David's Christian Tabernacle that doesn't always sit in the same area. And no matter where he sits, you are never more than a pew behind him."

April attempted to dispute the usher's claim. "I have no idea what you are talking about, ma'am. I also don't appreciate—"

"Whatever, child. Look, that man is married and ain't studying you. Like I said, all the ushers here see your mess, but as head usher, I was selected to speak to you about it. If your antics continue, I will be speaking to Pastor Abraham." After giving April the final part of her speech served with a healthy dose of finger-in-her-face, Ms. Daphne Gordon walked away, leaving April standing there with her mouth gaped open.

April finally moved from her living room to the kitchen to get a bottle of water, but her anger had not cooled as she slammed the door on her state of the art refrigerator.

April had always been a woman who used men to take care of her and to get what she wanted. She could spot a wealthy and vulnerable man from a mile away. Married or single mattered not to her. She was usually only in it for what they could offer her. There had been more than a few who wanted something more stable from her. That was usually the time she would replace him with a fresh face. She had also had her share of stalkers, but they would usually go away after being introduced to her cute nickel-plated .32-caliber pistol. This was Arizona, after all, and it seemed as if everyone was packing heat. She would not have been able to get away with having the gun as easily if she still lived in Chicago.

About four months into their affair, April found herself falling in love with William. This was so very different for her. The only emotion April ever allowed herself to feel for a man was that of greed. William, however, was unlike all the men she had been with, both in Chi-town and Arizona. William was a very intelligent businessman, serving as a director of finance for USA Bank. While most of the men she associated with only respected her beauty, William recognized her intellect as well, and he spoke about it often. Although April made a great living from the men she dealt with, she also held a master's degree and worked as a design engineer for an architectural firm. A lot of the time April and William were together was spent just talking and sharing. Many of their dates ended without sex.

William did not speak about his wife, good or bad, too often. The other married men she dealt with in the past always moaned and complained that their wives spent too much money. Their wives were no longer interested in sex. Their wives were lazy and unadventurous. On and on they went about their wives' negative qualities. William, however, hardly ever mentioned his wife when he and April were together. The only memorable thing April could remember William saying about his wife was that she was the only person that called him Billy.

On the other hand, William spoke about his son, William Jr. or B.J., short for Billy Junior, often. He was very proud of his little boy. His love for him was very obvious. April had never met William's son of course, but simply by the way he spoke so enthusiastically, she knew that once she and William were together for good, she would care for the child as her very own.

It was about six months into her relationship with William that April stopped seeing other men and set her heart on one day having William exclusively. She knew without a doubt that William had deep feelings for her, feelings that extended well beyond the physical. He made her feel important, needed, wanted, and safe. He was expressive, generous, and humorous. Despite the fact that the relationship did not hinge on it, he was also an extremely attentive lover. And as strange as it may sound under the circumstances, the fact that William attended and participated in church and its various activities was also a plus in April's eyes. Though she was not a Bible-thumping, scripture-quoting holy roller, she did believe in God and His Son, Jesus Christ.

April had no real idea why a man like William was cheating on his wife or what kind of wife William had, but it was her estimation that she must be lacking in some area. April could not imagine any woman who would not find William to be a wonderful man worth holding onto at all costs. Apparently he was married to one, however, and April appreciated whatever shortcomings Mrs. Rucker possessed. They gave her the opportunity and ammunition to show him she would be all the woman he needed.

Chapter Two

As William drove his family home from church, his nerves were completely frazzled. He walked past head usher Gordon as she spoke with April. Though he could not get a good ear on the conversation without obviously stopping to listen, he could tell that Sister Gordon was none too happy. April's facial expression showed animosity as well. So as to not draw attention, William walked past the ladies as if their conversation meant absolutely nothing in the world to him. From his peripheral vision he could see other congregants slowing to get an earful. He was beyond a doubt certain that April was very unhappy about being approached in front of an audience.

Even under duress April was absolutely stunning to William. Her beautiful face kept flashing before his eyes as he drove and his wife, Aujanae, sat in the passenger's seat singing along softly to the gospel music that played. Their son, fourteen-month-old B.J., slept peacefully in his car sat in the back.

The fact that April was from the Midwest was one of William's biggest attractions to her initially. Though he met his wife in college at the University of Michigan, Aujanae was originally from Mobile, Alabama. He found her southern charm new and refreshing. Her honesty and humility quickly endeared her to him, but he still enjoyed the sassy flavor of a Midwest woman.

Up until the day William initially laid eyes on April fourteen months ago, no one could have ever told him he would be cheating on his wife. He loved her. He loved her when he met April three days before his son was born. He loved her and his son now. Their courtship and marriage had been marred by very little drama, but as with all relationships, there was some. Coincidently, one of those few periods in his marriage to Aujanae was happening on the very day William met April.

Aujanae had never been what some would call a sex kitten, but William found their sex life satisfactory. This changed, however, when his wife found out she was pregnant.

They celebrated her pregnancy announcement with a nice evening of lovemaking. Shortly after that night, Aujanae began to represent herself as anything but sexy as she began suffering from the effects of her first trimester of pregnancy. The morning sickness was almost unbearable for her, as it lasted all day for the duration of those first three and a half months. Once the morning sickness passed, Aujanae felt too fat, unattractive, and undesirable. No matter how often William would assure his wife he wanted and needed her physically, she could not be convinced. In the nine months of the pregnancy, William and Aujanae made love three times; those second two times only after an impeccable amount of begging. William knew his wife had not enjoyed either encounter.

Then along came the beautiful, sexy, smart, and interested April, and as the saying goes, that was all she wrote.

William called April one week after she gave him her phone number.

"Hello," April answered, unsure of the number on her caller ID.

"Hello. Am I speaking with April?"

"Yes. This is April."

"Hello, April. This is William Rucker. You gave me your phone number a few days ago while I sat eating my lunch."

"Hello, Mr. Rucker. I'm not surprised you called, but I am wondering where is Mrs. Rucker on this early afternoon?"

Wow! William thought. He didn't know whether or not April noticed he was married. "So you know I'm married. Why, then, did you want me to call you?"

"After spying your wedding band, I noticed the pained look in your eyes. Anyone radiating that much sadness could not be happily married, so I decided I had to do my civic duty to help relieve you of the marital blahs from which you were obviously suffering."

To be honest, William was somewhat put off by her forwardness, yet still intrigued as he remembered her beauty. His desire to see her again after hearing her voice could be likened to that of an addict needing a hit of drugs. They arranged to meet for their first date three days later. Exactly one week after the date of his son's birth. In essence, April had been a part of his life for virtually as long as his only child.

When April joined the church a few weeks ago, William was bothered by her antic, but was strangely turned on and flattered at the same time. When he asked her about it a couple days after she joined, she admitted that she did it to be closer to him and to see Aujanae. She told him several months prior that she had fallen in love with him and wanted him all to herself. She had yet to repeat those words, but she had since begun performing to show him she meant it. April never threatened him or gave him an ultimatum. She just worked hard to prove she was the better woman for him.

William, poor William, could not be certain she wasn't.

Aujanae Rucker continued to sing along with the gospel songs that played from her iPod through the car's music system. She sang and concentrated on the lyrics to keep from having to concentrate on her husband, who sat pensively beside her as he drove them home from church.

For the past few months, probably about three or four to get closer to being accurate, she had been concentrating on a bunch of different things in an effort to keep her mind off the eerie feeling she had that William was seeing another woman, having an affair, cheating on her.

William had begun spending a lot more time at work since B.J. had been born. He explained to her that he had been putting in more hours so that he could get a promotion, move up in the company, and make more money to take better care of his family. In essence, he had actually received a small promotion about four months ago. No one was more proud of him than Aujanae. With the additional money he received, they opened an additional savings account as a college fund for their son, but that seemed to only prompt him to work even harder. His fifty-hour a week job now had him working up to seventy hours a week as he worked toward a vice presidency.

Aujanae believed her husband's claims of working ridiculous hours wholeheartedly, until just after he received the initial promotion. Then something in her changed.

Because she never doubted her husband before, she had never done any snooping behind him. She had no evidence of any betrayal. She attributed his absence from her presence to exactly what he said: his striving to rise in his career. However, Aujanae woke up in the wee hours one morning, 4:35 A.M. to be precise. She looked over at her husband, who had only come to bed four hours earlier and was sound asleep. At that precise moment, something stirred in her, giving her reason to believe there was another woman in his life—and not just some snippy little hussy he was only physically involved with either. This was a woman of some significance to him.

Though she was certain in her spirit there was something unsavory going on with her husband, she was less than certain that she wanted to know it in her flesh. William had been her life from the moment they started dating in her senior year of college six years ago. In her mind, they had a wonderful courtship and an even greater marriage. The birth of their son, William Jr., only increased the joy of their happy life.

Aujanae remembered William being extremely excited when she told him she was carrying their child and he was tremendously supportive during the difficult months of her pregnancy. Sure, their sex life suffered a bit during that time, but the emotional love the two shared kept them bonded beyond the physical intimacy they lacked.

Aujanae silently left the bed that morning, went downstairs to the family room, and began praying. After her talk with God, asking Him to give her strength and to show her what to do to hold onto her man and her marriage, she returned to their bed with one edict in mind. She would not accuse him or nag him with her revelations. Aujanae would just do what she could do to be a better wife. She would continue to listen to God and allow Him to lead her on the decisions she should make concerning her family.

Today, when the gorgeous woman who always seemed to be in the vicinity of wherever her family sat on Sunday morning again sat near her and her family in church, that same Spirit rose up in her. Aujanae, who was already very distressed with the idea that her husband was spending time with another woman, did not want to make assumptions about the unease she felt as a result of this woman's presence today or her remembrance of her constant company for the past few weeks. But it was difficult not to wonder why this woman made her so uneasy, and if she was indeed the woman who was stealing her husband's time and attention.

As the family walked past Sister Gordon looking as if she was giving the woman a piece of her mind about something, Aujanae had to restrain herself from running over and giving the head usher a big hug. She instead watched her husband as he watched the scene with painful eyes.

As they pulled into their driveway, Aujanae had decided that after she put her son down to sleep, she would run herself a relaxing bath and have another talk with God to see what she should do next.

Katrina Hartfield sat at her desk daydreaming about how handsome David looked standing in the choir stand at church yesterday. David sang the solo as he led the choir in a beautiful rendition of Donnie's McClurkin's song "Speak to my Heart." Every time she laid eyes on him she fell just a bit more in love with him. When he sang, her feelings doubled, so at this point she was truly head over heels crazy for the man. Katrina wanted David in the worst way, and she was sure David knew exactly how she felt about him too.

David Mathis stepped into Katrina's life for the first time eight months ago when he came to the church to meet with her boss, Pastor Calvin Abraham. David was new to Phoenix. His former pastor in Detroit was a good friend of Pastor Abraham. He recommended King David's Christian Tabernacle as a church home and Pastor Abraham as a mentor for David. This worked out great because this was the same church his cousin William Rucker attended.

When Katrina received the call from the receptionist to inform her that Pastor Abraham's appointment had arrived, she went to personally greet David and to escort him to the pastor's office. When she arrived at the reception area, Stacey, the receptionist, was openly flirting with him. Upon getting a look at him, she could totally understand Stacey's inappropriate behavior. One look at the handsome stranger and Katrina wondered if the church was named for him and his beauty instead of the biblical king.

As Katrina led David through the halls to the office she asked, "So how will it feel to attend a church with the same name as you?"

David chuckled and responded. "It will be interesting, I'm sure."

The magnificent timbre of his voice made the hairs on the back of Katrina's neck stand at attention.

"Wow! What a great voice. Do you sing, Mr. Mathis?" Katrina could hear the swoon in her voice only after she asked the question, and she felt quite embarrassed.

David laughed his sexy laugh again, as he too noticed the emotion in the voice of the pastor's pretty assistant. "I'm sorry. I don't think you told me your name."

Now Katrina was thoroughly embarrassed. "Oh my goodness. I was so busy admiring your voice and your face that I forgot to introduce myself."

Oh God! Please tell me I did not say that out loud. The look on David's face told her she had. Now completely humiliated, she meekly offered him her hand in introduction just as they reached Pastor Abraham's office.

"Hello. My name is Katrina Hartfield. Please forgive me for my juvenile, unprofessional, and even un-Christian behavior."

"No harm. No foul. This has been one of the best receptions and introductions I have ever received," David said just before he rewarded Katrina with a prize-winning smile.

Katrina smiled shyly in return, as she was still a little disgraced. She knocked on Pastor Abraham's door to let him know David was there.

Pastor Abraham opened the door and immediately received David with a smile and an affectionate hug. He greeted him as if they were old friends reuniting after many years, instead of a young man he had never previously seen.

"Come into my office, young man. It is so nice to meet you. I am Pastor Calvin Abraham."

"It is very nice to meet you too, sir." David began to follow Pastor Abraham into his office but stopped just on the other side of the threshold. "Thanks for everything, Katrina. And by the way, I do sing. If I decide to make this my church home, I hope to join a choir." He again smiled and walked into the office.

Katrina's affections toward David began that day and continued to build with each encounter, until they bloomed into full-blown love.

Now, here she sat daydreaming eight months later, like practically every other single female in the congregation, about a man who had been nothing more than kind to her.

For the past eight months every time Katrina would meet a guy who showed any interest in her she would compare him to David. If he was not tall like David or as gentlemanly as David or if he could not sing like David or as was not as good a conversationalist as David, she could not be bothered for too long. The only area in which she would cut a guy some slack was looks because there was no other man as handsome as David. In Katrina's opinion, even Denzel Washington came in a distant second.

The only man Katrina wanted was David Lorenzo Mathis. The only thing that kept her from having him was his girlfriend, Toriyana Kent, who still lived in Detroit.

Katrina's musings were interrupted by her ringing cell phone. Checking the caller ID, she realized the intruder on her thoughts was her best friend, Maleeka. "Hey, Mal," Katrina greeted as she answered the phone.

"Hey, Kat. What you up to other than work?"

"What am I always up to when I'm not bogged down with work? This happens to be one of those times, by the way."

"You are daydreaming about David Mathis. I have never seen anyone pine away for a man they have never even made a move on the way you do. You act as if he was your man once upon a time and he broke your heart." Maleeka was a little exasperated by her best friend's infatuation.

"I know. I have got it bad."

"What gets me is you refuse to do anything about it. Why won't you let him know how you feel about him?"

"You do know why, because I have told you a million times. He has a girlfriend, Mal. Besides, the man is supposed to pursue the woman, not the other way around."

‹ - "Okay, Kat. I can appreciate that. But there is no harm in letting him know you are available and willing to be pursued."

"Well, I am glad you can appreciate it. I am sure, however, that his girlfriend won't appreciate me making myself available to her man."

"When David's girlfriend came to visit a couple of months ago, do you remember how he introduced her to us?" Maleeka began excitedly answering her own question before Katrina could respond. "He said, and I quote, 'Katrina, Maleeka, this is my girlfriend from Detroit, Toya.' End quote."

"Well, so much for your quote being accurate. Her name is Toriyana, not Toya," Maleeka replied sarcastically.

"Whatever! The important part of that quote was 'his girlfriend from Detroit.' He didn't say his woman or his wife-to-be. Heck, he even signaled that she was a girlfriend relegated to a certain region of the country, which happens to be almost two thousand miles away."

Katrina quietly considered what her best friend said. She had not paid much attention to how David introduced his girlfriend when she visited several months back. The only thing she noticed was the fact that he said "girlfriend" and that Toriyana was a very pretty woman. Perhaps the only reason she was even thinking about it now was because she wanted to believe there was maybe some logic to what Maleeka said, or some sort of loophole in David and Toriyana's relationship.

"Katrina, are you still listening to me?"

"Huh? Oh yeah. I'm here. I was just thinking about what you said."

"Well, knowing you, Kat, that's all you will do: think about it."

"Maleeka, I don't want to be one of those women who hang out with a guy, pretending to just want to be his friend because I know he has a girlfriend, when the truth of the matter is I'm actually plotting all along to steal him away and make him my man. That is just so deceitful to me. Then you can add the fact that if I do successfully make him mine, I may always be wondering if he will cheat on me like he did his former girlfriend."

After Katrina's explanation, she began to feel remorseful, almost as if she had actually done what she described to Maleeka.

"Katrina, stop it. The bottom line is David Mathis is a single man. He is not engaged to that Toya—"

"Toriyana."

"Whatever!" Maleeka yelled a little too loudly. "He is not even engaged to what's-her-name."

"Calm down, please. Look, the true bottom line is this: I will never, ever pursue David or even do anything to let him know I am open and available to him. Though I'm sure he is aware of my crush on him. If anything were to ever happen between us, it would have to be initiated by him."

Maleeka found a glimmer of hope in her friend's statement. "What if he showed interest, but didn't profess to you that he broke up with what's-her-name?"

"If David Mathis showed me that he was interested in me, I would not be able to resist him . . . even if he and what's-her-name were married." Both women laughed. Both women also knew that Katrina was only half joking.

Chapter Three

Darrin Osborne looked at his caller ID and saw his fiancée, Maleeka, was calling. He hit the reject button on his phone and sent the call to his voice mail.

Darrin had spoken briefly with Maleeka yesterday when she called to tell him she needed to see him because they had something very important they needed to discuss. Darrin was sure Maleeka would get on him about setting a wedding date. He was not in the mood to have that conversation, so he made up an excuse to get out of meeting with her last night, promising to call her today. Certain that was the reason for her most recent phone call, he ignored it as well. Darrin knew he would have to see Maleeka soon. He just needed to buy himself a little time.

Darrin truly loved Maleeka. That was why he proposed to her. He enjoyed being with her. She was beautiful, smart, funny, and a good cook. She was the kind of woman who would make a great mom someday. And surprisingly enough, he even liked her church-girl persona. Even though she had yet to ride the threat out, she was always talking about the two of them becoming abstinent until they were married. Though Maleeka had all the qualities Darrin wanted in the woman he married, he was afraid to take the final plunge.

Growing up in the church and being raised by Deacon and Deaconess Thomas and Shirley Osborne, Darrin understood that marriage was supposed to be permanent. Forever! Till death do you part! His parents had been married for thirty-seven years. He knew what was expected of him as a husband. Quite frankly, it terrified him.

Four years ago, before Darrin proposed to Maleeka, he allowed his head to be turned by a pretty new receptionist on his job. Darrin secretly began dating the young woman behind Maleeka's back. The young woman knew full well about Maleeka, however. She initially did not care that he was involved with someone else; that is, until about three months into their tryst. On New Year's Eve, Ms. Receptionist refused to play second fiddle to Darrin's girlfriend. She demanded he spend the evening with her at her cousin's party instead of at church with his square, Ms. Goody Two-Shoes girlfriend. Darrin refused. On New Year's Day, Maleeka received a phone call from Ms. Receptionist, informing her of Darrin's ongoing fling. Apparently Darrin had inadvertently left his cell phone at Ms. Receptionist's disposal, during which time she found and copied Maleeka's phone number.

"Hello?" Maleeka answered.

"Is this Maleeka?" Receptionist asked aggressively.

"Yes, this is. How can I help you?" she asked warily.

"I'm actually calling to help you. I have some information for you. Your little boyfriend, Darrin, well, we have being seeing each other *and* sleeping with each other for the past three months. I don't want him or nothing like that—at least not anymore—but I just wanted you to know the type of guy you are involved with. I'm going to let you go now, but if you ask him about it and he tries to lie to you, I want you to know I've got recent pictures and other stuff to prove I am not lying. All right, bye."

Darrin had been sitting right beside Maleeka on her sofa when the call came in. He could hear Trisha's nasal voice as if the phone were on speaker.

After the call disconnected, Maleeka simply stared at Darrin for more than a minute. Not an sound came from her lips. Darrin was the first to attempt to break the contemptuous silence. The moment he started to speak, however, Maleeka calmly asked him to leave.

"Darrin, please get up from my sofa and get out of my house."

If Maleeka had been yelling, cursing, and crying, Darrin would have tried to calm her down, asking her to allow him to stay and talk about it. The composure and quietness of her demeanor under the circumstances frightened him a little, making him believe that leaving was the better option.

Darrin slowly but carefully extracted himself from the sofa. Once he had both feet planted firmly on the floor, he quickly walked to and out of the door.

The next time he heard Maleeka's voice was three days later. He had been calling her, leaving her voice mail messages and texting her for the entire time of her silence, but she had not bothered to respond, until early in the morning on the third day.

"Maleeka, I'm so glad you finally returned my call," Darrin said as he answered the phone after seeing her name on the caller ID. "I'm so sorry for the phone call you received the other day from Trisha. I'm even sorrier you had to find out about her that way. I don't want to lie to you anymore, Maleeka. I was seeing Trish for a couple of months, but it was never anything serious.

"I know you want to know if I slept with her. The answer is yes, but it was like a 'friends with benefits' type of situation. You are the only woman I'm in love with, Mal. Trish was just someone to play around with, baby.

She touched me only in my ego. You are a part of my heart. Please, please forgive me, Maleeka. I promise I haven't seen or spoken with Trish since before she called you. I also promise to never see her or any other woman like that again."

Darrin rambled out the entire speech before Maleeka had a chance to say hello. This had been the first opportunity he had to truly express himself since he left her apartment. He did not want to miss the opportunity to confess his mess and ask for forgiveness.

"Are you done?" Maleeka asked in the same calm tone she used when Darrin last saw her.

"Uh, yes. I guess."

"Good. I called to say I'm not going to hold your . . . whatever you had with Trisha against you. You and I are not married or engaged; therefore, we are both single people, free to date whomever we choose. I love you, Darrin, but I guess that wasn't enough to hold on to you exclusively. So I have to be realistic and understand you are not my husband; therefore, I don't have any claims on your time, your body, or even your heart."

Darrin sat for several seconds, silent and confused. He truly did not know what to make of Maleeka's speech. After finally finding his voice, he asked, "So are you saying we are breaking up and you don't want to be with me anymore, or are you telling me you want us to still see each other, but as single and not monogamous people?"

"Clearly, as evidenced by your little thing with me and Trisha at the same time, you were not in a monogamous relationship to begin with. I'm just saying I acknowledge it now and accept it. You are free, as a single, unmarried man, to date whomever you choose. We both are seeing that I am also unmarried."

"Wait, Maleeka. Are you saying you are now going to date other men?" Darrin could feel himself becoming irate, but he caught himself and tried to keep his voice as calm and relaxed as hers.

"I haven't started seeing anyone, nor is there anyone I am interested in right now, but I have to face facts. This is the state we are in, Darrin."

"Well, I don't like this state, Maleeka." Darrin had a bit more trouble controlling his voice with that statement. Maleeka remained steady and cool, however.

"It doesn't matter whether we like it or not. We are not married, Darrin; therefore, we have no right to demand exclusivity from one another. Our *state* is what it is."

There was silence for several more seconds as Darrin tried to digest what Maleeka said to him.

"Darrin, look. I accept your apology. I forgive you for lying to me. But I also have to thank you for showing me how misconstrued I was about our relationship and relationships in general. After praying about us, I realized that God didn't have much to say about us, because He had already given me a clear mandate and I chose to live outside of it. So, like I said, we are both single people who have been spending time together. We can continue to do that, but there will be no more sex between us. I don't expect anything from you other than respect and honesty. I have to go now. I'll talk to you later."

Darrin continued to reminisce and remember how confused and empty he'd felt after Maleeka hung up the phone. He knew he should be grateful she had forgiven him and still agreed to see him, but he could not get past the fact she would also be seeing other guys.

Darrin thought for a moment that perhaps Maleeka was trying to strong-arm him into marrying her. He then remembered Maleeka was not the manipulative type. She was usually a straight shooter. He dismissed the thought. It was his last thought that made him truly realize what a gem he had in Maleeka.

Maleeka had not written him off completely, so he decided to use that fact to get back in her good graces. Darrin painstakingly gave Maleeka a two-day reprieve by not calling her. On the third day he sweetly, innocently asked her to have dinner with him at her favorite restaurant. For the next several weeks he was the most perfect and generous gentleman, hoping to win her heart again and prove to her how much he loved her. As far as he knew, she had not actually seen another man as she initially insinuated, so he made sure she had no time to even think about anyone else. He had flowers delivered to her office once a week. They spent at least two nights a week together doing whatever she desired. He became her knight in shining armor. And on Valentine's Day after he was sure she had totally forgiven him for his indiscretion with Trisha, he asked her to marry him. She happily said yes.

That was four years ago. He had been exhaustively running from his commitment ever since.

He knew he had to face her sooner or later. More importantly, he knew if he wanted to hold on to her he would have to rid himself of his fear of failing in his obligation as a married man and marry her—or let her go, and thusly, forever be a prisoner of its terror.

"I miss you, Tori. I can't believe you have to reschedule your next visit here. I was so excited about seeing you in just a couple of weeks."

"So was I, David, but my mother's surgery came up suddenly. I have to be here to help her recover, which will take about six weeks according to her doctor."

David blew out a breath that held more frustration than he intended it to. Of course he understood Toriyana's reason for having to postpone her trip to Arizona, but he truly missed his girlfriend. It had been a long two and a half months since he had last seen her beautiful face.

Toriyana responded to his reaction. "David, I understand your disappointment. I miss you too. I also need you to understand the position I'm in with my mom. The hysterectomy is unavoidable. With her diabetes, her recovery will probably be more difficult than normal."

"I understand perfectly, Tori. I truly didn't mean to sound so frustrated. I guess my missing you got caught up in my understanding and support. It all came out in a harsh way."

There was silence on the telephone line for several seconds, each party caught up in their own thoughts. Toriyana wondered how much longer their relationship would be able to survive the distance, while David contemplated whether or not it would be rude to question when she would be able to get to Arizona for a visit. David decided to just ask what his heart wanted to know.

"So when should we reschedule the trip?"

"Well, the week I was taking off from work was all the vacation time I have available. I'm going to use that week plus an additional week of FMLA time to spend with mom taking care of her. I could use the Family Medical Leave Act for two weeks and preserve my vacation time, but I wouldn't get paid for the two weeks I'm off work. I really can't afford to take that much time off and not get paid for it."

David closed his eyes and very carefully refrained from letting out another frustrated breath. From the way things sounded with Toriyana, it would be at least another three months before he was scheduled to physically see her again, when he returned to Detroit for Thanksgiving.

When David initially decided to leave his hometown of Detroit, he thought the distance that separated him and Toriyana would pale in comparison to their love for one another. He was certain they could handle the separation of the miles when he decided to take his cousin William up on the offer to come and work alongside him as a non-profit director in the bank where William served as director of finance.

In an effort to avoid saying something hurtful out of his frustration, David decided to end the call. "Tori, sweetie, I'm going to get off the phone. I'm a little upset, and I don't want to speak negatively. I will think about some things and try to figure out a way for us to see each other before Thanksgiving. I'll call you tomorrow." He hung up before giving her a chance to reply.

David and Toriyana had been together for only two years before he decided to move to Arizona. They met when Tori joined the choir soon after she joined his church. Toriyana had actually been the one to initiate their formal meeting after her very first choir rehearsal. David had performed a beautiful solo in practice. He appreciated her boldness and her beauty. The two of them hit it off immediately.

The relationship was virtually drama-free up until he was offered the job in Arizona. They did their best to practice abstinence and were quite faithful to their commitment for an entire year. It was actually on the anniversary of their first date that they slipped and had sex for the first time with each other. The two had maintained their stance on abstinence since then, but had "slipped" more than once. They differed in their opinions on very few things; that is, until David decided to move to Arizona. Toriyana absolutely despised his decision on this.

In the back of his mind, David knew Toriyana wanted to get married. She had not too subtly mentioned it more than once. He also knew Toriyana was purposely giving him a hard time about visiting him in Arizona because he had not yet, or ever, mentioned the subject of marriage.

David loved Toriyana. She was truly a great woman inside and out, but before he popped the big question, he wanted to be sure she was the one for him. His marriage would have to last forever, whether he was happy or sad in it. He accepted the fact that God created marriage for holiness, not happiness, so he certainly did not want to stoke the odds in the favor of sadness by marrying the wrong woman. He hated the thought of being married to one woman and later finding himself emotionally attracted to another, which is kind of where he found himself now.

His love for Toriyana was strong and solid, but there was a chemistry developing between Pastor Abraham's executive assistant and him. Katrina was sweet, cute, and obviously attracted to him. He found himself reveling in her subtle attention. The distance between him and Toriyana, coupled with his own subtle, even if understated male ego, enjoyed Katrina's attention, and David could see himself hanging out with her in a more than *friendly* manner.

David prided himself on usually making sound decisions about his life. Before jumping into anything, he would often mull the idea over in his head, doing his best to be sure it was not too far off from the standards he had set for himself, which were usually based on God's Word. So he tested the thought of asking Katrina out against his natural feeling and his spiritual knowledge. In the natural, he felt like he would be doing Toriyana wrong if he took out Katrina. However, he and Toriyana were not married. They were not even an engaged couple, so how wrong could it actually be? He could not immediately come up with any biblical premise that governed the institute of boyfriend/girlfriend relationships. Admittedly, at the moment he was not trying very hard to come up with any scriptures that stated it would be wrong to ask Katrina to have dinner with him, because he really wanted to go out with her. So he followed his immediate sense of spirit and made the decision to do just that.

Chapter Four

Sunday morning at King David's Christian Tabernacle

It was the first time William had laid eyes on April since last Sunday's embarrassing incident with Sister Gordon. He had not even spoken to her. He spied her as she took a seat on the second row pew on the opposite side of the sanctuary, far away from where he and his family normally sat.

He attempted to call her on Monday while he was at his desk, but his call was answered by her voice mail. He left a generic message for her to give him a call when she had an opportunity. He tried again on Wednesday, and the same routine played itself out. On Friday when she had not returned either of his previous calls, he called her again. This time when the voice mail picked up, he was a little more specific in what he said.

"April, I would truly appreciate a return phone call. It is not like us to go this long without at least conversing. I know last week at church was awkward for you. It was for me as well. Please, baby. Call me so we can talk about it, preferably face-to-face."

And still William heard nothing from his beautiful mistress. He was beginning to believe something terrible had happened. He had made up his mind to go to her home unannounced on Monday if he had not heard from her by today. He had even considered going Sunday evening, but he never saw April on Sundays. William always spent the holy day with his wife and child, choosing to at least not participate in his affair with April on the Lord's Day.

But now that he had seen her face and knew she was all right, at least physically, he relaxed. However, no matter what, he was determined to go to her on Monday.

As April took her seat in the sanctuary, she could feel William staring at her from across the room without having to actually even see him looking. She was willing to bet her life savings that usher Gordon was looking as well. Sitting away from William and his family today served two purposes. She eliminated the chance usher Gordon would be in her face after service, and she could continue to make William squirm, wondering why she had not been in touch with him at all in the past seven days.

April had decided to put William's loyalty and desire for her to the test. After last week's humiliating episode, April no longer wanted to continue to play the part of William's sneaky, albeit sexy, other woman. She resolved it was time to begin making moves to either be his one and only, or to begin getting him out of her heart for good. So she had purposely avoided William for the past week. She needed to know how not seeing her or even hearing from her for longer than ever before would affect him. April felt she had the upper hand after listening to the three voice mail messages he'd left for her this past week. The one she heard on Friday spoke of just the right amount of desperation she needed to hear. She understood it would not happen overnight, but from here on out, she would step up her game by having him make choices she never before demanded of him.

Aujanae sat next to William in the pew as he stared obviously across the room at the beautiful woman who usually sat near them. He appeared to be completely lost in his observation of her appearance in the sanctuary. It was as if everything and everyone, including her, was non-existent at that very moment. Aujanae began to believe that if she asked William where he was at that very moment, he would be completely unable to give her a rational answer.

"Billy!" Aujanae called to him in a loud whisper in hopes of breaking the trance the beautiful woman had on him. As she figured, he was so lost in his thoughts he did not even hear her initially. "Billy!" she repeated a bit louder. This time she got his attention as he jumped slightly at the sound of her voice.

"Yes, baby. What's wrong? Why are you so loud in church? You startled me."

Aujanae realized William knew he had been caught staring at April, but he was not ready to concede in his gawking, so instead he was going to try to make her believe something was wrong with her for being so aggressive in the sanctuary.

Aujanae really wanted to give her husband a not-so-pleasant piece of her mind right then and there, but she would not dare humiliate him or herself in that way. She remembered her vow to do all she could to keep her suspicions to herself and to keep things good between them.

"Honey, I'm sorry, but you seemed so far away. I just wanted to pull you back into the service and into the presence of God. Work, since I'm sure that's what you were thinking about, can wait until tomorrow. This time belongs to the Lord."

William nodded his head in concession to her suspicion about him thinking about work and apologized. "I'm sorry, Aujanae. I was consumed with thoughts of work. Forgive me. You are right. This time belongs to God."

William righted himself in the pew and stared straight ahead. Aujanae looked away from the side of his face slowly, knowing he had just lied to her—and in church, no less. She began silently praying for the strength to not, at the very least, get up and walk out of the sanctuary so that she could release the tears that began building in her broken heart.

Maleeka began looking for Darrin the moment she and Tammy stepped into the sanctuary. The loud huff from her cousin let her know she saw her scoping the place for her man and that she was totally through with her. Maleeka did not know why she rode with Tammy to church today. The two of them had not spoken since last Sunday when Maleeka announced she was going to ask Darrin to move in with her. But it had been their tradition for the past couple of months. Maleeka's car was having issues at that time, so Tammy agreed to pick her up for church. Even since the car had been repaired, the cousins continued to ride together, usually enjoying their time together.

Tammy had berated her for her decision on the entire ride to church. Maleeka took her verbal lashing with very little retort. Her mind was made up, and there was really no use in discussing it any further with someone who was not a party to her decision or her actions thereafter.

Maleeka spotted Darrin talking with his parents, Deacon and Deaconess Thomas and Shirley Osborne. "Tammy, I will talk to you after church. I'm going to sit with my fiancé and my future in-laws. Hopefully I will be catching a ride home with Darrin, but don't leave until I let you know that for sure." Maleeka kissed Tammy's cheek and walked away before her cousin could give one of her famous sarcastic remarks about Darrin.

Maleeka approached Darrin from the rear, getting to him just before he sat down in the pew. She tapped him on his right shoulder while he faced left in conversation with his father. He turned, surprised to see her appear so suddenly.

"Hey there," Darrin said as he grabbed her in an embrace.

"Hey yourself," Maleeka responded while still in the hug. As Darrin released her she asked, "Do you mind if I sit here with you and your parents?"

Darrin replied with a shaky, "No."

The two of them took a seat on the pew, Maleeka sitting very close to Darrin. She heard the unsteady answer, but ignored it. Darrin had been avoiding her all week. She was sure he was dodging her because he assumed she was going to pressure him about setting a wedding date. She decided to allow him to squirm for a few moments. It was no less than he deserved for playing silly games with her.

Just before praise and worship got underway, Maleeka leaned in and whispered in Darrin's ear, "I would like to ride home from church with you this afternoon. There is something important we need to discuss. I know you have been avoiding me all week, but today I am not standing for it. And for your information, this is not about setting a date for our wedding, so there is no need for any further games or excuses."

Maleeka then sat back in her seat and took Darrin's hand in hers. She sang along with the praise team as they began their first song, not giving Darrin a chance to reply one way or the other. As far as she was concerned, the matter was settled. She and Darrin would talk about living together on the ride home from church.

Darrin knew he would run into Maleeka in church today, so he was prepared to have the dreaded conversation with her about their wedding date. Though he was still unsure of what he would say, he knew he could not continue to avoid her.

When she approached him, she startled him a bit, but instantly he realized how much he had missed seeing her this week. He grabbed her in a hug and reacquainted himself with her. When she returned his embrace wholeheartedly, he was again surprised. He was sure she would be a little stiff because she was upset with him for his avoidance tactics.

Once they were seated and she began whispering in his ear, he understood why she was so calm. She spoke with a determination that was unlike her, and he felt compelled not only to listen, but also to do as she said. He felt relief in hearing that she did not want to discuss a wedding date—but only a little. Something deep inside of him told him that whatever it was she wanted, he would not be pleased with it.

Chapter Five

Katrina sat in her usual seat, second pew, close to the west side of the sanctuary, watching mesmerized as David led the praise team in song. She could barely concentrate on the lyrics to the song because she was too busy concentrating on the singer himself. After several moments of gawking and lusting after David, Katrina became convicted of her actions. She realized that instead of singing along with the praise team in praise and worship to God, she was sitting and worshiping David Mathis, making him a god in her spirit. She tried to reign in her wayward thoughts and put her focus back where it belonged, on Jesus. She was determined to get a grip on her emotions.

Katrina said a quick prayer of forgiveness and then began singing aloud with the choir, deliberately giving her all to God. All was well until just a few moments into the next song, when she opened her eyes to find David looking directly at her. The look only lasted a second, or at least she had only caught the last second of the look, since her eyes were closed. But however many seconds it actually lasted was one second too long. She was again lost in adoration for David for the duration of the time allotted for praise and worship.

David looked out into the congregation as he sang lead on the song, "The Lord Is High above the Heavens," to make eye contact with the crowd. As he spotted Katrina Hartfield sitting in the seat she occupied Sunday after Sunday, his eyes lingered a little longer than on the rest of the people situated in the sanctuary. Her eyes were closed and she appeared to be in total praise to the Savior. She looked really cute in her peach-colored skirt and blouse. The color complemented her caramel complexion very well, making her skin glow. When she opened her eyes, David felt as if he she had caught him paying her special attention, so he looked away quickly.

A few days ago, David had made up his mind that he would ask Katrina to go out with him. As time passed, however, he began to feel a little guilty because he was supposed to be in a relationship with Toriyana. The guilt made him begin to waiver in his decision. Seeing her standing there praising God to his voice just now, however, strengthened his resolve. He made up his mind to not only ask Katrina out, but to ask her if she would join him for a meal right after church.

After telling his mother and father good-bye, Darrin went to the car to wait for Maleeka, while Maleeka went to tell Tammy she would be riding home with him.

"Tammy, if you don't hear from me until tomorrow, then you can assume my conversation with Darrin went well. Otherwise I will call you tonight because I will need your shoulder to cry on," Maleeka explained with an unemotional quiet.

Tammy's reaction was the polar opposite to Maleeka's statement. She threw her one hand on her hip, the other in Maleeka's face, rolled her neck, and spoke loudly.

"I cannot believe you are going to be all broken up if this man tells you he doesn't want to live with you, but you can tolerate him not wanting to marry you."

Maleeka looked around, embarrassed by her cousin's outburst, to see if anyone was paying close attention to them. She then addressed her cousin with a hushed, angry reply.

"You know what, Tammy? I am sick of you trying to run my life, or least my relationship. This is really none of your business. This is between me and Darrin, my fiancé, so please, from here on out, keep your nasty, sarcastic comments to yourself."

Maleeka's last word came out a little louder than she wanted it to. She again looked around to find the scene between her and her cousin had drawn the stares of the few people left in the sanctuary, which included her admirer, Gerald Miller. Gerald left the conversation he was having with one woman and bravely approached the two feuding cousins.

"Hello, beautiful ladies. Is everything all right between you two? I thought I heard some tension," Gerald asked smoothly.

Maleeka immediately straightened herself out in an effort to hide the issue between her and Tammy. Tammy, on the other hand, held onto the scowl that blanketed her features from head to toe. As Maleeka stared at her cousin, she could almost swear Tammy looked as if she was about to tell Gerald Miller everything about their conversation—every private, dirty detail. Maleeka knew Tammy wanted her to give in to Gerald's incessant flirting and allow him to take her on a date. She would not be surprised if Tammy did not tell Gerald the whole truth about their little argument; therefore, she quickly spoke up before Tammy had a chance to say a word.

"Hello, Gerald. My cousin and I are having an unpleasant moment, but nothing we cannot work out, right, Tammy?"

Tammy truly did want to tell Gerald what a fool Maleeka was being and beg him to rescue her cousin from the pain-pit she called a relationship.

On Gerald Miller's first visit to King David's Christian Tabernacle about six months ago, he inadvertently sat next to Maleeka, who sat alone. He noticed her beauty immediately, but he also noticed the huge ring she wore on her left hand. The disappointment he felt was instant and strange considering he had not even had a conversation with the woman.

Gerald continued to sneak glances at Maleeka during the entire worship service. Once or twice he thought she actually caught him when she was not truly caught up in the service. The fact that she enjoyed church so much, at least that day, attracted him to her all the more. Despite the fact she wore the ring, he still initiated a conversation at the end of service just before the two of them got up to leave the sanctuary.

"Hello. My name is Gerald Miller. I'm new here to the Phoenix area. I hope I'm not being too forward, but I wanted to say that I think you are beautiful. I enjoyed watching you enjoy church today," he finished as he extended his hand to Maleeka for a shake. That had always been Gerald's style—straight up, no chaser.

Maleeka looked at Gerald's hand for a quick second, then, deciding not to be rude, she gave him her own to shake. "Hello, Mr. Miller. My name is Maleeka Davis, soon to be Maleeka Osborne. I am engaged to be married. My fiancé's name is Darrin Osborne." Maleeka realized Gerald was flirting with her. Though he was quite an attractive man, something she noticed during service, she wanted to make it plain to him that she was not available to receive this kind of attention from him. She ended her introduction by wiggling her engagement ring in Gerald's face.

"I noticed the ring, *Miss Davis*," Gerald said, emphasizing the fact that Maleeka was still single at the moment. "However, I still felt compelled to introduce myself and hope for the best. Perhaps the ring meant something else. May I ask why your fiancé isn't here with you today?"

Maleeka was caught off guard by Mr. Miller's forwardness. Part of the reason, she admitted to herself, was how embarrassed she felt knowing she could not offer him a good explanation for Darrin's absence from church. He simply decided he did not feel like going, so he stayed home in bed, which left her annoyed with him after their phone conversation that morning. She was also a little shook by Mr. Miller's confident aggressiveness.

Unwilling to tell a flat out lie in church, Maleeka answered as honestly as she could without making Darrin look too bad. "My fiancé was a bit tired this morning, so he decided to take the day off from church, Mr. Miller."

Gerald noticed Maleeka's uneasiness as she explained Darrin's nonattendance. His observation led him to believe that she was covering for a man who either did not regularly attend church, a man who was lazy, and/or a man who was selfish and paid little concern to the desires and wishes of his woman. For Gerald, all of those scenarios worked in his favor as far as he was concerned.

"Well, if you were my fiancée, it would take more than a little fatigue to keep me from coming to the House of the Lord and sharing in praise and worship to our Savior with you. I would anticipate and savor this time together. I believe Sunday morning church service is one of the most intimate ways a couple can spend time together, at least for a couple who are right-fully practicing abstinence until they are married."

Maleeka did not even bother to hide the shock that crossed her features. "Mr. Miller—"

"Please, call me Gerald."

"Mr. Miller, I think you are being quite offensive and perhaps even a little invasive. You know nothing about Darrin or about our relationship, so please don't presume anything about him or our level of intimacy. That is just plain rude." Maleeka was obviously taken aback by Gerald's forwardness, but more so by his ac-curacy. She hoped she had not given that away in her reprimand of him.

"I never actually made any verbal assumptions about you, your fiancé, or your relationship. I simply stated how I, personally, would handle it if you were going to be my future wife. I'm very sorry if you found anything I said rude, offensive, or invasive. I did not mean to im-ply anything. I was only trying to share my views about me." Gerald was actually not too sorry. He only apolo-gized because he offended Maleeka with his comments.

Maleeka could sense that Gerald's apology lacked sincerity. She in turn stormed off without uttering an-other word. She decided that she did not particularly care for Mr. Miller and would from then on out steer clear of him. Gerald, however, made that very hard to do. For the past six months, each time Maleeka was in earshot of him and Darrin was not, Gerald would openly flirt with and flatter her.

On several occasions, after realizing the familial relationship between Maleeka and Tammy, he would even approach Tammy about the best way to get Maleeka to go out with him. Tammy, however, would always respect Maleeka's engagement as best she could and simply respond to Gerald by telling him it was not her place to get involved. But now, more than ever, Tammy wanted to tell Gerald about the stupid decision Maleeka was making by asking Darrin to move in with her; however, she smoldered her anger and put aside her concern for her cousin and agreed with what Maleeka said to Gerald.

"Gerald, this is just a disagreement between female cousins. You know how we women can get. As Maleeka said, we will work it out." To Maleeka she said sarcastically, "I hope to hear from you later today." She then left Gerald and Maleeka standing together as she exited the sanctuary.

"Are you sure there is nothing I can do to erase the scowl from your beautiful face? It would be my pleasure to kiss said face until all the pain went away," Gerald stated with mild mirth in his eyes.

"Thank you for the very forward and inappropriate offer, Gerald, but as I said, Tammy and I will be just fine. I'm going to leave now and join my fiancé so that we may go home. You have a nice week." Maleeka shook her head slightly as she walked away from Gerald.

Maleeka had become pretty accustomed to Gerald's bold flirting. She too began to find it somewhat humorous. She even found herself wishing Darrin would be as attentive and flattering as Gerald. As she walked to the car, she also found herself wishing and hoping that her proposal about the two of them moving in together would motivate him to do a lot more than flatter her more often.

Darrin sat in the car waiting for Maleeka, becoming annoyed that it was taking her so long to say good-bye to her cousin. When he saw Tammy come out of the sanctuary and get in her car a moment ago, he became a little angry. What on earth was taking her so long?

Darrin's nerves were already on edge as he waited to find out what Maleeka wanted to talk to him about. Sure, she said it was not about finally setting a date for the wedding, but what if she just said that to get him to have the conversation with her? He then tossed that thought aside. Maleeka had never before been manipulative. As far as he knew she was always honest with him. That thought, however, did little to assuage his curiosity. Having to sit and wait for her to come out of the church only added to his irritation and disconcertment. When he finally saw her approaching the car, his exasperation was turned way up on high. As soon as Maleeka sat in the passenger's seat, Darrin unleashed his annoyance.

"What took you so long? How long does it actually take to tell your cousin I am taking you home?" Darrin's voice was raised and filled with the frustration of all his thoughts.

Maleeka stopped midway through putting her seat belt in place and stared at Darrin for several seconds. So much for expecting more flattery and positive attention from him, she thought silently. Rather than respond to his verbal tirade right away, Maleeka took a moment to finish the task of putting on her seat belt. Her silence only served to further upset Darrin.

"Oh! So you don't hear me talking to you? Are you just going to ignore the fact that I asked you a question?"

"Well, the truth of the matter is, Darrin, you asked me two questions. You asked what took me so long, and then you asked how long it takes me to tell my cousin you were taking me home." Maleeka's response was calm but filled with irksome sarcasm.

"Don't get smart with me, Maleeka," Darrin replied venomously.

"And don't you dare scold me as if I am your child, Darrin. How dare you speak to me so rudely and expect me to respond to you in any other way?"

"You know what? Now I'm wishing you had just ridden home with your cousin," Darrin yelled.

"So do I," Maleeka yelled in return.

Up until that moment, neither of them noticed they were yelling loudly enough for the people in the parking lot to hear their argument. Gerald's knock on the passenger's side window clued them both in to the fact that their argument had been witnessed by others.

"Maleeka, are you okay?" she heard Gerald ask through the raised window.

Maleeka stared at him for several seconds before responding. She was so embarrassed that she was tempted to tell Darrin to just pull off to avoid having to face her handsome admirer. She instead lowered the window and answered him.

"I'm fine, Gerald. My fiancé and I were just having an unpleasant moment."

"Are you sure? If you need a ride home, I'd be happy to take you," Gerald replied as if Darrin were not sitting in the driver's seat.

Maleeka remembered Darrin's comment about wishing she had ridden with Tammy. She seriously considered leaving Darrin's car and taking Gerald up on his offer. It would serve him right for being so rude to her.

"Excuse me, partner, but my fiancée has already told you once that it's all good. She does not need you to take her anywhere. But, uh, thank you anyway." Darrin's words dripped with spite and mockery.

Maleeka did not know Gerald Miller very well, so she was unsure how far he would take things with Darrin; however, she knew Darrin well enough to know he would not back down unless Gerald did. She figured it was up to her to stop this little ruckus before it turned into a heated verbal battle, or something worse, between the two men. Darrin, Maleeka believed, was unaware of Gerald's flirtatious banter with her, so up until now, the two men had not been adversaries.

"Gerald, really, I'm fine. I don't need a ride. Everything is under control."

Maleeka rolled up the window without another word, hoping Gerald would take the hint and just leave. She silently thanked God when he began walking in the direction of his car.

"What's up with dude? Why is he trying to be your knight in shining armor? Is he trying to get with you or something?"

"What? Darrin, no. Let's just leave. Please take me home." Maleeka was so aggravated she had to fight with herself to keep herself under control and not begin yelling again. She was embarrassed enough. She just wanted to get away from the church as quickly as possible. She was relieved when Darrin put the car into gear and began backing out of his parking spot.

The first few moments of the drive to Maleeka's house were done in complete silence. No voices; no music. The couple could barely be heard breathing. The both of them simmered in quiet anger, each for their own personal reasons.

Darrin was still unnerved by the angst he felt over Maleeka's pending unknown topic of conversation. If he were completely honest, at least with himself, he would realize that was the reason behind the whole argument he and Maleeka just had. The time he waited in the car for Maleeka to say good-bye to Tammy was actually only a few minutes. It was the tension of not knowing what Maleeka wanted to discuss with him and not wanting to discuss setting a wedding date that had him in a tizzy. Old boy showing up to the car acting like he needed to come to Maleeka's rescue just added fuel to a smoldering fire.

Maleeka, of course, was angry because of the tone Darrin took with her the moment she got in the car. She had not seen him all week, and he barely had time to even converse with her on the phone. She knew her and Tammy's little tiff had come while he sat waiting for her, but she knew he had not waited long enough to warrant his reaction.

After the unpleasant exchange between the couple, Maleeka was unsure if she still wanted to have the all-important conversation with Darrin. In truth, she was unsure if she even still wanted to marry Darrin at this point. Of course, she let that thought leave her mind as quickly as it entered. She had felt this way several times before during their engagement, but her heart always, always led her back to wanting, almost needing to be Mrs. Darrin Osborne.

"What is it you wanted to talk about today, Maleeka?" Darrin's voice caught Maleeka off guard. The level of it had lowered, but his tone continued to spew irritation. Maleeka fought down the urge to respond in kind.

"I know you have been having some issues with taking that final step toward marrying me. I don't necessarily understand why. I don't understand why you even asked me to marry you if you were not completely ready—"

"Maleeka . . ." Darrin attempted to interrupt, but Maleeka continued while she still had the nerve to do so.

"Darrin, let me finish. I don't even want to hear your excuses or reasons right now. The bottom line is I still want to be your wife, so I will continue to wait a little while longer for you to pull yourself together. In the meantime, however, I have a proposition." Maleeka's tone was smooth and even, not too emotional and not harsh. She paused for a moment to purposely gather herself and make sure she kept on an even keel.

Darrin began to shift in his seat at the word "proposition." While he was not sure if he was ready to walk down the aisle, he knew he loved Maleeka. He did not want to lose her again. The last time she gave him a proposition, it was to see other people. He then began quickly wondering about that guy, Gerald. With the way he came running to his car today, trying to be Maleeka's hero, Darrin was certain he would love to have an opportunity to date his beautiful fiancée.

Instead of voicing his opinion, Darrin decided to let Maleeka finish what she was saying. He would decide what to do once he heard all she had to say.

"Darrin, I think that we should move into together. I believe once you see how well we get along living under the same roof, it will lessen whatever anxiety you have about us being married. Now, there has to be a time limit on our co-habitation. The lease on my apartment has six months left on it. I figured we could try living together for that amount of time, sharing in living expenses of course, and see how it fits for us. If it works out, which I'm sure it will, we can look for a new spot that we both choose together as husband and wife."

Wow! That was the only word that exploded into Darrin's brain at the conclusion of Maleeka's spiel. He truly was at a loss for any other words. He hoped that Maleeka was not waiting on an immediate response, because his brain was stuck on straight stupid at the moment.

Maleeka knew her proposition to Darrin would throw him for a loop, so she sat in silence as he processed all she had said to him. They actually rode the rest of the distance to her apartment in complete silence. She was prepared for his reaction. She had known her man for six years, during which she was studying him, his ways and his thought processes. At that moment she was reminded of the old Betty Wright song, "No Pain, No Gain." Betty sang, "I was earning my man while I was learning my man; something you young girls might not understand." Maleeka chuckled to herself as she reminisced about the old classic.

She had to admit, though, she was unsure what his answer would be. She just knew it would not be one made in haste.

When the couple arrived at Maleeka's apartment, Darrin was unsure whether he wanted to go in or just go straight home. Maleeka saw the confusion in his eyes as he sat behind the wheel, not making a move to get out of the car.

"Aren't you going to come in, Darrin?"

"I think I need to go home, sweetie. I've got a lot to think about, and I think it's best if I do it alone. I am really surprised by your request. I mean, it sounds logical and all; I just need a little time to really go over it all in my head. I also need to speak with David. If I do decide to take you up on your offer, I need to know if he will be able to swing the rent on our place by himself. Or he may have to find another roommate. I mean, there are a few variables that have to be taken into consideration. I just need time to think them all through."

Darrin got out of the car and came to open the door for Maleeka. He then walked her to her apartment. At the door he gave her a chaste kiss.

"Like I said, Mal, I'm going to go on home, think about what you said, and discuss options with David. I will call you tomorrow, I promise." Darrin then turned to leave without another word.

Maleeka entered her apartment still unsure of how Darrin would respond to her proposition, but the fact that he was going to discuss it with David gave her hope. She was sure he could afford the rent alone. David had a great job. Heck, according to her friend Katrina, everything about David Mathis was great.

David jogged to catch up to Katrina just before she left the sanctuary. "Katrina, can I talk to you for a moment?"

Katrina turned to find the man of her dreams, literally, standing before her a little out of breath. "Sure, David. What's up?"

The other day David was certain he would ask Katrina out today. He had rid himself of the guilty feelings he was having about his relationship with Toriyana and convinced himself there was no harm in asking this lovely lady out to dinner since he was not married. Standing before her right now, however, his conscience was singing an entirely different tune. His stomach became filled with butterflies and his mouth felt as if it were stuffed with cotton. He stood before Katrina unable to utter another syllable.

Katrina was confused by David's silence. He was the one who stopped her, after all, so why was he standing there looking as if he did not understand why they were in the same space?

"David, did you want something?"

"Huh? Ah, yeah. Yes, Katrina. I was wondering—" David stopped and cleared his throat, still fighting the nervous guilt that suddenly attacked him. "I wanted to know if you were going to be busy this afternoon," David finally choked out.

Though she had never seen David this jumpy before, Katrina was sure she heard David correctly. She did not want to jump to any conclusions on why he would ask her such a thing, though. She figured she would just ride the conversation out and find out where he was headed.

"I don't have any immediate plans. I was just going to call Maleeka to see if she wanted to catch a movie or something. Why?"

David took a deep, concentrating breath then said, "I was hoping you would consider having dinner with me this afternoon. If you'd like we can catch a movie as well, since that's what you wanted to do with Maleeka." He allowed the words to come out as he exhaled.

Where she was sure she previously heard him correctly, she now stood in awe, wondering if her ears were actually playing tricks on her. Before she made a fool of herself and leaped into his arms with a resounding yes, she needed to know for certain she was standing in the church listening to David and not lying in bed dreaming this scene.

"I'm sorry, David, but did you just ask me to go to dinner and a movie with you? Today?"

"Yes, I did. Considering the time, I guess it would be more like a late lunch and a movie. Or if you prefer and our timing is correct, we could do the movie first then grab a bite to eat. That way it will be closer to dinner time." David rambled because he was nervous.

Katrina stood frozen in her spot. She saw David's lips moving. In a distant fog, like the vapor that appears around people when they are simply illusions, she believed she could see the words he spoke that confirmed what she heard the first time. Somehow, though, she still could not believe this all was actually happening. Perhaps if she just said yes things would take their natural course into the next step. She would either wake up from her dream, or she would actually be preparing to go on a date with the beautiful man and singer, David Mathis.

"Yes," Katrina uttered breathlessly.

"Cool," David said with a relieved smile. "So do you want to eat first or go to the movies first?"

Finally realizing David and his invitation to take her out were real, Katrina began trying to focus real hard on what he was saying. Reality brought on a full course of nerves. "Um . . . I . . . think I would prefer the movies first. That way we can discuss it over dinner. I hope that's okay with you."

"No, that's fine. Why don't we check the computer in the ministry office to see what's playing and when and we can decide from there."

Chapter Six

The text message alert went off on William's phone about a block before he and his family arrived home from church. Since he was so close, he figured he would just check it once they arrived.

William pulled the car into the garage and unfastened his son from his car seat while Aujanae headed into the house to start dinner. William took Billy, Jr. to the great room and placed the wide-awake child in his playpen. He then remembered he had a text message he needed to check, so he sat on the sofa to do so.

As soon as William saw the name Adam appear on his phone, he became a little alarmed. Adam was the pseudonym William created in his phone for April just in case Aujanae ever decided to go snooping. It was Sunday, for goodness' sake. Sunday, they both agreed at the beginning of their time together, was a day reserved strictly for his family. William realized he had not spent time with April in over a week, but surely she could not have forgotten the rules that quickly. Why now was she being so obstinate and insubordinate? This was the first time in their fourteen-month history that she had broken that rule.

William took that into consideration and decided he would not jump to conclusions or make assumptions about her reasons until he actually read the text message:

Have you missed me? Of course you have. Or at least that's the impression the tone of your voice mail messages give. I need to see you. TODAY!

So much for him trying to give April the benefit of the doubt.

Aujanae stood in the kitchen pulling together ingredients for this evening's dinner, seemingly not paying any attention at all to William or his phone. Yet, he felt as anxious as if his wife were sitting only inches away from him, able to read every word of April's text and all that they implied.

William toyed with the idea of simply ignoring the text message and sticking to the rules of the game as they had been initially set; however, April seemed to have ramped up the game when she ignored all of his texts and calls last week. She mentioned William's tone in the voice mail messages he left. Admittedly, he remembered he probably sounded a little desperate.

April was obviously smarter than he. She cleverly sent him a text which gave no indication whatsoever to her own tone. For all William knew, April was asking that he come by to end things with him. Maybe she had become tired of being the other woman. William knew she had fallen in love with him. Perhaps their illicit affair had become too much for her to handle and she wanted out of it. Well, there was only way to find out for sure. Instead of returning April's text message, he decided to call her so he could get a feel for her vibe.

"I'm going into the bedroom to change, baby. Keep an eye on B.J."

"Sure, but hurry up, honey. I want to change also before I actually start cooking."

"All right. I'll make it quick." William rushed to the other side of their spacious home and into their bedroom. The moment he crossed the threshold, he dialed April's number.

"Hello, William," she answered.

"April, what is with this text? You know we agreed that we would never hook up on Sunday. Why are you saying you want to see me today?" William's current tone was just barely below hostile.

"Apparently you didn't read it very carefully. What I said was I *needed* to see you today," April replied coolly.

"Whatever, April. What is this about?"

"Aren't you at home with wifey now? Are you sure you're in a position to have this conversation over the phone?"

William realized April was right. He did not want to stay on the phone with her too long. Aujanae had asked him to hurry so he could watch B.J. while she too came in to change clothes.

"William, things between us are at a very odd place. I need to see you to see if there is any possibility we can sort them out. Besides, it has been over a week. While we have never broken our no-Sunday rule, we have also never gone that long without spending time together. I miss you." April almost purred the second half of her statement.

William's near hostility quickly turned into concern with the first part of April's account. He suddenly became very aware that he did not want to end things with her. Primal lust was the emotion that dictated his emotions in conjunction with April's last two sentences.

"April, I will be at your place in about an hour or so, but we will talk about you breaking the rules when I see you. This cannot happen again, no matter what the circumstances," William said quickly in an effort to end the conversation; or at least that is what he tried to make himself believe.

"Okay. I will see you when you get here." April disconnected the call without another word.

William tried to come up with a story to tell Aujanae about having to leave while he hurriedly changed his clothes. He usually used work as an excuse to spend time with April. He knew that would not fly on a Sunday. Just as he hung up his tie, he came up with the perfect lie to get him out of the house.

"Aujanae," William called as he went back to the great room after completely changing his attire. "I checked my text message while I was in the bedroom. David texted me while we were in the car on our way home, asking me to give him a call. I just spoke with him, and he really needs to talk to me. He didn't give any real indication what he wanted to talk about, but I think he is really bummed about the strain the distance is causing on his and Tori's relationship." David had spoken to William earlier in the week about Toriyana not visiting as they had previously planned. He did seem pretty depressed about it at the time.

"Billy, it is Sunday. Sunday is family day, remember. You are the one who came up with that rule just after B.J. was born. On Sundays it is supposed to always just be the three of us unless there was a special occasion involving our friends or family."

"I know, baby, but you didn't hear David at work the other day. And he sounded even worse on the phone just now. I know it's not really a special occasion, but I think it qualifies as special circumstances. I mean, I kind of feel responsible. I'm the one who convinced him to move here to Phoenix in the first place." William surprised even himself with how easily the lies were rolling off his tongue.

"I have an idea," Aujanae said. "Why don't you invite him here for dinner tonight? That way he might not feel so alone."

"Sweetie, I think seeing us here together in our home may just rub salt in his wounds. Remember, he's depressed because he is not with his woman. How would that look for me to ask him to come spend time with me and my wife?"

Aujanae responded with only a quiet thoughtfulness.

"Look. I'll go over there, talk with him for a little bit, maybe take him out to get a beer or something. I promise I won't be gone for more than a couple hours, three tops." William knew Aujanae was acquiescing, but he did not want to make a move until she said she was cool with him leaving.

"Okay. I won't be selfish. You can go and have some male-bonding time with David. But let's not make this a habit, Billy. You work so much; I look forward to our Sundays."

"I won't, baby." William kissed his wife, kissed his son, who was still playing quietly in his playpen, and grabbed his car keys to leave.

"Wait just one minute, Billy."

William froze, knowing his wife had quickly come up with some great reason for him to stay home, but he tried to remain calm as he asked, "What's up, baby?"

"Why are you in such a rush? Remember I told you I wanted to change clothes? I need you to keep an eye on B.J. David can wait a few extra minutes, can't he?"

William exhaled the breath he did not even realize he was holding before he responded as he sat on the sofa to wait for Aujanae to change. "Oh yeah. I forgot that quickly. Go ahead. Take your time, baby."

Aujanae walked back to the bedroom feeling very uncomfortable with William and his story about going to see David. She remembered hearing his text indicator going off while they were in the car. The hairs on the back of her neck stood up at the sound. She immediately began to think that perhaps it was his possible lover trying to contact him. Her nerves had on been edge since she saw him staring at the pretty woman at church.

She really wanted to believe William, and the story about David did make sense, so she tried to put the negative thoughts out of her mind and not assume or accuse him of anything.

April began preparing her apartment for William's arrival as soon as they hung up the phone, starting, of course, in the bedroom. She lit scented candles, powdered the fresh sheets, and pulled together everything they would need and put it on the tub for a nice relaxing bubble bath later. She then went to the kitchen to slice strawberries and mangos for a sexy snack while the homemade lasagna she prepared yesterday and the garlic rolls warmed in the oven. The tossed salad and the perfect bottle of wine chilled in the refrigerator.

April began plotting her efforts to become the next and forever Mrs. William Rucker, Sr. on Friday, after hearing William's last voice mail message. The seductive scene she was putting together today was nothing out of the ordinary. This was usually how the two of them spent their time together. It would be the conversation today that would be quite different. Today April wanted to hear William tell her how he really felt about her. Oh, she had hinted about it in very obscure terms while they played tiddlywinks, and he was always just as obscure with his answers and reactions. Today, though, April wanted to hear more definitively about William's feelings for her. She would be direct but not too blunt. She knew she was not yet in a position to give him an ultimatum, but she needed to be more assured that it was more than just an assumption on her part that he cared for her deeply.

The doorbell chimed just as April was slicing the last piece of mango. She removed her apron and tossed it on the granite island. She was dressed to kill in a sexy blood-red dress that hit every inch of her hour-glass figure in just the right spot and landed just above her knees. The V-neckline showed just enough cleavage to make it alluring but not overtly sleazy. When she saw this Calvin Klein number in the store at Dillard's two months ago, she knew it would be something William would enjoy seeing her wear. Today gave her the perfect opportunity to test her theory.

When she opened the door, William stared at her for several moments before he even attempted to step into the apartment. Apparently she had been absolutely correct.

"Are you going to come in and kiss me, or are you going to stand out there and gawk at me?" April asked seductively.

William responded by walking into the living room, grabbing her in a greedy embrace, and planting an even greedier wet kiss on her opened mouth.

"I gather from your reaction that I was missed," April teased as they ended the ninety-second kiss.

William answered by kissing her again for another ten seconds. When their lips parted this time, he said, "Yes! You were missed, April Colston."

Oh yes, April thought. *I am finding out things this evening and I haven't even asked a serious question yet.*

"I assume you're hungry, William. I'm guessing you didn't have time to eat dinner with your family because of the timing of your call. I have a very special meal prepared for you."

April's statement reminded William that he had left his family on a Sunday to come to her, and he became slightly agitated. Only slightly, though. How could he be truly mad at her when she went out of her way to look this good for him?

"April, what is up with you beckoning me to come over here on a Sunday? We talked about this from the very beginning. In order for me to be okay with this thing between us, I had to establish some rules and boundaries and you were cool with it. So why now are you demanding that I come see you on a Sunday?" Where William was only mildly aggravated, April instantly became strongly irritated at William's comments and question.

"Are you serious, William? Boundaries and rules?" April began pacing the living room floor with her hands on her hips. "Are there really any such margins for a man who is cheating on his wife? Are you really going to stand there and try to infuse some integrity into our relationship? I can't believe you have the nerve to stand here and utter those words to me as if they truly make some kind of sense." April finally stopped walking and stared at William through eyes that had sharpened into mere small slits.

William, who remained standing in the same spot he had been in since entering the apartment, was taken aback by April's reaction to his inquiry. Like he said, initially April had no issues with what he required of her in this relationship. There were actually only two rules, one spoken and one implied. Rule number one: Sundays were off limits. It was the day reserved for God and his family. Rule number two, which they never verbalized, but seemed to have an understanding about, was that they never discussed Aujanae. Things were changing in this thing he and April shared. William was not sure if he liked the direction they were going.

He then took a moment to examine April fully, even in the angered state she was in right now. He looked at her, and in her beauty he could see all that made her that way: her outer appearance, her intellect, her strong will, her pride in her education, and her work ethic on her job. He combined all that with her desire to make him happy and the sheer pleasure she derived from doing it. He stared at April and realized in that moment that he was not prepared to allow her to leave his life, even though she had changed the game.

William took a couple of steps toward April and reached for her. She initially bristled at his attempted touch. She was still angry with him.

"Come here, April," William demanded softly as he gently pulled her to him despite her protest. The two stood in the middle of the floor embracing while William spoke.

"I'm sorry if what I said hurt you. This past week without you has been rough on me. I'll admit that. That is the real reason I have stepped outside of our normal box and come here today. Yes, I was not happy with you asking me to do that, but I would have been more unhappy about going another day without seeing you."

April relaxed in William's arms as he soothed her with his words. She nuzzled her nose into his broad chest and allowed herself to fall deeper in love with him. Before she even realized what happened, she said, "I love you, William."

Though this was not the first time she had told him that, she was still not supposed to say it to him tonight. Tonight was supposed to be about finding out how he truly felt about her. But it was out there now. She looked up into his eyes to see if they revealed a reaction. What she saw was confusion compiled with many emotions. She saw compassion and uncertainty. She saw trepidation and excitement. She saw respect and dilemma. She saw lust and passion. She then heard his response.

"Oh April," he said as he held her closer, tightly, and without restriction or even regret. It was not exactly what she wanted to hear, but she would take it for now.

The pair stayed like that for what seemed like the longest time to them both. April was the first to break the passionate silence that was pregnant with so many emotions.

"William, look. This evening has already taken us in so many different directions and you haven't even been here ten minutes. How about we let go of the heaviness? We can start by eating this fabulous meal I've prepared and just enjoy the rest of our time together. What do you say?"

"I say I agree with you wholeheartedly. I am starving in more ways than one, if you know what I mean," William said suggestively and honestly.

"Oh, I know exactly what you mean and how you feel. I feel the same way. After dinner, I have a beautiful bubble bath planned where we can sit, relax, and let nature take its course from there."

April and William started their evening together in the kitchen with their meal and ended it waking up from a sound nap more than six hours later. It would be 10:45 P.M. before he arrived home, more than three hours later than the three hours he promised his wife he would be gone.

Chapter Seven

David returned to the rented house he shared with his friend Darrin after his early morning jog and quiet time in nature with God. He was about to hit the shower and get ready for work when Darrin appeared in the kitchen to grab a bite to eat as he too prepared for work.

The two gentlemen had moved in to the house together when they were offered a great deal by one of the members of their congregation at King David's Christian Tabernacle. David was staying at his Cousin William's house with William's wife and son when he first moved from Detroit to Phoenix, until he found an affordable, suitable place to live. Darrin's lease had expired one month prior, and he was paying an enormous month-to-month rent increase because he had decided not to renew his lease, but still had yet to find another apartment that he liked.

Darrin and David were in the midst of a conversation at the end of a Men's Ministry meeting at the church when William approached David to let him know one of the congregants told him he had a house he wanted to rent on the west side of the valley. The church member had just purchased a new house but wanted to hold on to his old house that he had purchased at such a great deal when the housing market crashed. The current mortgage on the house was $529, and the congregant was willing to rent it for only $100 above the mortgage payment. Though William was speaking to David, Darrin thought it could be a great opportunity for him as well. Not wanting to fight over the place, they decided to become roommates and take even greater advantage of the phenomenal blessing presented to them by God.

That was about eight months ago. In the interim, the two men had become really good friends. They had lots of common interests, such as sports, with both holding a special fondness for basketball. They enjoyed the same types of movies and only slightly different types of music. Darrin's favorite genre was hip-hop and David's was rhythm and blues. But they mutually had their favorite artists in each genre. They were both in committed relationships with what they would describe as pretty special women, and they were Christians. Darrin was slightly older than David. Darrin was thirty-three. David was thirty.

"Morning, David. Can I have a word with you for a quick second?"

"Sure, man. What's up?" David grabbed a bottle of water from the refrigerator then sat at the table to listen to Darrin.

Darrin leaned on the kitchen counter, waiting for his frozen waffles to pop up from the toaster. "I was wondering how you would feel about me moving out. I mean, would you be able and willing to handle the rent and responsibilities on this place without me?"

"What, man! You're thinking about moving out? Is it something I've done?" David asked apologetically.

"No, no, man. It's nothing like that. We are cool. We will be cool even if I do move out of here."

"Oh. Okay. Then what's really going on? Why are you thinking about moving and where are you thinking about moving to?"

Darrin was a little hesitant to tell David about Maleeka's offer. He did not want David, or anyone else for that matter, to criticize him about shacking up with his fiancée before they were actually married. And while he was pretty sure David would not openly judge him, he still did not want to deal with the lecture he was sure he would receive.

David was a man truly after God's own heart, just as King David in the Bible. As a matter of fact, Darrin considered earth David to be even godlier than King David. King David's mistakes and mess-ups had been well known and chronicled for the entire world to see. Earth David seemingly led a life dedicated to living by God's Word. David was always praying. He loved singing in praise to God. He openly loved being a Christian. Darrin, of course, knew he was not perfect, but David took his faith very seriously.

Darrin, on the other hand, was a very carnal Christian. He did believe in God, Jesus, and the Holy Spirit, but he was a participating Christian more out of obligation and tradition than a heartfelt desire to be like Jesus. Darrin's parents were church deacons, and he grew up knowing and learning about God his entire life. His parents were also very serious about their faith, but Darrin just was not feeling it like that. He led a decent life—no drugs, no criminal activity, no addictive habits. He just did not look to live his life according to every word quoted from the Bible. His church attendance on Sunday was his reasonable service to God. His minimal participation in the Men's Ministry gave him an outlet and an opportunity to be involved with the church and not have his parents harping on him every five minutes about showing no outward service to God. Therefore, his uneasiness about sharing his thoughts with David about moving in with Maleeka were more from his own sense of inferiority than his view of David's superiority.

He decided to reveal his reason though, knowing, as he figured, that David would not judge or try to condemn him.

"Maleeka asked me yesterday to move in with her. She figures that if we live together for a while, it will help me get over my apprehension about us taking that final step to forever."

David's eyes did grow a little bigger on his face as Darrin told him his news. "Wow, man! That's a deep one. You said this is what she thinks and feels. Obviously you are considering it since you brought up possibly moving out to me. But tell me, how do *you* really feel about it?"

Darrin let out an audible breath as he retrieved his waffles as they popped up from the toaster. He sat at the table with David, where the rest of the stuff he needed to complete his breakfast was already placed.

"Man, I'm not really sure. I mean, I think it makes sense to at least give it a try. I do love Maleeka. I don't think I will ever find anyone better than her out there. I just have this fear of getting married and having it not work out for whatever reason. Maybe taking a trial run at it will help me to see that we can actually make it work. I do know this: I would rather be just living with her and simply have to move out than to be married with children and have to get a divorce if we can't keep each other happy."

"Well, it sounds to me like you have already made up your mind about this. You already know all the rules about fornication and living in sin and all that, so I'm not going to give you a lecture. As far as me being cool with handling this place alone, don't worry about that. I'll be fine," David said evenly as he finished off the last of his water. He purposefully made sure he did not come across as condescending or judgmental.

"Thanks, Dave. I appreciate that. I'm still not one hundred percent sure, but if I'm honest with myself, I have to say I am definitely leaning in that direction. I will give myself another forty-eight hours to make a final decision."

"All right, brother. And if you do decide to go that route and it doesn't work out, you can always come back here, no questions asked. I will either live here with you or live here alone."

The men shook hands and then stood for a manly hug.

"So what was up with you yesterday afternoon? What direction did you take that led you away from home after church?" Darrin asked curiously.

David smiled as he reminisced about the time he spent with Katrina after church yesterday. Their date had been absolutely perfect. Their timing to catch the next Tyler Perry movie could not have been better. They decided to go to the theater downtown in the Arizona Center. The landscaping of the small outdoor mall was absolutely gorgeous.

The two decided to leave her car in the church parking lot and ride together in David's car the short distance to the mall. After thoroughly enjoying the film, they decided to have dinner at The Cheesecake Factory in the Biltmore Area, another beautiful spot in Phoenix.

The two laughed about the movie and conversed about some of the folks at church and a host of other topics. They were very natural and at ease with one another. During their time together, David did think about Toriyana a couple of times, but there was no guilt; however, when he dropped her off at her car, they shared a lingering hug and a chaste kiss. When he got back in his car to leave, a little shame began to rear its head.

"I hung out with Katrina Hartfield after church yesterday. We went to see the Tyler Perry Movie, *Good Deeds,* and we had a bite to eat at The Cheesecake Factory," David answered matter-of-factly.

Darrin's fork stopped midway between his plate and his mouth. After holding it suspended for a few seconds, he dropped it back into his plate. "My fiancée Maleeka's best friend, Katrina Hartfield? Katrina Hartfield that works at the church? Katrina Hartfield that is fine as frog hair? Katrina Hartfield that is *not* your girlfriend, Toriyana? That Katrina Hartfield?"

David shook his head at his roommate's silly but thorough depictions of Katrina. "Yes. That Katrina Hartfield, goofy."

It was now Darrin's turn to shake his head. "Wow! You cheating on your girl, dude?"

David was unprepared for Darrin's point blank question. He visibly jumped in reaction to Darrin's bluntness. The guilt he felt yesterday at the end of their date was nothing compared to the dishonor he felt right now. He tried to rationalize his actions using the same theory he had used before to explain himself to Darrin.

"Man, I am not cheating on Toriyana. Tori and I are not married or engaged, which makes us both single people," he answered weakly.

"Now you sound like Maleeka. That's the same line she gives me when she keeps trying to get me to hook you up with Katrina." Darrin also recalled when Maleeka used that logic on him when he got busted going out with Trisha behind her back.

David felt a wee bit better after hearing Darrin say Maleeka and he were on the same page, but only a little. Darrin obviously was not convinced that David was not cheating.

"Okay. So since you are not 'cheating,'" Darrin said, using air quotes over the word cheating, "are you going to tell Tori about your date with Katrina?"

"I'm not sure. To be honest, D, I do feel a little guilty about going out with Katrina. I love Tori. She is my heart. I only considered going out with Katrina because I was upset that Tori wasn't going to be able to get here to see me as we planned. Don't get me wrong, I think Katrina is great also. I have been attracted to her ever since the first time I met her. And while I don't think she has done it intentionally, she has made it obvious she's attracted to me as well."

"Wow, D." The men called each other D on occasion. "I'm not going to judge you just like you didn't judge me when I gave you my news. You are a grown man and you make the rules for your life and your relationships. But I will say this: I would be devastated and pissed if Maleeka was going out with any guy other than me."

"And you would have every right to be. Maleeka is your fiancée. The Bible considers an engagement a covenant with one another. You two have pledged and committed to get married—some day," David threw in jokingly. "But there is nothing in the Bible that speaks about boyfriend/girlfriend relationships or significant other couples who are dating." David was speaking to Darrin, but he was sure his words were more for himself than his roommate.

"Okay. I hear you. Now, let me get out of here and get to work before you break out in a sermon with a praise song and three points to your message," Darrin joked with his roommate and friend in return.

David laughed. "Yeah, I better get out of here too. Like I said, I got your back on whatever you decide to do with Maleeka."

"Thanks, D."

***

Aujanae moved around her kitchen, preparing breakfast and packing a lunch for her husband like a zombie. William was in the shower getting ready for work. He had not come home until after 11:00 P.M. last night. When he left the house under the guise of going to console his cousin David, Aujanae fought every voice in her head that said he was lying. She pushed down every instinct that told her he was going to see the pretty woman at church. But when 7:00 P.M. came and went; then 8:00, 9:00, and 10:00, she began to believe she had been the fool and her gut had gotten the painful glory—an oxymoron if she had ever heard one.

There were several times last night that she picked up the phone to call her husband, but her fingers refused to dial the number. She would not have been able to stand hearing his voice mail because he chose to neglect her call. Nor could she have stomached hearing him possibly lie to her if he did bother to answer. So she suffered in silence as she sat up mindlessly staring at the television, her mind conjuring up images of William and the pretty woman in various sexual embraces. Those images replaced those of the folks that were actually on the television.

By the time she climbed into bed at 10:30, she had exhausted herself with worry, sadness, and anger. She fell asleep so quickly she was not exactly sure what time William came home. She just knew he was there when she awakened at 3:30 A.M. from a dream that included him and the pretty woman. She got up from the bed, went to the bathroom, and decided to spend the rest of the night on the sofa in the great room. She did not trust herself in the bed with her husband. She still wanted to keep true to her vow to not accuse him of anything when she still had no solid proof.

When he made his way into the kitchen to retrieve his coffee, he said, "Good morning", and kissed her on the cheek.

The kiss he planted on her cheek felt like sharp needles stabbing her skin. The cologne he wore, a brand she picked out for him especially for her pleasure, now made her feel nauseated. The sight of his face, which she normally deemed beautiful, was provoking her to smack him with the hot spatula she used to turn his pancakes. Aujanae continued to prepare his breakfast and did not utter a word, afraid of what she might say.

William felt the tension in Aujanae when he kissed her. He also noticed she did not respond when he said good morning. He knew she was more than likely upset about the time he came in last night. He could not blame her. He was just relieved that she only had his lateness to be angered about. *If she really knew everything* . . . He let the though slip from his mind. He could not bear to think about what the truth would do to her.

"Aujanae, I know you're upset with me about last night. I'm so sorry, love. David was worse off than I thought. We ended up staying at his apartment and talking instead of going out as I had mentioned we might. Before I knew it, he was drowning his sorrow in the first beer, and then he switched to wine. I was only supposed to talk to him and have a beer, no more than two myself. Somehow I obviously lost track of how many I had and we both ended up falling asleep in his living room. I woke up about ten thirty and made my way home. You were already asleep when I got here. I didn't want to wake you to apologize and explain my tardiness, so I let you rest, figuring I would just talk to you this morning."

Aujanae prepared William a plate of pancakes, turkey bacon, and scrambled eggs. She took the plate to the table and set it before him. She then sat in the chair on the corner of the table with nothing to eat for herself.

"Aren't you going to have breakfast with me?"

"I'm not hungry, Billy. I was pretty upset last night when you were out so late after first leaving me on a Sunday and then being out much longer than you said you would be without at least calling me. I have to be honest with you. I eventually ended up thinking you were with another woman."

William began coughing and sputtering on the piece of pancake he had just swallowed. Aujanae quickly got up from her seat to get him a glass of water. He was silly enough to try to wash it down with hot coffee. William took several gulps of the water, finally able to get himself under control.

Aujanae was unsure what exactly to make of William's reaction to her declaration. Was it guilt or astonishment that made him choke? Did he feel shame or indignation? She had never been so unsure of anything in her entire life. Her belly told her it was the former. Her heart begged that it be the latter.

William pushed the plate away from him, unable to eat another bite. "Aujanae, why would you think I was cheating on you? Don't you believe I love you?" His fake indignation could have garnered him an Academy Award.

"Yes. I'm sure you do, but I have become so uncomfortable lately." Aujanae stopped short of saying she was uncomfortable about the pretty woman at church.

"Baby, there is nothing for you to be uncomfortable about." William got up from his seat at the table and stood behind his wife's chair, gently massaging and

kneading her shoulders as he spoke. "I love you and
B.J. far too much to ever consider doing anything to
upset you or our household in such a devastating way."

Aujanae allowed William's slow fingers to soothe her
aching heart. She willed that he infuse in her the confidence she needed to trust him. She loved her husband,
and she wanted their marriage to last forever.

"Honey, I've got to get out of here and get to work.
We have a lot of things going on at the bank right now.
You know I'm still working my way up that corporate
ladder, trying to build a better life and a more secure
future for us. But guess what? In light of what you just
admitted to me, I am going to be sure to leave at five
o'clock tonight. I will be home at a decent hour so we
can spend some quality time together. How does that
sound?"

"It sounds great, Billy. And I do understand how hard
you are working for our family. Really I do. I just want
you to know that the money and the material things
mean far less to me than our marriage and our family.
Please understand that your time, our time together, is
priceless. Even if it means I have to get a job in order to
help fulfill your dreams for us, I am willing to do that.
As long as we work similar hours and are home around
the same time, I really would not mind working. I've
got my primary education degree. All I have to do is get
my teacher's certificate and I'm sure I can get a job that
will have me home by four o'clock. I will do whatever it
takes to make our marriage work, Billy." Aujanae was
nearly pleading with her husband to understand how
desperate she was to keep their marriage intact.

"And who is supposed to take care of our son while
you're off teaching other people's children? We have
talked about this, Aujanae. I don't want B.J. raised by
daycare workers. You already have a job here that you

are perfect for. No one, and I mean no one, can be my wife better than you can. You are the best wife and mother I could ask for. I thank God for you each and every day, sweetie. So no more talk about me cheating, okay? It's just me and you, Aujanae. We will work through this insecurity you are having together, okay?"

Aujanae focused her mind on relaxing in William's words. She refused at that moment to allow any doubt to creep into her spirit. She wanted to believe William, so she would. She exhaled an unwinding breath and simply said, "Okay."

William lifted Aujanae from her seat and kissed her passionately on the lips. Their intimacy was cut short, however, by the sounds they heard on the baby monitor coming from their son's bedroom. Aujanae broke the kiss, shaking her head in disappointment.

"I have to go and get your son before he starts to yell his head off. I'm sure he's hungry and wet now that's he awake. Thank you, honey, for the reassurance and for not getting upset with my foolishness." Aujanae gave her husband one last long peck on the lips and then headed to tend to their baby.

William stood in the kitchen for a few minutes after Aujanae left and hung his head. His stomach was in knots, his head began to pound, and the perspiration from his armpits had begun to stain his shirt. He had no idea until today that Aujanae had suspected anything was amiss in their marriage. William loved his wife; he truly did. Seeing her in such distress this morning over a simple suspicion was more than he was prepared to handle. He did not even want to imagine how she would react if she found out the truth.

Under normal circumstances, it would be time to end the affair with April, or at least he assumed that would be standard procedure. He had never done this kind of thing before. But the mere thought of giving up April was as distressful as seeing Aujanae suffer this morning.

William had no idea what he was supposed to do now, but he knew for sure that he would not see April tonight. Tonight he would keep his promise and be home at a decent hour to help ease some of Aujanae's worries.

William followed Aujanae in the direction she had gone. He wanted to kiss his son good-bye, change his shirt quickly, and then get out of the house before he became more of an emotional and confused wreck than he already was.

Chapter Eight

Katrina sat at her desk beaming and singing. The effects from her date with the most fabulously handsome, perfect singing, overall wonderful man in the world still lingered from last night. The spot where he kissed her cheek, very near her lips, still tingled. Her body still involuntarily swooned at the memory of his good night embrace. Yes, last night was nothing short of magic for her.

Katrina took a moment away from her joyful reminiscing and began remembering all the protesting she had done to her cousin against going out with David because of his relationship with his girlfriend. In light of all she had said to Maleeka in the past about not trying to get with David, she felt as if she should feel guilty about being a party to him cheating on Toriyana. But as she searched her heart, she could not conjure up one ounce of remorse.

On a couple of occasions, she did think about how Toriyana would feel if she knew she and David were out together. Her senses were especially heightened during the movie, *Good Deeds*, which closely simulated her and David's situation. But as the evening wore on, thoughts of David's girlfriend were pushed to the back of her mind as she began to pray that she and David's story would end much like the movie.

David was so considerate. She told him about her love of the scenery surrounding the Arizona Center, so he took her to that theatre. She told him how she loved hanging out in the Biltmore Area, and he took her to a restaurant there. David was funny, fine, intelligent, fine, sweet, fine, and a man who was proud of his relationship with God. And fine. Taking all of that in caused her to once again think about Toriyana during their date. She thought about what a blessed woman she was to have such a great guy who cared about her.

Katrina considered *courteously* asking about Toriyana just to see what David's response would be. But she did not know if she could pull the charade off without him realizing she was being phony. Besides, he never brought up her name, so why should she?

As she sat at her desk now, a thought occurred to her. What if the two of them had actually broken up? What if they mutually and amicably realized the distance was too much for either of them to handle? What if he was now a single man, free and clear to date her and make her his one and only?

"Yes!" she exclaimed softly, but out loud to herself. Just then her desk phone rang. She had to pull herself together and put on her professional persona and get back to work.

"King David's Christian Tabernacle, Pastor Abraham's office. Katrina speaking," she recited as she answered the call.

"Hey, girl," Maleeka sang into the phone. "What you doing?"

"I'm at work, Maleeka. What do you think I'm doing?" Katrina replied humorously.

"I think you are thinking about David Mathis like you are always doing." Maleeka laughed at herself while both of them knew she was only half joking.

Katrina was just about to tell Maleeka how right she was when Maleeka spoke again.

"Kat, I called to tell you something. I have already shared this with my cousin Tammy. I felt I should share it with you too since you are my best friend. Yesterday I asked Darrin to move in with me," Maleeka said with a false calmness.

"You did what?" Katrina's response was genuinely calm, but she was still shocked.

Maleeka went on to explain why she did what she did. Generally, Katrina never judged Maleeka and Darrin's relationship. She was so unlike her cousin Tammy. Where Tammy felt it was her job to protect Maleeka from herself when it came to Darrin, Katrina's job had always been to just love Maleeka through all the problems in her relationship. Maleeka hoped Katrina's persona would hold up under the gravity of what she had just told her.

"Wow, Maleeka! Are you sure it's going to work?"

"I really do think so, Kat, but only time will tell. The truth of the matter is he hasn't even given me an answer yet. He's supposed to call me sometime today."

Katrina thought about the movie again. Tyler Perry and Gabrielle Union lived together while they were engaged, but that did not end as either of them thought it would. Katrina considered sharing that information with Maleeka, but decided against it. She did not want to seem like she was judging her best friend. In all the time Maleeka and Darrin had been together, the only time Katrina ever advised Maleeka on her relationship was when she found out Darrin had been sneaking around and seeing someone else behind Maleeka's back. Back then she told Maleeka she should get rid of Darrin and find someone else. Maleeka instead got engaged to Darrin. From then on out, she decided she would stay out of her relationship until Maleeka needed her for whatever reason.

"Well, I'm not sure if this is sacrilegious or not, me praying for your living in sin to work out, but I will be praying that things turn out the way you want them to, Mal. I love you and no matter what, I never want to see you hurt."

"I appreciate that, Kat. You are the bestest best friend."

The line went silent for a minute. Katrina knew it was because Maleeka was having one of her mushy moments. She started to break the silence by telling her all about her date with David last night. But again, just as she started to open her mouth, Pastor Abraham buzzed her on the intercom.

"Katrina, can you come into my office for a moment? I need you to help me sort through this credit card bill and put in the correct account numbers for this reconciliation."

"I will be there in just a second, Pastor," she replied to her boss. To her friend she said, "Mal, I've got to go, but I have some news of my own I want to share. Can you meet me for lunch at La Canasta at twelve thirty?"

"Of course, but give me a hint about your news."

"Nope. You will have to wait till I see you." Katrina hung up the phone before Maleeka had a chance to start begging and whining. She then headed in to Pastor Abraham's office.

Maleeka stared at her phone, unable to believe Katrina left her hanging like that. While she was looking at the phone cross-eyed, it rang again. She assumed it was Katrina calling back to apologize for being so rude; however, the caller ID showed another friend's number.

"Hey, Aujanae. I haven't heard from you in a while. What's up?"

"Hi, Maleeka. Uh, girl. I just need a little girl time. What are you doing today?"

"Well, I'm actually just pulling into the parking lot at work. What do you need, Aujanae? You sound stressed."

"Stressed is probably a really good word. But I don't really want to talk about it in detail. I just need to get out of this house and perhaps stop thinking about things for a while. I was hoping we could meet for lunch today or something. My treat."

"Um, I actually just made a lunch date with Katrina. I'm sure she won't mind you coming along with us, though. And each of us can pay for our own meals."

"Okay. That sounds good. Like I said, I just need to be in the company of some girlfriends. I would love to join you guys. Where and what time are you hooking up?"

"We are meeting at the Mexican restaurant, La Canasta, near downtown at twelve thirty."

"Sounds good. I will see you ladies there. And don't worry about it. It will still be my treat. Since my husband enjoys working so hard to make the money, I will enjoy spending some of it on my friends," Aujanae said spitefully.

Maleeka took Aujanae's response and tone of voice to mean that her troubles were in her marriage, but she would not push. Aujanae said she did not want to talk about it, and she would respect her wishes.

"Great. Thanks on behalf of both of us. We will see you at twelve thirty."

***

"What do you mean we won't be able to see each to-night? We always see each on Mondays because of your Sunday rule." April was livid and indignant.

William called April in his car through his Bluetooth on his ride into work.

"Well, if I remember correctly, we were not together last Monday because one of us had an attitude and re-fused to take the other's call," William replied a little loudly and very sarcastically.

"Don't be a smarty pants, William, and don't take that tone with me. Why can't we see each other to-night?" April was positive she knew the answer to that question, but she wanted to hear him say it aloud.

William was silent for several seconds. He was un-sure if he should tell April about Aujanae becoming suspicious. Something inside told him that April would somehow find a way to use that information against him.

"Look, April, I was away from my son yesterday. I don't like the idea of doing that to him two nights in a row." He decided using his son was safer than being completely honest about his wife's distress.

"William, that is crap and you know it. The boy is only fourteen months old. I remember because he is the same age as our relationship. He doesn't under-stand the concept of time and days yet. It's your wife, isn't it? Aujanae is tripping, isn't she?"

William should have known April was smarter than he had given her credit for a moment ago. "Listen, April, she is a little upset. I was able to appease her this morning about taking off and leaving her yesterday and then coming home so late last night, but I need to go home tonight to keep things on an even keel. We can resume our regular schedule next week, and I will see you on Wednesday as usual. I need you to understand

and be okay with this." William tried to sound stern and not pleading. He knew he needed to take back some of the power in this thing with April.

"No! I will not understand and be okay with this, William. I am tired. Do you hear me? I am tired of playing second to your wife. I thought we had a breakthrough last night. I thought you understood that I need you, William. I thought . . ." April paused as her voice began to crack. "I thought you and I were on the same page."

William heard the tears in April's voice and his resolve weakened. He was so torn at that moment. He remained silent.

"How about I make this easy for you, William? Why don't you go home to your wife tonight and stay home? I can't do this anymore. I love you. I want to be the one who looks forward to you spending your entire day with me on Sundays and coming home from work to me on other days. I want it all from you. I refuse to continue to settle for less. So how about I eradicate you completely from my life? I can go back to who I used to be when it came to men, with no risk of heartbreak on my part, and you can go back to being Aujanae's faithful husband."

April had willed herself not to cry so that she could give her speech. When she was done talking, she let the pain pour from her heart through the tears from her eyes. She cried loudly as she continued to hold the phone, wanting badly to hang up, but not as prepared as she made out in her oration to break the connection from William.

William felt like crying himself, but knew tears would not solve anything for him right now. He guessed the easiest thing to do would be to do as April suggested and just end this thing right now with her, leaving while it was her choice. The easy was far more difficult than it sounded in reality. He warred in his head as his eyes stayed on the road. Trying to maintain focus under these trying circumstances was as difficult as everything else he had going on at the moment. Then he had an idea.

"April, why don't you call in sick to work? I'm about to do the same. We can spend the day together." He almost said "and I can get home in time to make Aujanae happy," but he did not think April wanted to hear about his wife right now. "We can talk about us when I get there."

It only took April a moment to decide. "I'll make the call now. I'll be here waiting when you get here." She hung up the phone.

William allowed his phone to disconnect from April. He then gave the voice command to dial his job.

"USA Bank. This is Analeisa. How can I help you?"

"Hi, Analeisa. This is William Rucker. Is Dale available?" Dale Rollins was his boss.

"No, William. He's on a conference call with some folks on the East Coast."

"I see. Do me a favor, please. Tell him that I'm not feeling well and I'm going to take the day off."

"I'm sorry to hear you're under the weather. I'll pray for you to feel better, and I will give the message to Mr. Rollins as soon as he's off the call."

"Thank you, Analeisa, on both parts." William hung up, jumped off the freeway at the next exit, and detoured his car to head to April's house.

Chapter Nine

Katrina arrived at the restaurant first and sat waiting in the small lobby for Maleeka to show up. When she saw Aujanae walk through the door she was pleasantly surprised.

"Aujanae." Katrina stood and waived Aujanae in her direction.

"Hi, Katrina." The two friends embraced then sat back down together.

"Do you eat here often? I've never seen you here before, and Maleeka and I come here at least once a week. We love the food here."

"Oh," Aujanae said, a little embarrassed. "Obviously Maleeka didn't tell you that I would be joining you two this afternoon. I hope it's not a problem."

Katrina was again surprised and again not unpleasantly so. Although she wanted to tell Maleeka all about the evening she shared with David, she did not think it was anything she could not share in front of Aujanae. But then again, David and Aujanae's husband, William, were cousins. She was sure Aujanae had met and knew all about David's relationship with Toriyana. Perhaps she should reconsider saying anything about it during lunch.

"No, it is not a problem at all. It is really good to see you," Katrina stated a little shakily. She hoped Aujanae did not notice or take her sudden apprehension the wrong way.

"Thank you, Katrina," Aujanae said as she hugged Katrina again.

Aujanae was so bogged down with her own issues she did not notice a thing. She was just happy Katrina and Maleeka welcomed her in her opportunity to get away from the house for a while. She took Billy, Jr. to her mother's house, promising to pick him up in a few hours. She thought she would do some shopping for herself after lunch when the two ladies returned to work, again taking more advantage of spending the money William enjoyed spending so much time making.

Maleeka walked in the door seconds later, giving the two ladies hellos and hugs. The trio was then seated immediately. The waitress took their beverage orders of Coca Colas all around and left to get them prepared. Maleeka and Aujanae sat on one side of the table, sharing a booth. Katrina sat on the other side alone.

"So, what have you been up to lately, Aujanae, besides looking fabulous? I see and talk to this chick all the time, so I pretty much know all of her business already," Maleeka said, pointing at Katrina once they were seated.

"You look marvelous yourself, Maleeka. Thank you so much again for letting me tag along with you two for lunch," Aujanae answered. "I saw you both in church yesterday, but I didn't have a chance to make my way over to say anything to either of you. It is always so crowded in the sanctuary after service. Billy usually just rallies me and B.J. out right after the benediction."

"How are William and that cute little son of yours doing?" Katrina asked politely.

"B.J. is great. He's so smart. He amazes me with something new every day." Aujanae beamed as she spoke about her child. "Billy is good." This time her expression changed drastically and both women noticed.

Maleeka quickly changed the subject in hopes of changing the vibe as well.

"So, Katrina, what had you so perky when I spoke to you this morning? Girl, your voice was all sing-song and whatnot. What's the news you wanted to share? I know it has to be good judging by the way you were talking."

Katrina had kind of hoped Maleeka did not bring up that subject while they were at lunch, but not saying something now would make Aujanae know she was the reason she had decided not to talk, since she was not originally invited to lunch. Katrina considered telling a little white lie, but nothing would come to mind. She then remembered Maleeka's opinion on her dating David. She figured if Aujanae did have something negative to say, it would be two against one. She just hoped it did not turn into something too unpleasant. Besides, she was anxious to share her great news with her best friend.

"Okay, I'll tell you since you won't stop badgering me about it," Katrina said in jest. "It happened. It finally happened," she said, grinning as she paused for dramatic effect.

"Girl, if you don't stop sitting over there with that goofy grin on your face and tell us what happened . . ." Maleeka said only half teasing.

Katrina finished her news. "Yesterday after church I went to the movies and then to dinner with David Mathis." Saying it out loud made Katrina feel as if she were reliving it all over again. She did a little dance in her seat then covered her face with her hands, acting like a teenager who just shared the news of her first date.

If there were ever polar opposite reactions, the two women sitting at the table with Katrina were perfect examples of it. Maleeka was grinning and beaming as hard as Katrina, while Aujanae stared at Katrina as if she said she had gone on a date with her husband.

"Oh my goodness, Katrina. No wonder you are so excited. Girl, I am so happy for you I could just bust. Now give me all the gritty details. Don't leave a single—"

Maleeka stopped her raving as she noticed the panicked look on Katrina's face. As she stared at her, she realized Katrina was staring at the horrifically pained and shocked look on Aujanae's face.

Katrina looked panicked because she thought Aujanae might not be as understanding as Maleeka about her going out with David, but she never imagined it would upset her to this degree. Now she was wishing she had just conjured up some lie. Aujanae looked like she was ready to kill her.

"What's wrong, Aujanae?" Maleeka asked, very concerned.

Just then the waitress returned with their sodas and asked if they were ready to order. Maleeka and Katrina always ordered the same thing whenever they ate there, so they had no need to look at the menu. And with the look on Aujanae's face, both Katrina and Maleeka were sure food was the last thing on her mind. Even the waitress looked a little skittish now.

"Uh, why don't I give you all a couple more minutes and I'll come back." She quickly left the table.

"What time did your date with David end last night?" Aujanae demanded of Katrina in the most unfriendly voice either of the other ladies had ever heard.

They both thought the question to be strange under the circumstances, but Katrina did not hesitate to answer.

"David dropped me off at my car at between eight and eight thirty," she said hesitantly.

"Aujanae, sweetie, what is wrong with you, really?" Maleeka was frightened for her friend. Her facial expression looked almost demonic. She knew all of that anger and pain had not come simply because Katrina announced she went out with David Mathis.

Aujanae ignored Maleeka as if she had not even heard her. In her state, she probably had not. She directed her statement to Katrina again.

"And you said you went directly from church, right?" Her voice was still as dreadful as before.

"Yes." Katrina was also frightened now.

The waitress reappeared cautiously. "Are you ladies ready to order?"

Maleeka took up the charge of ordering for everyone. Maleeka would have the chicken chimichanga. Katrina would have the taco plate. She decided to order the taco plate for Aujanae as well. It was hard to go wrong with tacos, though Maleeka was sure Aujanae would not touch a morsel of her food.

When the waitress left their table with their order, it seemed as if she had taken Aujanae's soul with her. She now sat at the table staring at nothing with a look of nothingness as well. Gone was the anger. Gone was the original joy she brought with her to the restaurant. She now just looked empty—empty and lost.

Maleeka scooted over just a bit in the booth she shared with Aujanae. She started off cautiously by first lifting Aujanae's hand and rubbing it softly. When Aujanae did not protest, she got bolder and put her arms around her to embrace her.

Aujanae then broke. She released the terrible hurt of just finding out that William lied to her yesterday in order to be with another woman. She cried right there in the restaurant. Right there in Maleeka's arms.

"I'm going to find our waitress and tell her to make our orders to go."

Katrina left the table for the few brief moments it took to locate their waitress. When she returned, she found both her friends still seated in the same position. She squeezed in on the opposite side of Aujanae, who sat on the outside, and placed her arms around her too. Neither Katrina nor Maleeka knew for sure what caused Aujanae's misery, but each assumed in their own heads it had something to do with her husband.

Katrina looked up to find the patrons in the restaurant staring at them. She supposed they did make an odd-looking trio. "Hey, girls, why don't we step outside while we wait for our food? We can sit in either one of our cars. I'll pre-pay for our food while you two go out and get settled," Katrina offered.

"No. I'll pay for it, Katrina. I told Maleeka lunch would be on me today," Aujanae said softly through her sobs.

Katrina started to protest, but Maleeka shook her head slightly to ward her off. Katrina got the hint that arguing with Aujanae about anything right now would probably not be best.

Aujanae cleaned her face with one of the napkins from the table. The ladies then headed toward the cashier's station. Maleeka told the gentleman what they were waiting for. He looked at the sadness surrounding them with pity and rang up their order without any further questions.

"Thank you, sir. I will come back in about five minutes to see if it's ready."

The cashier nodded his head.

The three ladies ended up sitting in Maleeka's Ford Explorer SUV. All three climbed in the back seat, with Aujanae seated in the middle. Maleeka opened the armrest in the front seat, took out some napkins from her stash, and silently offered them to Aujanae. Aujanae accepted the offer and again attempted to clean her face and compose herself.

"Do you want to talk about it, Aujanae?" Katrina asked compassionately. To both the other women's surprise, she began speaking immediately.

"Billy is having an affair. He's cheating on me. Billy left me and B.J. yesterday, telling me he was going to be with David, who was upset about his relationship with Toriyana. Sundays are usually the day reserved for the family because Billy has been *working* so much lately. I have been suspicious about it for a little while now, but Katrina just confirmed it when she said she was with David yesterday."

Katrina put her head down and closed her eyes. She felt horrible and responsible for the distressed state Aujanae was in now.

"Oh, Aujanae, I feel so awful for opening my big mouth. I can't believe I'm the one who made you feel this bad because I wanted to share how great I felt about my date. I am so sorry."

Aujanae looked at Katrina and saw the sincerity of her words and the guilt she felt. "No, no, Katrina. This is not your fault. I guess I needed to hear and find out for myself what I have been denying and avoiding for a few weeks now. Trust me, Kat. God wanted me to know the truth. There was no way any of us could have orchestrated this. This news came to me through divine revelation. God just used you to confirm what I have known but tried to ignore." Aujanae then began to sob again.

Maleeka reached across Aujanae from the back and grabbed Katrina's hand, giving her encouragement and hopefully assurance that this was in no way her doing.

Neither Katrina nor Maleeka said a word for a few moments. They just sat and allowed Aujanae to vent her grief.

"I'm going to go in and get our food. When I come back, why don't we go back to the community room or the chapel at the church, where we can have some privacy? We can talk or pray or whatever," Katrina suggested.

"Oh, no!" Aujanae protested softly. "You ladies are on your lunch break. I don't want to intrude or impose on either of your jobs." Aujanae made the objection softly. The truth was she really did not want to be alone right now.

"Don't you worry about that, Aujanae. I'm going to just call them at the job and let them know I have an emergency I need to deal with. They will see me tomorrow. There is nothing so pressing that it can't wait till then. You need us right now," Maleeka explained.

Katrina nodded her head in agreement. She then left to get their food. When she returned, Maleeka and Aujanae were in the front seats of Maleeka's truck. They decided Maleeka would drive them both to the church, and she would return with Aujanae to retrieve her car later. Aujanae agreed without hesitation. She did not trust that she could concentrate well enough to drive right now.

Katrina took the food to her car and headed for the church. The other two ladies followed her the short distance there. When they arrived, Katrina went to let Pastor Abraham know she had a crisis with a friend, who was also a member, and she would return to her desk at soon as she could. He gave her his okay to take as long as she needed. She then went and found Maleeka and Katrina in the church's small chapel. No conversation had started. Aujanae was actually in one of her crying spells when Katrina walked into the room. Maleeka was holding Aujanae.

"Why don't we give her some space? Let's just move over here a few seats. Let her have a moment to just pour it out," Katrina advised Maleeka quietly.

Maleeka remembered the lesson from their Christian sensitivity training class. The instructor told them that oftentimes when someone was in distress and crying, the discomfort they try to relieve when hugging that person or giving them tissue to wipe the tears is their own. The instructor said, "It makes us uncomfortable to see someone in pain, so we rush to alleviate it. But that is what's best for us, not necessarily the person who is suffering. Sometimes they just need to get it out without feeling our pity."

So she and Katrina moved away from Aujanae just a few steps. She was so caught up in her grief, both women realized, that she did not even notice their slight absence. When the crying subsided, she began to talk.

"Katrina, Maleeka, I'm so sorry. I did not mean to ruin your lunch or your entire afternoon with my drama."

Maleeka and Katrina stayed in their seats and spoke from there. "We know, Aujanae, but it's okay. We are your friends and we love you. We are willing to help you in any way we can," Maleeka said soothingly.

"Yes, we are. I don't know how much we can do other than listen to you. If William is in fact having an affair, how you handle it will be totally up to you, Aujanae. Neither Maleeka nor I have any right to interfere in your marriage, no matter what. But we are here to support you today and from here on out in whatever choices you make, okay?"

Katrina was taking the same stance with Aujanae as she had with Maleeka. She would just listen and do what she could to help without giving advice or judging.

"I don't even know what choices I have, Kat. I mean, I don't have a choice as to whether or not I love him. I do, plain and simple. I love my husband. I love my son. I love my family." Aujanae fought the tears that threatened to choke her again. She wanted to talk. She needed to figure this out.

"I have been ignoring the warning signs because I did not want them to be true. The alarms were ringing loud and clear, and I kept turning them off because I did not want to be in this position. I did not want to be faced with the possibility that I could lose my husband, my marriage."

Katrina hoped what she was about to say did not constitute advice. "Aujanae, cheating does not have to automatically mean the end of a marriage. I mean, if it is proven that William is seeing someone else, maybe you two can work through this. I hate to sound so cliché here, but you know the Bible says we can do all things through Christ who gives us strength. God can fix anything and anybody, Aujanae. I'm not saying you should stay. I'm not saying you should leave. I just don't want you to feel pressured into doing anything. Please seek the Holy Spirit and allow Him to guide you through everything."

Aujanae left her seat and walked toward the small altar. She stood there wordlessly for several seconds.

"Aujanae, when Darrin and I were dating, I found out he was seeing someone else. It was before we were engaged. I was so hurt. I know our situations are different. I mean, we weren't married, or like I said even engaged at the time, but my point is, we were able to get past it and stay together. I honestly don't even think about that time anymore. Our love, time, and God truly did help us overcome that situation."

Aujanae turned around to face the ladies. "Really, Mal? He cheated on you and you were able to forgive him?" Aujanae asked wistfully.

"To be honest, I really didn't classify it as cheating because he was not my husband. But that did not make it hurt any less. I loved him," Maleeka answered honestly.

Aujanae came back to sit with the women. "Did you know the other woman, Mal?"

The tone in Aujanae's voice made both Katrina and Maleeka believed she knew who the other woman might be, if there was indeed another woman.

"No. I had never met her. She called me on my phone and told me all about herself."

"Why do you ask, Aujanae? Do you think you know who the woman is that William might be having an affair with?" Katrina asked.

"Listen, Katrina. Please stop saying *maybe*, or *might be* or *if*. Billy is definitely having an affair, okay?" Aujanae spat.

"I'm sorry, Aujanae. I didn't mean anything by my remarks," Katrina replied, understanding full well that Aujanae was not snapping at her directly, but speaking from her pain.

"No. It's me. I'm sorry. I know you didn't." Aujanae apologized sincerely. "And to answer your question, yes. Yes, I believe I know who she is. She is a beautiful woman who joined our church a few weeks ago. I don't remember her name, but since she's joined, she always manages to find a seat not too far away from Billy and me on Sunday morning. Yesterday, though, she sat on the opposite side of the sanctuary, and Billy spent the better part of service staring in her direction."

"What? She's goes to this church?" Katrina asked incredulously.

Aujanae nodded.

"You said she joined about a month ago, right? Do you think they were messing around before she joined the church, or do you believe it just got started?" Maleeka asked, joining in on the indignation.

"I'm not really sure. Billy started working crazy hours just after B.J. was born, but I trusted him, and he did get a promotion. My suspicions about him having an affair started about four months ago. There was nothing any more extreme than his working late to give me pause then, but I woke from my sleep in wee hours of the morning on this particular night with an eerie feeling that Billy was seeing another woman. Since then my senses have been on full alert. So if it is this woman who just joined the church, I believe she did so to be even closer to my husband more often," Aujanae said with a confidence she did not wish she had at the moment.

"I think I know exactly who you are talking about, Aujanae. She probably did it to get a closer look at you too. She wanted to spy out her competition. That sneaky heffa," Maleeka spat.

"Maleeka! We are in the church chapel, for goodness' sake. Watch your mouth," Katrina admonished. "Besides, we are not one hundred percent sure of anything," Katrina said a little softer this time. She did not want to chastise her best friend too much, especially since she was thinking the exact same thing.

"I know you keep saying that to make me feel better, Kat, but trust me when I say I know. Billy's lie yesterday gave me all the proof I need. I may not be as sure about Ms. Beauty Queen, but it is a fact that my husband is cheating with someone." Aujanae now had fire in her voice. Anger had managed to sneak in past the hurt, even if just for a brief moment.

"I guess the big question is not who Billy is sleeping with, but what am I going to do about it no matter who it is?" She was again back to being miserable. The tears and sobs started up again instantly.

This time Katrina and Maleeka did wrap themselves around Aujanae, both forgetting about their Christian sensitivity training. It was not long before Aujanae's bout with the blues ended again.

"Oh my goodness. I know I'm supposed to do something other than fall apart here," she said with all the humor her torn heart could muster.

"Aujanae, you are supposed to do exactly what you are doing. You are supposed to be hurt, sad, angry, and everything else you feel. God feels your pain, and He will dry your tears in His time, in His way. Do not beat yourself up for how you are handling your distress," Katrina said lovingly.

Aujanae gently untangled herself from the arms of her friends. She stood up again as she used the tissues handed to her by Maleeka to wipe her face.

"Well, even as much as I hurt, I do know that I am and must continue to be a mother to my child. I need to get back to my car so I can go and get my son from my mother. Maleeka, are you ready to take me back to the restaurant?"

"Certainly, Aujanae. No problem. Let me grab my purse from over there and we can get going."

Katrina noticed the containers that held their lunch that not one of them bothered to touch. She passed each person their box as they all made ready to leave the chapel.

"Let's pray before we leave," Maleeka offered. The trio went and stood in front of the altar as she said the prayer.

"Our Father in Heaven, we come right now, Lord, so glad that we know who we can turn to in our times of trials and trouble. Lord, we come blessing Your name because we know You are there for us at all times, no matter the situation, problem, or circumstance. Lord, we praise You for Your son Jesus, who has laid down His life so that we may have the privilege of coming to You in prayer. Father, right now we come praying on behalf of our friend and Your child, Aujanae.

"Lord, You know her troubles. She is in pain, Father. She is facing a trial right now Lord, in her marriage. Father, right now, in the name of Jesus, we offer up her issue to You. Lord, we place it at this altar right now and we give it to You. Father, we ask that You touch her heart, her mind, and her spirit. Lord, give her the strength to endure as she continues to look to You for the wisdom and guidance on how to handle her situation.

"Lord, we come praying right now for her husband, William. We come asking that You touch him as well. Lord, bring him back to the man that You have called Him to be. Lord, remove from him the desire for this unsavory behavior and let him remember the covenant he made before You to his wife.

"Father God, we even come praying for the other person, Lord, whoever that may be. We ask, Lord, that you open her eyes if she is unknowing and remove the stoniness from her heart if she is aware.

"Lord, touch all who are involved in this painful situation. Have Your way and let there be glory even in this to You. This is my prayer in Jesus' name. Amen."

"Amen," both ladies said together.

Aujanae had once again begun to cry, but the tears were silent. She hugged Maleeka and then Katrina.

"Katrina, I hope you don't think I'm out of line for what I'm about to say to you, but I just want you to be careful. You know David has a girlfriend who lives in Detroit, yet you are all giddy about going on a date with a man who is in a committed relationship. I don't think that's right. I just want you to consider Toriyana's feelings. Do you think she would be giddy if she knew you and David went out last night?"

Katrina and Maleeka both stared at Aujanae like deer caught in headlights, but with different thoughts running through their heads.

Katrina understood all too well what Aujanae was saying. She had often recited a similar speech to Maleeka whenever she brought up the matter of her going after David Mathis. The guilt she suddenly felt kept her silent.

Maleeka, however, felt offended on behalf of her best friend. She understood Aujanae's pain because of her cheating husband, but she would not allow her to take such a grandiose stand on Toriyana's behalf and hurt her best friend in the process.

"Wait a minute, Aujanae. We are talking about apples and oranges here. I know you are hurt. You have every right to be. William is your *husband*. The two of you stood before God and made a covenant to be faithful to each other. If the woman you believe William is having an affair with knows that he is married, and I think we all believe she does if it's who we think it is, then she is a low-down skank. David and Toya . . ."

"Her name is Toriya—" Katrina started to correct Maleeka, but the look she received from her stopped her.

Maleeka continued. "David is not married or even engaged to his girlfriend; therefore, he is deemed a single man. And in that case, David's girlfriend cannot claim exclusivity. Monogamy is reserved for marriage. That is the way God set it up. There are no biblical principles governing boyfriend/girlfriend or significant other types of relationships. There is no harm in two single people enjoying each other's company. Please do not put Katrina in the same category as the tramp that is cheating with your husband." Maleeka's intention was to be firm but gentle in her reproof of Aujanae's reprimand of Katrina. She hoped she had succeeded. She was not trying to inflict anymore pain upon her.

"Your opinion is noted and valid, Maleeka. I'm not sure I agree with it completely, but I hear what you are saying," Aujanae said evenly. To Katrina she said, "I'm sorry if I offended you. I was not trying to. My statement was meant to be one of simple consideration and compassion for someone who I'm sure loves David. And if I'm honest with myself, there was probably a little bit of my own scorn in there as well. Forgive me, please," she sincerely pleaded with Katrina for her understanding.

"All is completely forgiven and forgotten." All three women hugged again.

"Let me grab my purse so we can leave and get you back to your son," Maleeka said as she walked the short distance to where her purse sat. When she got to her purse, she felt her phone vibrating inside. She pulled it out and saw she had two missed calls, a voice mail message, and two text messages from Darrin. She read the text.

"Thanks again so much for your ears and your hearts today, ladies. It's embarrassing to have to go through in front of you all, but at the same time, I'm glad I wasn't alone when I found out the truth. You guys have been great friends," Aujanae said sincerely. One final hug to Katrina, and then she was headed to the door of the chapel to leave.

Maleeka gave Katrina a departing hug as well. While in the embrace, she whispered in her ear, "Darrin said yes." Out loud she said, "I'll call you later."

Chapter Ten

William arrived at April's to find her still dressed in her bedclothes. Or perhaps she had changed from her work clothes and re-dressed in her nightwear. Either way he sliced it, William enjoyed the display of sweetness, completely and raw sexy that beheld him when he entered April's apartment. "Hello" had barely gotten out of her lips before he had gotten her out of her gown and into bed.

On the drive to April's apartment, all William could think about was the fear and pain he saw in Aujanae's eyes this morning. He now realized he had not thought about his wife once until that moment in the hour and fifteen minutes he had been at April's. This woman who lay in his arms in the middle of the day captivated his thoughts, mind, and body whenever he was with her. If he was honest with himself, he had to admit she mesmerized him even when they were not in each other's presence.

While April slumbered lightly in his arms, William tried to again reason with himself on what was best for everyone involved in this mess he created when he started having this affair with April.

He knew the obvious. Aujanae was his wife, the woman he pledged to love, honor, cherish, and be faithful to for the rest of his life. She was the mother of his child, a child he loved more than life. He knew that it was his duty, his obligation, and in some small way, even his desire to cut himself loose from April and return to his married life—his life without the drama, stress, lying, sneaking and manipulating. Yes, the obviously right thing to do would be to end things now with April. He believed in his heart that he should tell Aujanae all about the affair, beg for her forgiveness, and rededicate himself to her and to God. As painful as it would be for April and even for him, he knew what he had to do—what he would do.

April stirred in his arms the moment he had come to his conclusion. She opened one eye, looked at him, smiled, and snuggled closer to his body. And in that small span of time, those two and a half seconds, his resolve nearly crumbled.

"So are we going to spend the remainder of our time together in bed, or would you like to do something outside the four walls of this room?" April purred as she stretched her legs beneath the bed sheets and intertwined them with William's.

William's libido stirred, and the thought of remaining in bed did not sound like a half bad idea.

"The idea of laying here with you for the rest of our time together sounds great, sexy lady, but I think we should at least map out a strategy for feeding ourselves."

"Aw, is my man hungry? Do I need to feed my baby? Did you work up an appetite, honey?" April grinned as she looked at William. Her excitement at having William with her was palpable. It permeated every square inch of her bedroom and her soul. This was actually the first time in their fourteen-month relationship that they had played hooky from work and spent this time of the day together. The earliest they had ever been together before was lunchtime on a Saturday. Their little tryst were usually reserved for the evening hours. April knew she could definitely get used to this.

"I am getting a little hungry. Besides, we were supposed to be talking about you and me, remember? So
let's get up and go into a room where we can think
more clearly," William said seriously as he began moving away from April in the bed.

April heard the grave set of his tone. She felt the
instant loss of heat as he extracted himself from her.
The giddiness she felt a few moments ago was now
replaced with trepidation. She did not want to make a
scene though, at least not yet. William was right. They
definitely needed to talk. She needed to know if there
was any chance of him leaving his wife to come and be
with her forever. The fact that he came to her yesterday
on command and that he suggested coming back this
morning were both signs in her favor, so she would not
let the starkness in his voice get the best of her, at least
not until she heard what he had to say once and for all
about the future of their relationship.

"You're right, William. We must talk. Why don't you
go on and take a shower while I whip up something for
you to eat? I'll shower while you are eating." April kept
her voice even, not sugary, but not salty either. She did
not want to play her hand one way or the other just yet.

"You're not going to eat?" William asked, concerned
as he made his way to the master bath.

"Maybe. Right now I'm not that hungry," April said
as she left the bedroom.

April decided against making a big breakfast. In
actuality, it was closer to lunchtime than breakfast.
She decided to whip up some scrambled eggs, slice a
mango, and reheat the leftover lasagna from yesterday.
This would be brunch versus breakfast or lunch.

While she worked in peace, she thought in turmoil.
Her heart was about as mangled as the eggs she was
beating. She loved William so much. She did not mean

to fall in love with him, but she did, and for her there was no turning back now. She refused to continue to share him with his wife. She knew that was smug and despicable on her part, but it was also the truth. April hated the thought of him doing what he had every right to do with her, with Aujanae. She could no longer stomach him kissing, making love to, or even sharing a meal with any woman other than her.

Today absolutely had to be the day. Today he either had to tell her he was leaving his wife to be with her, or he had to tell her he was leaving her life for good.

"Hello, Katrina."

"Hello, David," Katrina replied as she answered her cell phone. Hearing his voice caused Katrina's smile to stretch from one wall to the other in her office area.

David was pretty thrilled as well. "How has your day been so far?"

That question reminded her of the situation she was involved in earlier with Aujanae and her pain. She was then reminded of the critical remark Aujanae made about her seeing someone else's boyfriend. Her joy then plummeted a few levels. She did not want to upset David, so she debated as to whether she should mention Toriyana and if she should try to find out where he and she were in their relationship.

"I hope you had a great time yesterday. I had an amazing time," David said.

Katrina could hear the sincerity in his voice. His enthusiasm seemed to match hers—or at least what it was before she allowed her brain to see past her over-zealous heart. She was so caught up in her musings, the silence stretched between them after David's last statement.

"Katrina, are you still there?"

"I'm sorry, David. Yes. Uh . . . I'm at work, so I was splitting my concentration between two things." Katrina was happy she could at least be partially honest.

"Is everything okay, Katrina? Your mood seemed to have switched suddenly," David asked pensively. "Maybe it's a bad time. Why don't you call me when you get off work?"

Though Katrina was a little perturbed about his relationship status, she was not ready to end the call. She so enjoyed hearing his voice. She enjoyed the connection even though it was just through the phone lines right now.

"Uh . . . no. I'm fine. I deserve a quick break."

"You sure?"

"Yes," Katrina said as she attempted to put a little perk in her voice. "So how has your day been?"

"Uh-uh. I asked you first."

Katrina laughed. "Yes, you did. You probably don't want to hear my answer though."

"Why? What happened?" David asked, his voice laced with concern.

Katrina thought about the events that covered her lunch break. She realized she could not share too much with David because one, she did not want to blab Aujanae's business. Secondly, David was William's cousin, so telling him anything would cause a conflict of interest. So she answered carefully.

"Well, I'm not really at liberty to talk about it. It's kind of confidential, but I had to help a member, a friend, with a very painful, very personal issue today during my lunch break. She was dealing with an awful situation."

"I see. I'm sorry you had to deal with that. I'm even sorrier for your friend. I pray she gets through whatever it is."

Wow. David is an extraordinary man, Katrina thought. She simply swooned as she held her small phone. "Thank you, David. That's sweet of you."

"Speaking of sweet, I was calling to find out when we can go out again. Like I said, I enjoyed myself a great deal yesterday. I look forward to hanging out with you again."

Katrina could not believe the mixed emotions she was experiencing at that moment. She loved how David made her feel: excited, happy, warm inside. She hated how knowing about Toriyana made her feel: deceitful, duplicitous, unjustified, and guilty. Maleeka invaded her thoughts, saying words like "justified," "fair," and "no ring on his fingers."

"Katrina, either you are very busy or very uninterested in what I am saying to you. I'm going to let you go now so you can get back to work. Hopefully I will hear from you soon," David said disappointedly.

"No, David, wait. Please don't hang up. It's not that I'm all that busy with work. I am honestly just a bit distracted by my friend's issues and some things she said this afternoon. I would love to hang out with you again very soon. Just say when." Katrina knew she sounded a bit desperate, but she was more concerned with David hanging up the phone thinking she was not interested.

"Wow. It must be pretty serious. Look, I was thinking about us going out again on Friday, but in light of your very tough lunch, how about I take you to dinner tonight? Maybe I can help you take your mind off your friend's sadness for just a little while. What do you say?"

Without any further hesitation or delay, Katrina said, "Yes."

David chuckled at her quick response. "Okay. What time do you get off and do you want to meet someplace or do you want me to pick you up?"

Katrina's first thought was to have him pick her up straight from work, but she re-thought that. She did not want anyone who may be at the church to see the two of them together on a Monday evening. Someone else may be thinking the same way Aujanae was earlier. Just about everyone at the church knew David had a girlfriend back in Detroit.

"Why don't you pick me up at my apartment? I live on McDowell and Seventy-fifth Avenue." She gave him the address and apartment number.

"That will work. I'll be there about six thirty. Is that all right?"

"That's perfect. Thanks, David."

"No. Thank you for agreeing to hang out with me again. Think about what you want to eat, and we'll decide when I see you tonight. Bye, Katrina." He then hung up.

"This looks wonderful, April. Thanks." William came in and sat at the kitchen counter where April had placed his food.

April kissed William's cheek. "You are quite welcome. I'm going to take a shower and we can talk when I'm done. Enjoy your food while I'm gone."

"Have you already eaten?" William asked as he began digging into his food.

"No. Like I said, I'm not really hungry right now. Maybe later. Maybe while we are conversing." April left the room and went to take her shower.

She returned approximately fifteen minutes later. William knew that had to be the fastest shower and dressing expedition on record for this woman. He was quite familiar with April's normal routing of getting ready for just about everything. And no matter what the occasion she was getting ready for, it was never less than a forty-five minute routine.

"That was quick, but as usual you smell great," William said in surprise.

"Thank you. I just want to get on with this, William. We both agree that we need to talk, and we both know what we need to talk about. I guess I'm kind of anxious to find out what you have to say."

April sat in the second seat at the counter next to William. After sitting for about three minutes, just long enough for William to finish his food, April decided they needed to move to the living room sofa. The bar chairs that decorated this area were built for beauty, not for comfort. April headed to the living room first. William put his plate in the dishwasher then joined her.

They both sat on the sofa, close together, hand in hand. They sat quietly, both afraid. William was afraid of what he needed to say. April was afraid of what he was going to say. They remained quiet for several moments, just holding hands and silently thinking of what the future held for them both. Finally, April got restless waiting for William to speak.

"William, let me lay this on the line. I will not continue to be your mistress. I can't. I love you too much to continue to watch you leave me, knowing you are going home to be with your wife. Sharing you has become impossible for me, and I won't do it anymore."

There. She had said it. Period. Point blank. April stared at William, who had now hung his head. April took that as a not-so-positive sign. She wanted to tear her heart from her chest in an effort to ease the mounting pain.

William began rubbing the hands he held, taking deep breaths, preparing himself to respond to April's declaration. April removed her hands from his, using one to lift William's bowed head and then placing them both on her lap.

William looked into her face. She had on no makeup. Her hair was pulled into a ponytail at the back of her head. She was fresh-faced and void of any of the trappings that supposedly made her glamorous, and right then she was more gorgeous than when she went through all the rituals to beautify herself.

"April, I care for you so deeply. I think it's even fair to say I love you."

April smiled for the first time since she left the bedroom to make breakfast. William had never before said he loved her. The pain in her chest lessened just a bit at hearing those three words.

William saw the smile and his heart flipped in his chest. He knew that she loved him, but it did something to him to be able to see how much those words from him meant to her. A knot formed in his throat, causing him to nearly choke on what he was about to say.

"I hear what you're saying, April, about not wanting to be second or to share me with my wife. But the truth of the matter is you are second—"

Before he could finish, April visibly recoiled. She moved to the far end of the sofa and pulled her legs beneath her, balling herself up in that corner. But she did not say anything. William continued.

"What I mean by that is Aujanae was in my life first. April, she was my wife before I ever laid eyes on you. She is the mother of my child. She is the woman I committed my life to forever. I'm not ready to leave her. I can't leave her."

April slowly closed her eyes as the anguish she had no power to stop gradually washed over her, invaded her soul, and caused her temples to pound. The head-ache that came fast and hard caused her ears to ring. She moved her hands quickly to cover her ears in an attempt to stop the ringing—or perhaps it was to stop herself from hearing what William just said play over and over again. She held her hands so tightly to her ears it took her a moment to realize that William was still speaking.

"I understand your all-or-nothing stance. You defi-nitely deserve better. I wish I could be the man to give you better, but I'm not. All I can do is apologize for the pain I have caused, because I can't be that man." Wil-liam attempted to reach for April, but she shooed his hand away. He did not press the issue.

April had known it was possible that William would choose his wife over her. She knew it would hurt if it came to this. She just was not prepared for the level of pain that she was experiencing. She was so hurt by Wil-liam's refusal to give up his wife that she almost con-sidered rescinding her ultimatum. If having only part of William in an effort to keep him in her life would eliminate some of the grief she was feeling, perhaps that made more sense than losing him altogether.

"William . . ." Just saying his name made her hurt more, and she started to cry. "William, I've played this game a hundred times before . . . and as far . . . as I was concerned, I had . . . always won. Never before had I put my heart . . . my heart on the table. I played dirty . . . and I played until . . . my opponent ran out of chips. Never before had I gambled anything . . . of my own. But with you . . . I gambled everything. Every-thing!" April paused to catch her breath, but she stayed put. She made no attempts to wipe the moisture that poured from her eyes or nose.

"I gambled it all, William, and I lost it all: my heart, my soul. Heck, I'm sitting here wondering if I am even losing my mind. I have come up completely empty."

When April stopped talking, William considered trying to touch her to console her once again, but stopped himself. Something in her slumped posture told him her body was now off limits to him in any way, shape, or form. He just watched as she hung her head, hugged herself, and cried. He sat still, feeling completely helpless and responsible for her turmoil. When she began to speak again, he pulled himself from his self-pitying revelry to pay attention.

"I messed up, William. I made a mistake. But what are mistakes other than weights that we lift in an effort to make us stronger? I heard that in a movie I watched as I sat here alone this past Saturday."

April got up from the couch and stood directly in front of William. It was now her turn to reach for his hands. Unlike her, he did not resist. She pulled him to his feet and wrapped her arms around him strongly, fiercely. He returned her embrace with the same fervor as she sobbed on his shirt front.

April began speaking again as she looked up from the front of his shirt directly into his eyes. "William, you apologized a moment ago. I think I owe you an apology also. I pressured you to put more of yourself into this than you wanted to. I selfishly played with your chips as well so that I could hit the jackpot. I played on your weakness to resist. But I guess this game is over now, right?"

William was not sure if the question was rhetorical or if she wanted him to give her a finite answer. He stayed silent until she prodded him again for an answer.

"It is over, isn't it, William?" April asked as she licked her lips, making one last desperate attempt to get him to say the words that would eradicate all of her pain.

William hesitated and questioned his own pause. Did he pause because he was not eager to hurt her again, or did he stall because he was unsure of his answer?

"It has to be, April. I can't give you what you really want, and I won't keep hurting you like this." Regardless of whether he knew exactly how he felt, he did know right from wrong for sure, so he gave the *right* answer.

April stepped completely out of the embrace, but continued to look in his eyes. There she saw uncertainty, skepticism even. She then checked herself, wondering if she was just seeing what her heart wanted to be there.

No, William was right. It was time for this to end. William would probably always remain in her heart, but he would no longer control her existence. It was time for her to let go of William and perhaps to let go of her way of dealing with men in general. This incident had her so afraid, too scared to ever risk this kind of pain again.

She knew this would require some major changes in how she lived and viewed her life. In fact, she would begin by continuing to attend church on a regular basis. April was not sure if she would remain at William's church and give him the pleasure of still being able to look at her at least once a week, but she knew church would be a part of the new life she would start.

April straightened her spine and added some bravado to her voice. The boldness was something that she would fake more than she would actually feel.

"Then it's time for you to go. I hope you find nothing but happiness in your marriage from this day forward. Now, please leave. Let yourself out." She turned and left him standing in the middle of her living room floor as she headed to her bedroom.

William stood there for several seconds, wondering if it was even possible for him to now just go home and have a happy marriage after what he had experienced with April. Could he possibly forget about April? Forget the joy they shared, their passion, their commonality? He even wondered, as he finally decided to walk out the door, in his heart of hearts, if he even wanted to.

Chapter Eleven

At 6:28 P.M. David rang the bell to Katrina's apartment.

Katrina had spent the rest of her afternoon at work in anticipation and in bewilderment about her date with David this evening. She was excited about the chance to be with him again, just the two of them. She was also confused about whether she should be, considering he had a girlfriend. She then tried settling her mind on the fact that perhaps he and Toriyana had broken up. She was also plagued by whether she should even bring up the question, or she should just be happy with the fact that he wanted to spend time with her. When David arrived to pick her up, Katrina was no less perplexed. She answered the door vowing to keep her mouth closed on the subject.

"Hey there. You made it and right on time. I like that," Katrina said happily as she let him in the door.

"Yeah. And it looks as if you are ready right on time. Now that's a rarity for a woman." David laughed as he reached for Katrina for a hug.

She returned his embrace and instantly all insecurities about his relationship status vanished from her mind to be replaced with her best friend's edict of "if he is not married, then he is single. Single means datable."

"Have you decided where you would like to eat?" David asked after releasing Katrina

"No. I thought we could decide together once you got here. We have quite a few choices right up the street from here. There's Olive Garden, Red Lobster, and Texas Road House on Seventy-fifth Avenue. Then a little further west you have Red Robin, Carrabba's Italian Grill, a Hawaiian barbecue spot . . ."

"Okay, okay. You are making me dizzy here," David joked. I love Italian food. Are you cool with Olive Garden, or would you prefer the Italian Grill spot?" he asked

Katrina thought for a half second then said, "Olive Garden works for me. It is literally only forty-five seconds from my apartment."

Katrina and David left the apartment and headed for the restaurant. David found Katrina was absolutely right. The drive from her place to Olive Garden was less than a minute. That left no time for talking. They were unable to have any real conversation until they were seated at their table.

"So, Mr. Mathis, you love Italian food, huh?"

"I do. I do. I dare even say it's one of my favorites. Steak is actually my favorite food."

"Interesting. I'm surprised you didn't choose the Texas Road House then."

"I ate steak at The Cheesecake Factory yesterday, remember? I try not to eat too much red meat, even though I love it."

"Health conscious. Cool."

"Don't get excited. My stomach does more protesting than my doctor, trust me."

They both laughed. Just then the waiter came over to take their drink orders. They gave him their selections, peach tea for Katrina and Coke for David.

"So, while we are on the subject of favorites, tell me a few of yours," David asked.

"Okay. My favorite pastime is reading. Any reading—the Bible, fiction, self-help, whatever—but my favorite genre is romance."

"Now it's my turn to say 'interesting,'" David replied with a head nod. "Are you a romantic?"

"Oh, yes. I love the books, the movies, the poems, the couples who are open to public displays of affection. I love it all. I am definitely a romantic." Katrina blushed as David smiled at her enthusiasm about romance.

"Being that you are so in love with love, I'm surprised you are not in a relationship or married, *Miss Hartsfield*."

He did have to go there, Katrina thought. Now she was back to thinking about his relationship with Toriyana. Ironically, David's mind automatically switched to that gear as well. They both sat in the booth, eerily quiet, until their waiter returned to take their order.

"Have you all decided what you are having this evening?" he asked politely.

"I'll have the classic lasagna," Katrina replied mechanically.

David looked over the menu quickly. "And I'll have the uh . . . Tour of Italy," David answered blandly.

The waiter asked the typical soup or salad, etc. questions and left the table, leaving the couple drowning in their silence.

"So . . . speaking of relationships, what's up with you and your girl in Detroit? Toriyana, right?" Katrina's voice shook as she pretended like she was not sure of his girlfriend's name.

She knew she was being silly. She knew this was only her second date with David. She knew part of her wanted to know what was really going on with him, but another part of her was worried about what the truth was. But the question was out there now, so she had to just ride out the answer.

"What do you mean exactly? What do you want to know?" David asked feebly.

Katrina heard his hesitancy, but she needed to know. She could not handle this obscure view of his circumstances any longer. She needed to know exactly where she stood with him because she was in love with him. She needed to know if there was room for allowing this to grow, or if she should stunt it all right now.

"I mean, does she know that we were together last night or that we are together right now?" Katrina could not believe how nervous she was.

"No," was his one-word, non-emotional answer.

Katrina expected a little more, but that was all she got without further prodding.

"Is it that you are hiding it from her, or that it no longer matters to her?" Even in her anxiety, Katrina thought her questioning to be clever.

David thought her to be shrewd with her curiosity as well. He gave her a slight smirk. Before he decided whether to respond with a cunning retort or to just answer her seriously and straight up, the waiter returned with their food.

He placed each of their meals in front of them. "Is there anything else I can get for either of you?"

"Could you please refill our drinks?" David asked.

"Certainly." The waiter left and returned almost instantly with a fresh peach tea and Coke. "Is there anything else?"

"I think we're fine for now. Thank you." This time it was Katrina who replied.

David said a quick blessing over their food and the two began to eat before the subject at hand was brought up again.

"The truth of the matter, Katrina, is Toriyana doesn't know about last night or tonight because I haven't told her," David began suddenly. "The answer to the flippant part of your question is yes. Yes, it would matter to her if she knew we were together last night and again tonight."

"So you are hiding it from her?"

"I don't know if I'm hiding it. I just haven't told her yet," David stated, trying to sound more casual than he actually felt.

"Yet! So you do plan to tell her, correct?"

Katrina realized she was being snide, but she did not like feeling like the secret other woman. Her thought reminded her of her friend Aujanae's situation and how Maleeka referred to the other woman in that case as a skank. Katrina did not want to be seen as or feel skanky.

Both parties took a moment to consume more of their meals. Though Katrina was a little uncomfortable with the conversation, she found herself to be grateful they were having it. Now that they were talking about the big pink elephant in the room, she realized she was better off knowing the truth about everything than assuming that her fantasy of the situation was real.

"Katrina, can I be totally honest with you?" David asked seriously.

"Please do, David. I never expect anything less from you."

"Toriyana is my girlfriend. We have tried very hard to make this long distance relationship work. It has been difficult, but we have managed to do an okay job of it. We do our best to see each other as often as our time and finances will permit. We were scheduled to see each other in a couple of weeks. She was supposed to fly out and spend a few days here in Phoenix, but her mother had an unexpected health challenge that will prevent her from coming as planned. This means we will probably be unable to see each other again until Thanksgiving when I go home." David took a breath to take a bite of his meal and a sip of his drink.

Katrina continued to eat her food while also trying to digest David's first line. *"Toriyana is my girlfriend." Not was, but is,* she thought.

David resumed his dialogue. "Don't get me wrong. I totally understand Tori having to postpone our plans due to her mother's illness, but it just made me start to wonder if I can continue to deal with the distance between us."

Katrina felt her heart perking as she intently listened to David speak. Maybe the *is*, is not currently a *was*, but maybe he will finally decide he can't deal as he stated.

"I mean, there are crucial times in a relationship when one party needs to physically be able to support the other party, and that is missing from our relationship because we live on opposite sides of the country from one another. I don't know. I just think that perhaps she and I are being overly optimistic about our ability to sustain our relationship under the circumstances."

Katrina had to consciously stop herself from grinning as she listened to David speak about the possibility of his relationship with Toriyana ending. She also had to stop herself from reading too much into what he was saying. She said she wanted the truth, so she would not assume anything, even if what she was hearing sounded ridiculously close to definite demise to her.

"Do I love Tori? Absolutely. But unless one of us is willing to make the concession and she either move here or I go back to Detroit, I don't see it lasting between us. And I know Tori. She will not relocate to Arizona unless she does it as my wife, or at least my fiancée."

Whoa, Nelly! Did this speech just take a very sudden and dramatic turn in the opposite direction? Love? Fiancée'? Wife? Where did those words come from? Katrina thought.

Before she could stop it, a piece of the bread she had just put in her mouth went down the wrong pipe and she began coughing uncontrollably. She picked up her tea and drank to push down the bread. David immediately left his side of the table and joined her in her seat. He removed the tea from her hand and then pushed both of her arms above her head until the coughing subsided. He then gave her back her glass.

"Now drink this slowly, okay?" Katrina did as she was instructed.

"Are you okay, ma'am?" the waiter returned and asked.

Katrina nodded her head. The waiter accepted her affirmation and went to check on another table. Realizing that the waiter had heard her antics, she thought that the other patrons who sat near her must have been witness to the small fiasco as well. She looked around to see people staring at her with sympathy and became a little embarrassed. Her embarrassment, however, paled in comparison to the contempt she felt over David's last few sentences.

"Are you sure you're okay?" David asked as he slowly rubbed her back.

'I'm fine, David. I hope I didn't embarrass you as much as I did myself," Katrina said warily.

"Of course I'm not embarrassed. I'm just glad you're good. You scared me for a moment." David gave Katrina a tight hug then returned to his side of the table.

Katrina felt his closeness and absence, both in an instant. She knew she really wanted David Mathis all to herself. Tonight the realization of just how badly slammed into her like a ton of bricks.

"Well, that is the truth about my relationship with Toriyana."

David picked up the conversation where they left off, but it took Katrina a moment to get back on the same page. She was still a little shaken by her choking episode, but even more so by his unclear statements about his relationship. At the end of the whole thing, she was unsure if David wanted to be with Toriyana or not. Yes, he loved her, but he was unhappy with the distance that separated them. He seemed pretty certain she would move to Phoenix if he married her, but he did not sound as if he was ready to make that leap. So at the end of the day, where did that leave her?

"Okay, David. You and Toriyana are still in a relationship. She is still expecting monogamy from you, at least until you tell her different. So why are you here with me behind her back?"

Wow! Straight up and blunt, David thought. But he really could not blame her. She deserved to know the truth and how all of that truth affected her.

"Katrina, you say it's behind her back, and I can acknowledge that it is, but it's not so much that I'm hiding this from her. I just don't think there's anything to really tell her just yet. I mean, I'm here with you because I think you're pretty, sweet, and generally a very nice person. What would be the point in telling her that? I think it would only serve to hurt her. Why would I want to intentionally do that?"

David knew he was grasping at straws. What he told Katrina was a watery version of the truth, because he did not want to readily admit he was in fact hiding their dates from Toriyana because he did feel a little guilty about seeing her. Katrina's next question drove that point home.

"Well, if taking me out will hurt her, then why do it, David? Especially if you say you love her."

That David could answer in complete truth. "I like you, Katrina. I have known for a while that you have been attracted to me."

Katrina blushed so bright she was sure the entire restaurant was as aware of it as they were of her choking incident. And the compliments continued.

"But you were never overtly flirtatious or disrespectful to my relationship. You are classy, spiritual, intelligent, and beautiful. Without realizing it, you made it very difficult not to open my heart to you just a bit. Add all of your beautiful qualities to the fact that the distance was putting a strain on my relationship with Toriyana, and it totals up to an irresistible desire to spend time with an amazing woman."

David's answer did nothing to strengthen the case she was trying to build against him. If it were possible, she was even more attracted to him now than she was initially. If he kept talking like that, she might slip up and tell him she loved him.

"Wow. Thank you for saying all those nice things about me, David," she said longingly.

"What I said about you were honest things, Katrina."

David stared at her so intently. She stared back. In his eyes he saw truth, compassion, and respect. In her eyes he saw a passionate innocence, admiration, and something he might dare liken to love.

"Katrina, I'm not trying to make you out to be my rebound chick or a substitute for Toriyana. You are too good for that. I have a sincere attraction to you, and I acted on it. I have convinced myself that because I am literally a single man, I am free to go out with you, and I'm going to stand on that."

"Wow," Katrina said again. "You sound like you have been talking to Maleeka. That is her philosophy about couples who are unmarried or unengaged."

David laughed. "That is exactly the same thing Darrin told me about her this morning."

David reached for Katrina's hands across the table. She obliged. "But you are right. I do need to be honest with her, with both of you. Tonight I've told you how I feel. Tomorrow I will tell her. It's too late in Detroit to call her tonight."

"Thank you for sharing with me tonight, David. Sharing your time, your thoughts about me, and what you are going through in your relationship. I must admit I was a little wary of what to think about all of this knowing you have a girlfriend. I tried to be progressive like you and Maleeka, but I was kind of challenged with that." Katrina snickered. "But I like hanging out with you, and I wouldn't mind continuing to do that if it's still cool with you," she said hopefully.

"I would like that very much," David responded happily.

"Will the two of you be having dessert tonight?" the waiter asked as he reappeared.

"Yes," David replied quickly to the waiter. To Katrina he said, "This just gives me an excuse to keep you out with me longer."

Chapter Twelve

After being dropped off at her car, Aujanae went straight to her mother's house to pick up her son. When she got there, however, she realized she was too emotionally drained to handle Billy Jr. She decided it would be best if she left him there. She cleared it with her mother, who was all too thrilled to have her grandson spend the entire night with her. Aujanae praised God for the blessing of her mother and headed home.

On the drive to her house she decided to call William at work. She wanted to know what it would now feel like to hear his voice—the voice of the man who had been lying to her and more than likely cheating on her. She attempted his cell phone first, but when it went straight to voice mail, she assumed he had turned it off because he was in a meeting of some sort. So instead of leaving a message on his voice mail, she decided to call his assistant and see if she could pull him out of whatever he was doing for just a moment. She was sure this move would totally catch William by surprise. The only time she ever did this before was when she went into labor with Billy Jr.

"USA Bank. This is Analeisa. How can I help you?"

"Hi Analeisa. This is Aujanae Rucker."

"Hello, Ms. Rucker. It's been a little while since I have heard your voice. William must be pretty sick if he has to have you call to check in for him. When he called off work this morning, I was kind of surprised that he would actually take the day off, even though he is sick. Tell your husband not to worry about what's going on here at the office. We can manage one day without him. He just needs to concentrate on resting and getting better."

Aujanae was initially confused by Analeisa's statement, but it quickly hit her like a ton of bricks. William had taken the day off by telling them at the office that he was sick. It did not take her as long to figure out where he went when he left the house this morning, however.

"Uh . . . you know what, Analeisa? You're right. I am going to hang up this phone and tell Billy he can just wait until he returns tomorrow to discuss the dealings of the office. I will take good care of my husband, and I promise to send him back to you all in the morning." Aujanae quickly disconnected the call.

"Wow! This day just keeps getting better and better," Aujanae said out loud sarcastically.

To her surprise, when she arrived home, William's car was in the driveway. Aujanae was stunned. Could it possibly be true? Maybe, just maybe, William was home from work sick and had not been with his little hoochie mama.

No. No. She was not going to do this to herself this time. She was not going to allow her heart to keep her naïve and in the dark. She was going in this house, knowing that her husband was involved with another woman, refusing to be lied to anymore.

Aujanae entered the house and found William sitting in the family room on the sofa, flipping through channels on the television. He turned when he heard her enter.

"Hey, baby. Where have you been? You didn't mention you were going out today."

"I could ask you the same thing. You said you would be home from work early, but I wasn't expecting you this early."

William got up from the couch and stood in front of Aujanae as she stood in front of the kitchen island.

"I missed you. Since we didn't get to spend yesterday together like we usually do, I found myself longing for your company, so I left the job early."

Wow! Aujanae thought. Her husband stood right in front of her, lying through his teeth, while she could smell the other's woman fragrance all over him. When he reached for her, she recoiled.

William lifted an eyebrow, wondering what could possibly be bothering Aujanae. He knew the possibilities, but could not fathom how she could really know anything. He began to play things cautiously.

"What's wrong, sweetheart? Have you had a rough day?"

"You don't know the half of it," Aujanae answered cryptically. "You smell . . . nice. Is that a new brand of cologne you're wearing?"

William's heart skipped a beat and his breath caught in his throat. Aujanae knew something. He could hear it in the foreign tone she was using. The woman standing before him did not sound like his wife. He was totally caught off guard by Aujanae's question and her demeanor. Since he was not sure how to handle her stance just yet, he decided to defer.

"Where's B.J., baby?"

Aujanae stared directly into William's eyes. There she saw confusion and fear. These were not emotions she was accustomed to seeing in her husband, but she recognized them still the same. She decided to play along with his little game of diversion for just a few moments to see how much more he would lie to her.

"He's at my mother's house. I took him over there while I went to have lunch with Maleeka and Katrina, my friends from church. After lunch I decided I needed a little time to myself so instead of picking him up, I asked Mom if she minded keeping him overnight." Aujanae kept her voice as even as she could, considering how angry she was becoming as she continued to breathe the other woman's fragrance.

"Oh. Sounds cool. Did you have a good time with the ladies?" William asked, still a little nervous about Aujanae's whole aura.

Aujanae had had enough. It was time for him to answer some questions. She walked into the family room, trying to put some distance between herself and the sickening scent on her husband. He followed closely on her heals, though. She was granted a little reprieve when she went to sit on the sofa and he chose the love-seat instead.

Aujanae crossed her legs and began bouncing her left calf up and down as she stretched her arms across the back of the sofa.

"It's interesting you should ask that question, honey. My time with the ladies was . . . fascinating, for lack of a better term. I'll tell you all about it in a minute. But first, tell me, how long have you been home?"

William was finding out that guilt was a horrible emotion. It made the senses overly inflamed when they did not necessarily have to be. William, knowing what he had been up to for over a year, sat with the sick feeling that his wife knew something simply because there was something to know. But how could she have found out the truth? He had been very careful to keep his tracks covered. He told absolutely no one about him and April's affair, so no one could have told her other than April, and he was fairly certain she had not said a word. The most lax he had been had been in the past two days by going to see April on a Sunday, the day he was supposed to be off limits to her, and today when he called in sick to work.

William knew he needed to say something to Aujanae. His hesitation was surely making an already uncomfortable situation even more awkward.

"I . . . uh . . . came home about an hour or two ago. Like I said, I missed you. I told them at work that I was going to take a half personal day so I could come home to you."

William's lie sounded sick even to himself. He hoped it was only because he knew the truth, not because he was being a terrible liar right now.

"So you went to work for half a day, and then came straight home? Is that what you're saying, Billy?" Aujanae sounded like a district attorney on cross examination.

"What is with this third degree, Aujanae? Why are you speaking to me like I'm a child who missed curfew?" William's guilt and nervousness was now turning to frustration because he felt himself losing total control of this situation that was obviously brewing with his wife.

Aujanae sat quietly for a few moments, just staring at William through eyes that had been reduced to mere slits. She had never before been a violent woman, but something inside of her made her want to pick up the lamp from the end table and hurl it at his head, hoping to hit him in his lying mouth.

"How, Billy? How can you sit there and just keep stringing those lies together?" Aujanae's voice sounded foreign even to herself. Anger had taken up residence in her bones and it propelled her to want to hurt and humiliate William as she had been hurt and humiliated. She, however, would do it with her words instead of her body.

"What are you talking abou—" William again tried to deflect Aujanae's dead-on-point observation.

"Don't you dare! Don't you dare trying to make me think I'm crazy. You know exactly what I'm talking about. Now, I want you to tell me exactly where you were today, where you were yesterday, and who you were with during those times." She did not yell, but there was viciousness in her voice that left no uncertainty about how she felt at that moment.

It was now time for William to stare at Aujanae. His stomach knotted and flipped. He began to perspire from his armpits and upper lip. His distress was visible and palpable. He was lost as to what to do or what to say right then. It was apparent that Aujanae knew he had lied, but was he really ready to concede, to admit that he had been cheating on her for fourteen months? Was he ready to openly destroy her with what he had been doing secretly for more than a year?

William got up from his spot on the loveseat and attempted to move next to Aujanae on the sofa, but she moved when he sat down. She then stood hovering over him, glowering at him with spirited contempt.

"Answer my questions, Billy." Her voice was filled with all the malice she felt inside.

"Aujanae, I don't know what you are talking about, I told you I was with David yesterday, and you saw me this morning leave here going to work," William responded weakly.

"Well, tell me this then: Do you have more than one cousin named David Mathis that lives here in Phoenix? Because the one I thought you were talking about took Katrina Hartsfield to a movie and to dinner right after church yesterday."

William literally doubled over from the blow his wife had just delivered. He clutched his stomach as he hunched forward on the sofa. Before he could right himself from the first shot, she distributed another.

"Oh, and the job you say I saw you leave for this morning, told me just a few moments ago that you called in sick today. By the way, Analeisa says she's proud of you for taking the day off to take care of yourself, you lying skunk!"Aujanae yelled.

William knew the jig was up for sure now. Aujanae had hard evidence against him. There was not a thing he could say to refute what she used to counter his deceit, so he sat quiet, embarrassed, and afraid.

Aujanae had actually exhausted herself from her mini tirade. She dropped onto the loveseat and placed her face in her hands. She needed a place to rest her heavy head, which carried the weight of her heart. She sat like that for three or four minutes, neither she nor William speaking a syllable to each other. She was the first to end the hush.

"I want you to tell me who she is, and I want you to tell me every gritty and grimy detail of your affair." Aujanae's voice was calm, but not the least bit peaceful. She oozed such seriousness that William began explaining immediately.

"Her name is April Colston, and we have been seeing each other for fourteen months," he said softly and contritely.

It was now Aujanae's turn to feel the gut shot. She had suspected it for weeks now, had known it for sure after spending the afternoon with her friends, and had it signed and sealed when she called his job. Somehow, though, hearing it from his lips made it rawer than she realized she was prepared for. She jumped from her seat and ran to the half bath to vomit her misery.

William sat glued to his seat, tears pooling in the corners of his eyes. The guilt in his chest was threatening to pound itself into a heart attack. The pain between his eyes made him dizzy enough to believe he was about to have a stroke. The hammering in his ears had to surely be a symptom of a seizure or brain aneurism. And if any one or all of those medical malfunctions had occurred, they could not have made him feel any worse than he did at that moment. In fact, William believed they may be a relief compared to the agony he was going through.

The tears now fell from his eyes, landing on the caramel-colored carpet and forming a wet spot. How ironic that on the very day he ended his affair, his wife would find out about it. Under normal circumstances, William would pray when he was in this kind of misery. If there was ever such a time before, he could not remember it, but misery in general usually led him into prayer. Somehow, though, he felt that talking to God about this mess he had created would be blasphemous. He assumed Jesus was shaking His head at His child in censure.

Aujanae sat in the bathroom on the toilet with the top down after her dry heaving session was over. She wet several paper towels, one after the other, to cool her face, but they kept falling apart from the extra moisture her unyielding tears created.

She could still hear William's voice ringing in her ears, telling her he had been cheating on her for as long as their son had been alive. She told him she wanted to hear all the gory details, but she fled the room the moment he uttered the small amount of information he had shared.

April Colston, Aujanae recalled. That sounds like a name that could belong to the pretty woman at church.

Aujanae conjured up an image of the beautiful woman, and her heart sank further into her shoes.

How could I ever compete with a woman so stunning? she thought.

Just as quickly, she told herself out loud, "Why should I have to compete with her or any other woman? If William was not satisfied with me, then he should have never married me."

Hearing her own declaration gave her a little strength, at least enough to want to go out there and ask William if April Colston was indeed the pretty woman at church.

Aujanae was a bit taken aback by the scene she found in the family room when she returned. William was kneeling in front of the sofa looking like he was praying. In her anger, she said a silent prayer as well. She prayed that God was not listening to a word her raggedy husband had to say. Aujanae began speaking before he had concluded his conversation with God.

"Is April Colston the woman who has been sitting near us at church for the past few weeks? Is she the one who had the confrontation with the usher last week? Is she the woman you were staring at yesterday in church?"

William remained on the floor for another twenty seconds, as if finishing his prayer. He then rose slowly and sat on the sofa. Aujanae approached him and stood directly in front of him, awaiting an answer.

William continued to hesitate, unsure of just how much he should tell his wife about April and their affair. He looked up with bloodshot eyes into a pair of eyes that mirrored his own. It was the hurt, misery, and anger in those eyes that told him what he should do.

"Aujanae, sit down, please."

Aujanae continue to stand, glaring at her husband. Her emotional state really did have her exhausted, but she wanted to continue to stand simply because he had asked her to sit. Fatigue won out, however, and she sat.

William took a deep breath. "Yes. April is the woman at church. She joined the church in order to see you, the woman she deemed as her competition."

Aujanae shook her head as the sick feeling in her stomach returned. This time she stayed put, however. She willed herself to hear the rest of this horrible tale that had now become a part of her life.

"Competition! Funny you should use that word. While I was in the bathroom, I wondered about her being *my* competition. Then I wised up and realized I am your wife, not some snotty little chick you are just killing time with. Therein lies the difference between me being just your girlfriend and me being your wife. When you decided that you wanted to *marry* me, you made a legal and supposedly spiritual declaration that there was no one who could compete with me. Your decision should have eliminated all competition, as I was supposed to be your one and only. That's what marriage is, William."

William visibly flinched at Aujanae's very appropriate reprimand. Though his actions may not have shown it in recent months, William was a saved man, a man who believed in God, Jesus, and the Holy Spirit. At that very moment, he felt as if he had received a tongue-lashing from the Trinity themselves.

"Aujanae, 'I'm sorry' seems so inappropriate right now, but that is all that comes to mind. I don't know what else to say—other than it just so happens that I ended things with April this very afternoon."

Was that supposed to make me feel better? Aujanae wondered silently. Though she may not have said it aloud, the look on her face spoke volumes.

"I know that doesn't change what has already happened. I just wanted you to know it's over now," William said meekly.

"So that is where you spent your morning, with your little whore?"

"Yes," he replied in a raspy voice.

"Did you have sex with her this morning? Is that her scent that you brought home with you?"

"Yes," he answered again, contritely.

Aujanae really wanted to run screaming from the room, from the house even, but she forced herself to sit and find out the grimy details, as she had asked for them previously. She continued to question William as the sound of her shattering heart roared loudly in her ears.

"Why did you end it with her, if that is even the truth, and still have sex with her?"

William was more uncomfortable than he could ever recall being before in his life. He imagined that sitting in front of a firing squad would be less excruciating than sitting before his wife, telling her all about how he betrayed her, her trust, and their marriage vows.

"Honestly, it was not my intention for it to end today. April gave me an ultimatum, her or you, and I chose you."

William was not trying to win points with Aujanae; he was just giving her the facts. He felt so bad about the situation that he would not blame her if she never spoke to him again. In fact, in light of the pain this conversation was obviously causing her and the humiliation and guilt it was causing him, he almost wished she would stop talking to him forever.

Several more seconds of silence stretched between the couple. Tears began to silently fall onto Aujanae's cheeks. William saw them, and his waterfall started again as well.

Through a hazy fog of fear and pain, Aujanae asked the question that burned deepest in her heart. "Do you love her, William?"

Just as she pushed the question out, she began to audibly sob, even before she heard the answer. It was as if she was one hundred percent certain what his response would be, but she had to hear it spoken in order to exemplify the treachery.

Here again, William battled with whether he should continue to be brutally honest with his wife. He seriously considered minimizing his relationship with April, especially since it had now come to an end.

"My feelings for you are not affected by what happened between me and April, Aujanae." William knew his retort was shallow with regards to his wife's deep question, but stating the truth would be as painful for him to say as it would be for her to hear.

"Do I look stupid to you, William? Answer the question. Do you love April? Yes or no?"

"Yes."

The blood-curdling scream followed by the loud sobs that tore from Aujanae's throat could probably be heard by the neighbors in at least a four-house radius. William expected, at the very least, a knock on the door any moment. He would not be surprised if the police showed up to investigate.

William jumped up and rushed to Aujanae's side. He attempted to wrap his arms around her shoulders, but was met with violent opposition. He had to admit he was taken aback when his normally demure wife started swinging her small fists at him in an effort to keep him from touching her.

"Get away from me, you bastard. How dare you touch me right after you have been having sex with your whore? I hate you, William! I hate you," she screamed.

William could count on one hand the number of times he heard his wife call him by his given name and not Billy, and never before had it sounded so detestable. His ears burned, and the portion of his heart that had not been torn to pieces in his final farewell with April now seemed to virtually evaporate.

William stood in front of the loveseat, looking down at the crumpled heap on the floor that was his wife. He dared not reach for her again for fear of her knocking him out, or worse, somehow hurting herself in the process. He decided to speak to her from exactly where they were at that moment.

"Aujanae, baby, I know this is rough right now, horrible even, but we can get through this and past this. I want to try to somehow work this out with you. I don't want to lose you. I don't want to lose our marriage. Perhaps we can go and talk to Pastor Abraham for advice and counseling on how to overcome this thing," William said sincerely.

Aujanae looked up from her slumped position on the floor and stared menacingly at her husband. "Oh, so now you want to talk to Pastor Abraham. Did you think about talking to Pastor Abraham and asking him his advice on whether or not you should start sleeping with your whore behind your wife's back? I would be willing to bet my son's life that you didn't do that," she spat sarcastically.

"You know what, William, I don't want to go and see your pastor. Your pastor is Satan. Just like him, you lied, you tried to kill, steal, and destroy. I foolishly aided you in your efforts too."

Aujanae pulled herself from the floor, anger still radiating from every pore in her body, and she got in William's face. He backed up a few steps in an effort to be in a better position to protect himself if she started swinging again.

The fight had gone out of Aujanae, as she now began to blame herself.

"I knew something was going on, but I kept ignoring what my spirit was saying to me. I lied to myself to protect myself, and I only ended up making a fool of myself." She sat down wearily again on the loveseat.

William recognized that Aujanae was depleted, so he sat down next to her on the loveseat to continue his attempt to plead his case.

"Aujanae, listen to me, please. I know I messed up tremendously, but I love you and—"

"You also love your whore, too, remember? So your declaration of love means very little to me right now," she sniped.

William shook his head. He did not know why now, but when he sat down, he imagined this would be easier than it was turning out to be.

"Okay, Aujanae, what is it you want? What do you want me to say or do to help change this thing and get our marriage pointed back in the right direction?" he asked, exasperated.

"First of all, I would like you to acknowledge what has happened, William. You keep downplaying your mess by calling it a *thing*. I want you to call it what it is, William. I want you to say *affair*. I want you to say *cheated*. I want you to acknowledge that you lied and destroyed our marriage and loved another woman. It is not a thing, William. It is a disgusting display of your obviously horrible characteristics. You are a pig, and I want you to acknowledge it."

Aujanae sat on the loveseat with her eyes squinted and her arms folded. She looked at William with nothing but disdain and contempt, daring him to either apologize or trying to speak around the subject of his infidelity again.

Although Aujanae's new derisive posture was foreign to William, he knew better than to ignore her and risk who knew what kind of retaliation. The statement, *hell hath no fury like a woman scorned,* screamed in his head as he looked squarely at his wife.

"Aujanae, I acknowledge that I was wrong beyond measure for cheating on you with April. I acknowledge that I was selfish and showed no respect for you or our marriage. I even acknowledge that had April not given me the ultimatum, I may have even continued being a low-down, dirty dog and continued in the affair. I did it. It was horrendous. But I am really sorry, and I want to make an attempt to save our marriage."

Aujanae did not respond to William for a few moments. She stared off into space, as if contemplating what she wanted to do, what she should do, what she should say. After a while she spoke.

"William, the obvious question for me now would be to ask you why. Why you did this to me. But truthfully, I don't care why you cheated. There is no good explanation. I know I was a good wife to you, and I am a good mother to our son, so there is nothing you can say to justify this; therefore, there is no reason to ask why. And since you have no good reason to have done this to me, I can't think of a good reason to forgive you, at least not now. I mean, despite the fact that you are a jerk, I am still a Christian, and I still love God, so I know I have to eventually forgive you. But right now, I just want you out of this house and out of my life. Now! Tonight! Get out."

Aujanae got up from the sofa and headed for the bedroom. She went in and slammed the door behind her, giving William the impression he need not bother to gather anything that may be in their bedroom.

Chapter Thirteen

"How much more stuff do you have to move, Darrin? I pray this is a one day job, because I only took today off work for this," Maleeka huffed in annoyance as they were in the process of moving things from Darrin's former residence to her apartment.

The nagging is starting already, and I have not even gotten my stuff in the apartment yet, Darrin thought.

"This is a one day job, a job that I told you did not require you to take off work. All I needed was the spare key you have yet to give to me. Besides, I only have to make one more trip back to the house to grab my computer equipment. I'm leaving all the furniture, including my bedroom set, in the house for David."

On Monday, Darrin and Maleeka agreed to move into Maleeka's apartment together. They worked out the preliminary details of their cohabitation over a celebration dinner that evening. They would each pay half the rent and utilities. Darrin would pay the cable and internet bills, and Maleeka would purchase the groceries.

On Monday night, Maleeka was almost as happy as if she and Darrin were planning their wedding instead of just plotting their sin. Today, one week later, she was feeling a little irritated. She wanted to pretend she did not know why she was experiencing increased stress and pressure, but she could not fool herself. She knew God was not pleased with her actions; therefore, she found it hard to remain pleased with them.

While she was not happy with herself, she remained steadfast in her decision. Maleeka rationalized that this was a means to an end. She was not joyful now, but in due time she would persevere and receive a blessing in spite of her tribulation. She halfheartedly thought of the scripture in James 1:2-4 that says:

Dear brothers and sisters, when troubles come your way, consider it an opportunity for great joy. For you know that when your faith is tested, your endurance has a chance to grow. So let it grow, for when your endurance is fully developed, you will be perfect and complete, needing nothing.

She just hoped that God still spoke to people like her who were doing wrong through His Word.

"What's wrong with you, Mal? You seem uptight. This move was your idea. Now you're acting like I'm inconveniencing you." Darrin too was beginning to feel a little annoyed.

Maleeka could feel his irritation. She knew she should not be taking anything out on him. Darrin was right. This was all her idea. She just hoped he would come to his senses and decide they should get married quickly. She did not know how long she could handle the conviction of her choices on this matter.

"I'm sorry, Darrin. Moving is just not one of my favorite things to do. It always brings out the worst in me."

Maleeka decided not to talk to Darrin about the spiritual misgivings she was currently having. When they carried the loads they had in their arms into the apartment and put them in the spare bedroom, she gave her fiancé a hug to seal her apology.

Darrin returned the embrace, hoping to invoke some feelings of peace between him and Maleeka. He committed to this, praying that being with her full time, coming home to her after work, would eradicate his fears of marriage.

He had not told his parents about his decision to move in with Maleeka. They liked her well enough, but he knew they would not like the two of them living together without the benefit of marriage. As far as Deacon and Deaconess Osborne were concerned, Darrin still shared a house with his friend David Mathis. Darrin planned on keeping it that way.

Maleeka was raised by a single mother, who had actually only been living for God for a few years now. It was actually Maleeka, along with her cousin Tammy, who helped lead her mother to Christ. They urged her to attend King David Christian Tabernacle with them for years. She finally relented and attended when Maleeka was scheduled to be on the program one Sunday to give the altar prayer. Tracey Davis had given her heart to God that Sunday and had been a faithful servant for the past three years now.

Maleeka and Tracey had no secrets between them. Tracey knew all about Maleeka's decision to move Darrin in with her in an effort to prompt him to want to get married. She did not agree with it any more than David's parents would have, but had resigned herself to the fact that her daughter was a grown woman and had to answer to God for her own actions.

Maleeka did find a little solace in Darrin's arms. She loved this man with all her heart. She thought him to be brave when he consented to her request. She wanted to understand his fears, and she hoped to help alleviate them as they shared their lives together daily.

"Let's go and get the rest of my things so we can begin our new lives together, Miss Davis," Darrin said as he gently pulled from their hug.

"Okay, Mr. Osborne. Let us go and do that." Maleeka pulled her arms from around his neck and palmed the side of his face as she kissed the tip of his nose. "But don't get too used to calling me Miss Davis. I like the sound of Mrs. Osborne much better."

When Maleeka and Darrin arrived back at Darrin's former house to pick up his remaining things, Maleeka was extremely surprised to see Gerald Miller at the house with David. She was not aware that there was a friendship between the two.

"Hey, Darrin. Hello, Maleeka. Gerald and I were just passing through on our lunch break. We spoke in church yesterday and decided to meet to discuss some Men's Ministry business," David said.

David almost reminded Darrin not to start missing meetings now that he was moving in with his lady, but he stopped himself. He did not want to spread Darrin's business in front of Gerald.

"Even though I will be living with Maleeka now, I still want you to call and remind me about the meetings and events. I still plan to be a viable part of the ministry." Darrin was intentionally and shrewdly laying a possessive claim on Maleeka in front of Gerald Miller. Something in his gut told him that Gerald had an interest in his woman, and he did not appreciate it.

Oh my gosh! I am so humiliated, Maleeka thought.

So much for discretion, David thought.

Gerald Miller voiced his thoughts aloud. "Oh! So you two got married? What did you do, elope?" He directed his question at Maleeka. His surprise was only slightly more evident than his disappointment.

Maleeka's embarrassment quadrupled. She was too mortified to even answer the question, but she knew she had to. Gerald was waiting with glaring eyes.

"No. Not yet, Gerald," Darrin said, "but we will be setting a wedding date in the near future. We'll be sure to send you an invitation."

Darrin knew he was biting off more than he was prepared to chew by indicating a wedding was close at hand, but at the moment it was more important for him to put Gerald Miller in his place than to run the risk that Maleeka would be all over him about actually setting the date as a result of his statement.

"Wow!" was the barely audible response uttered by Gerald. He then trained a sympathetic eye on Maleeka, who looked like she wanted the floor in the kitchen to open up and swallow her whole.

"I'm sorry, Gerald. Did you say something, man?" Darrin asked, irritated.

"Not really. I was just expressing my shock. Maleeka is the kind of woman you marry, not shack up with, Darrin, but I guess you'll find that out soon enough," Gerald said as he continued to stare at Maleeka.

Gerald's sarcasm escaped Darrin completely because of his irritation; however, both Maleeka and David heard and understood Gerald's meaning completely.

"Well, how about you let me worry about that, all right? It is really of no concern to you." Darrin snorted at Gerald. "Come on, Mal. Let's get the last of my stuff. David, I'll talk to you later, guy." Darrin grabbed Maleeka's arm and practically dragged her from the kitchen into his old bedroom.

Once they were in the bedroom, Maleeka expressed her disappointment. "Darrin Osborne! I cannot believe you embarrassed me and yourself like that. Why did you have to play that pissing game with Gerald and tell him we are living together? Tell me! What did you accomplish?" Even though Maleeka did not raise her voice, her fury came across loud and clear.

"I don't like the way he looks at you, Maleeka. I get the feeling he wants you even if you are too naïve to see it for yourself." Darrin's voice was just a bit louder than Maleeka's. He sounded more whiny than angry.

Maleeka was definitely aware of Gerald's desires toward her. She just never found it necessary to share his sentiments with Darrin, and she reasoned that now would probably not be a good time to do so, either, as she tried to calm herself.

"Darrin, you do not have to worry about what Gerald Miller thinks of me or wants from me. Or not," she added as an afterthought to not arouse any more suspicion. "I am with you, engaged to be married to you. You don't have to defend my honor or your pride."

Darrin paced around the room, gathering his computer equipment in a hasty manner. It was obvious he was still boiling, even if only slowly. Maleeka approached him just as he threw an extension cord into a box. She grabbed his arm and wrapped it around her waist as she attempted to hug away his stress.

"Darrin, you have nothing to worry about from any other man, okay? I love you. I have been with you for six years, and I'm not going anywhere now, especially after hearing you declare that we will be setting our wedding date soon," Maleeka said soothingly. She knew Darrin well enough to know that he only said that to get at Gerald, but she was not going to pass up an opportunity to use it to her advantage.

Darrin suspected he would have to hear about his declaration from Maleeka, but he did not realize it would be this soon; however, he thought it best not to challenge it one way or the other right this second.

Still locked in his fiancée's embrace, he instead said, "Let's hurry and get the rest of this stuff, baby, so we can get back to your place. Scratch that. I mean *our* place."

Maleeka knew Darrin was stalling, placating her even, but she remained cool. She would definitely be pressing him again in the very near future.

***

April walked into her doctor's office behind his nurse on pins and needles. She had gone in for her annual checkup about ten days ago. Dr. Palmer contacted her on Friday to tell her he found some abnormalities on her pap smear and would like to talk to her as soon as possible about it. She spent the entire weekend thinking about the horrible possibilities. Add that stress to the stress of her still-wounded heart from the breakup with William, and it all equaled a terrible three days for her. She added those three to the four prior to that, and it all made for a mighty bad week.

April sat in the chair in front of Dr. Palmer's desk as the nurse instructed. The nurse left the office and the waiting game began.

Cancer! The word continued its blatant dance on the eyelids of her closed eyes. The doctor had given her no clues as to what the abnormalities were on her test, yet her pessimistic mind kept circling around the disease. *Cancer!* April had all but completely convinced herself that the deadly disease would be her diagnosis.

April did believe in God, even though she did not attend church much until she joined King David's Christian Tabernacle to spy on William. The only time she ever really went was for funerals, one of which was for her mother, who died from ovarian cancer, and the two weddings she attended.

Though she did not worship in the building or read her Bible often, she still knew God and believed in Christ. As a result, she also believed that this dreaded disease would be her punishment, her consequence, for the affair she had with William and all the affairs she had prior to him. She definitely believed her broken heart was a penalty from the Lord.

April missed William more than she ever thought possible. Had she known living without him at all would be this difficult, she would have chosen to continue to share him with his wife. She had picked up her phone to dial him on his cell or at his office on several occasions, but she always changed her mind before she entered the final digit of his phone number. She loved him. She missed him. She wanted him, even now, but she would not grovel or beg for him to come back to her. Her only option was to endure the horrific pain and learn to live without him—but live with the cancer she knew would be her fate.

Dr. Palmer entered while April had her eyes closed.

"Hello, April. It looks like you fell asleep. I'm sorry I took so long," she said apologetically.

"I wasn't sleeping, Dr. Palmer, just . . . thinking, trying to prepare myself for what it is we have to discuss regarding my test results." April almost said she was praying, which would have only been a half truth. She was indeed at least thinking about God and how, she rationalized, He was not happy with her.

Dr. Valencia Palmer had been April's primary care physician since she moved to Phoenix. All of April's professional contacts for personal care were female. Her dentist was a woman. Her gynecologist was a woman. Her hair stylist was a woman. She only allowed women to do her manicure and pedicure. If she ever found herself in need of an attorney, she would be seeking a woman. April did not trust men. William was one of the first men she allowed to get close to her. After the way things turned out between them, she was more certain than ever that she was correct in her mistrust of them.

"Well, I can imagine sitting in a doctor's office not knowing what he or she might say can be a little unnerving. And, April, I am not going to lie to you. What I've found is not so pretty."

April almost lost the contents of her nearly empty stomach. She had not eaten much since her breakup with William, but something threatened to come up and out of her mouth. She visibly fought hard to extinguish the feeling. She wanted to hear how bad Dr. Palmer's report was in its entirety before she wasted any time throwing up.

Dr. Palmer immediately noticed April's distress, but recognized it as normal under the circumstances. Since it was not extreme, she decided to press on with her report.

"April, your tests show that you have the human papillomavirus, which is a virus that can cause cervical cancer."

April gasped loudly as she felt her worst fears had been confirmed. She was going to die a painful and horrific death, a death that would be her punishment for sleeping with so many men, married and single.

"I knew it. I just knew it. I am going to die, and I brought it all on myself." April sobbed as she sat clutching her stomach in the chair.

This time Dr. Palmer did emerge from the chair behind her desk. She sat in the chair next to April and reached for one of her hands.

"April, this virus does not have to be a death sentence." Dr. Palmer pulled on April's arm a bit aggressively in hopes of pulling her out of her state of despair so that she could talk to her more effectively.

"April, look at me." Dr. Palmer put her free hand under April's chin to lift her face. "I said this does not have to be a death sentence. This is a very treatable disease."

April became embarrassed as she looked at Dr. Palmer in the face. She had never been one to show weakness in the presence of others. She was a private person, a person who always strived to be the epitome of control and class, even in the face of difficult circumstances. She pulled herself together. She pulled her arm from Dr. Palmer's grasp and began quickly wiping the tears from her eyes.

"I'm sorry, Dr. Palmer. You words just caught me off guard. I apologize for making a spectacle of myself."

Dr. Palmer handed April several tissues from her desk. She remained seated next to April versus returning to the chair behind her desk.

"April, there is no need to apologize or be embarrassed. I told you it was not going to be pretty, but as I said, this is a very treatable disease. Human papillomavirus, or HPV as it is commonly referred to, is a sexually transmitted disease. It is very common, and it has virtually no symptoms or side effects. Most times it usually clears itself up without a person even knowing they have been infected; however, there are more extreme cases where various cancers can occur. Unfortunately for you, April, your case is one of those."

Again April felt the effects of karma kicking in like a big dog, but she managed to hold herself together as she continued to listen to Dr. Palmer give her the facts.

"There are a couple more tests we need to run in order to determine the complete diagnosis and treatment. The first thing we need to do is called a colposcopy to confirm the presence of the abnormal cells. The next thing we do is called cryosurgery. This procedure allows us to freeze and hopefully destroy the cells. Neither of these procedures is painful. In fact, they are done right in the office, and you are free to go home the same day," Dr. Palmer said calmly.

"Will this cure the cancer?" April asked curiously and hopefully.

"Well, we have to first determine that there is cancer to cure. The first two procedures I mentioned will help determine that. All we know for sure is that you are infected with HPV. The fact that you are not experiencing any abnormal symptoms is a very good sign."

April visibly relaxed. The breath she released could have fanned Saudi Arabia. She still wanted to know as much as possible, just in case cancer was found.

"Dr. Palmer, if cancer is found, how curable is it? How can it be treated?"

"April, cervical cancer is a pretty curable cancer, but as with any other cancer, it all depends on how far advanced the cancer is. If cancer is found, it could be treated with radiation and/or a partial hysterectomy to remove the uterus, which is connected to the cervix. Chemotherapy may be necessary in more extreme cases."

"And you say my case is more than likely not that extreme since I have no symptoms, right?"

"That is what I said, yes." Dr. Palmer smiled at April optimistically.

April however found it hard to receive the doctor's enthusiasm, because she remembered something else Dr. Palmer said.

"You also said this is a sexually transmitted disease, right?" April's nervousness began to show again as she asked that question.

"Yes. Yes, April, it is. Because we cannot specifically determine how long you have been infected, I recommend that you inform any sexual partners you have had in at least the past two years so they can be examined."

April knew exactly who she had been sexually active with in the past two years: Jordan Mitchell and William Rucker. She started seeing William after breaking up with Jordan because he wanted to take their relationship to the next level and consider marriage. She was not interested. April considered asking the doctor to repeat the part about the disease curing itself, but she did not want to arouse Dr. Palmer's suspicion to her possibly not contacting either of the men in her history.

Then a terrifying thought struck her. What if William did have it and had passed it to his wife? April wanted to find out from Dr. Palmer what she needed to do next and get out of the office before she became unglued again.

"Dr. Palmer, what do I need to do now?" April asked anxiously.

"I need you to stop at the receptionist's desk and schedule the appointment for the colposcopy. Then we will go from there. We will take this one step at a time. The appointment should be scheduled as soon as possible."

April stood from her chair and made ready to leave. "I will do that, Dr. Palmer. Is there anything else I need to know right now?"

"I think we have covered everything for now. Please don't hesitate to call me or my nurse if you have any other questions or concerns. Otherwise, I will see you when you come in for the next procedure."

April shook Dr. Palmer's hand and left the office. She went to the receptionist's desk as instructed and made her next appointment for ten days later. She then went to her car.

April would normally listen to her radio or a CD when she drove, but this time she decided she needed complete silence as she thought about all she learned today from Dr. Palmer. She was grateful that she was not given an immediate death sentence. In fact, she felt very optimistic about her prognosis, but there was still the thought of having to inform William about her diagnosis, and he in turn having to tell his wife.

April had not spoken to William since they stopped seeing each other a week ago, so she had no idea whether Aujanae knew anything about their affair. She just assumed William left her apartment on that early afternoon and returned to the life he had before he met her.

Before hearing of today's news from her doctor, April's only desire for Aujanae finding out about her and William had been so that William would leave his wife and be hers and hers alone. She was not spiteful or vindictive enough for his wife to find out just for the sake of knowing and hurting her.

Now she was faced with the daunting task of having to not only face William again, but face him to tell him she may have given him an STD that he probably passed on to his wife. April seriously considered just letting this thing ride itself out in hopes that William and Aujanae were in the high percentage of people who never even knew they had the disease because it usually cured itself; but the more she thought of doing that, the closer the bile in her stomach came to rising up and spilling over. She knew, even in her usually selfish and uncaring mindset, that she would feel terrible if she somehow learned in the future that William's wife died from cervical cancer.

April knew she had to tell William the truth. Her only question now was if she should tell him now, like in the next day or two, or if she should wait until after she got the results from the colposcopy in ten days, when she would have more information to share.

Chapter Fourteen

William sat at his desk staring out of his office window, totally unable to concentrate on anything. This was day seven of his separation from both Aujanae and April. He was miserable, lonely, and confused. His confusion came because he realized he missed each woman equally. The only advantages Aujanae had over April were that she was his legal wife and the mother of his son, whom he also missed.

While he cared deeply for April, he knew the right thing for him to do would be to work to make things right between him and his wife to reconcile himself to his family. He had called Aujanae several times since he was kicked out of his home to make his new temporary dwelling at the Residence Inn. For the first four days, she would not answer either her cell or the house phone, but on day five she finally picked up the phone at the house.

"What do you want, William?" she answered and asked indignantly.

"You know what I want. I want my family back, Aujanae," William said solidly.

He did not whine or even beg. He understood his mistake, but he had to be strong in order to make his wife understand that he was sorry and wanted another chance to make things right between them.

"William, you had your family, completely intact and devoted to you, but it wasn't enough for you. You had to go out and get someone, something you thought was better than what you had at home. You had to go and get some hoochie tramp to satisfy something that you never bothered to communicate to me, your wife, was missing. So what has changed so much in the last five days? Why now are we suddenly all that you ever wanted?" Aujanae yelled.

William knew his first conversation with Aujanae would be difficult, but he was not prepared for the hardcore attitude of this new woman on the other end of the telephone. He did not even have an answer for her very basic question of why. Surprised and even a little stung by Aujanae's tone and demeanor, William responded defensively.

"Look, Aujanae, I know you still love me, and I would not be calling you, practically begging you to allow me to come home, if I did not love you. I could hang up this phone, call April right now and tell her that you and I have split up, and be back with her in fifteen minutes. But I'm not doing that, am I? No! In fact, I have not made one phone call to April; however, I have been calling you all week only to be ignored. I am on this phone with you, trying to get you to listen to reason and put our marriage back together."

"Guess what, William? I don't need you to do me any favors. I will be just fine without you. I don't want to be tied to anyone who doesn't think I am enough for him, so you can just stop beating yourself up about not calling April and give her a call. Then you can find yourself an additional whore, since one woman no longer seems to satisfy you."

William realized Aujanae may have meant every word of what she was saying. He knew it was still early in their separation, but she truly sounded like a woman who had grown stronger in the mere five days they had been apart. His defensive posture quickly changed to one of respect and perhaps even fear about how she may try to stick it to him in a separation or divorce proceeding. He rapidly quieted his stance as he continued to speak.

"Aujanae, what about our son? Where does he fit into all of this?"

Aujanae recognized the swift change in her husband. That attitude adjustment and the mention of their child also caused her to let go of some of her own hostility.

"William, Billy Jr. will always be your son. I would never do anything to intentionally ruin that relationship between the two of you," she said softly.

But then, with a little more flavor, she added, "I hope Ms. April has good maternal instincts. I would not want my child around a woman who does not want him around and only tolerates him because of you. So you be sure to be careful where my son is concerned, William Rucker."

Now William was completely afraid. From all the horror stories he had heard from his friends and co-workers, the one piece of bait a woman will hold onto as leverage is the children.

"When a woman plays games with you with regards to the kids, it's usually because she wants you back, but she wants to make you suffer for the way you have hurt her. She knows that getting another man might bother you, but only if you still want her. But if you are a good father, she knows she is guaranteed to hit you below the belt if she plays silly games with the kids." This was a paraphrased version of some of the things he had heard from his male associates and colleagues with regards to various levels of breakups with women.

Here, pretty much out of the starting gate, Aujanae had conceded that she would not attempt to keep B.J. away from him. She did not even bother to threaten him not to take B.J. around the other woman. She really did not care if he did. Her only concern was for her child. This had to mean she was truly done with him. William knew it was silly for him to rely on generalized information for his specific state of affairs, but he was a man in a desperate situation, not clearly thinking with his rational mind intact.

William sat silently holding the cell phone, totally confused. He almost wished Aujanae had continued to ignore him. That way he would still be clueless as to how she really felt. After speaking with her, he began to wish he could still hold on to the "no news is good news" theory. She seemed to have totally given up calling him Billy, the name no one aside from her ever called him.

"William, are you still there?" he remembered her asking.

"Uh, yeah. I'm here. Okay, Aujanae, thanks for not playing games with my son. Um, I'll call you a little later to arrange some kind of schedule for him." He then disconnected the call and tried to collect his thoughts and make some sort of sense out of the mess he had made.

That was two days ago. He was still no closer to making heads or tails of anything. All he knew for certain was that he had made a huge mistake in taking for granted Aujanae's goodness and hurting her the way that he had. He also knew that the conviction of the Holy Spirit was heavy upon his heart for his mistake. He prayed every night for forgiveness, knowing that God heard him each time, but each morning the guilt would return, weighing on him like a medicine ball.

William intentionally skipped church that Sunday. He just did not have the heart or the energy to go. He was pretty certain April would not be there, since her only reason for attending had been to be near him. He was not so sure if Aujanae went. If he had to say, he would assume that she did not, simply to avoid running into him.

The finality of the conversation William had had with Aujanae the other day gave him an excuse to think more and more about calling April. If he were entirely honest with himself, he would admit that she had never been far from his thoughts. Before his talk with his wife, he just worked harder at focusing on pushing those thoughts to the back of his mind. For the past couple of days, contacting April had been a constant, bombarding consideration.

William picked up the phone to call Aujanae to arrange to pick up B.J. after work tomorrow. He dialed the number, and after several rings, the voice mail picked up. When the beep sounded, he left a message.

"Hi, sweetie. I miss you, but that's not the real reason for my call. I actually wanted to arrange to pick up B.J. tomorrow after work. I should be at the house about five thirty. I'll bring him back about eight thirty. If this is a problem, please call me on my cell phone and let me know. Otherwise I will see you tomorrow. I love you, Aujanae."

William ended the call and began dialing again. This time the call's recipient answered.

"Well, well, well. I am really surprised to hear from you. The funny thing is I was just thinking about contacting you," April said seductively.

William initially could not pull himself together enough to speak. He had not heard April's voice in seven days. Because he had refrained from contacting her altogether, he had not even heard her speak on her voice mail. The impact her intonation had on his heart and his libido was startling. After several seconds of basking in the euphoria of it all, he finally found the ability to speak.

When William hung up from leaving the message on the voice mail for Aujanae, there was an overwhelming urge in his soul to contact April. *Why continue to keep depriving myself of all pleasure simply because I cannot get anything but hurt and pain from my wife?* he thought.

"Hello, April. Wow. I really missed you, lady." William spoke as if he was literally intoxicated.

"I can tell," she replied with more control than she actually felt.

April still loved William, but after being hurt by him so deeply, she decided she would play her hand close to the vest. Unless he was calling to say he finally decided to leave Aujanae and be with her forever, she would keep him at least an arm's length from her true feelings from now on. Besides, she had no idea how he would react once she told him her news.

"How have you been?"

"I have been okay. How about you, William? How have you been?" April replied, still in control.

"April, I have never been anything but honest with you, so I honestly have to tell you that I have had it rough for the past seven days. I have been missing you, and . . ." William hesitated, not sure if he should tell April about him and Aujanae separating. He then decided to just go for it. "Somehow, April, Aujanae figured out that you and I were having an affair. She asked me to leave."

"What! How? Wha—William, when did this happen?" April was stunned and totally unprepared for what William said to her.

"Ironically, it happened the same day you and I fell out. When I got home, Aujanae was not there. When she finally did come in, she told me she knew that I had spent Sunday and Monday morning with you."

April had a string of mixed emotions running through her soul, and surprising to her, guilt was the one taking center stage. It had never truly been her intention to hurt William's wife. She knew the woman must have been devastated to discover the truth, however that happened. April actually felt sorry for what Aujanae must have endured, must still be enduring.

She also felt fear that Aujanae may somehow retaliate, especially in light of the news April had yet to share. She quickly pictured William's wife standing in the pulpit at church on a Sunday morning, telling everyone about her and William's affair and how the two of them managed to infect her with an STD that could prove to be deadly.

She also felt a little excitement at the possibility that now she and William could possibly be together forever. That was probably the reason for his phone call, she thought with a half-smile—a smile that disappeared quickly when the reality of today's doctor's visit came back to her remembrance. April continued grilling William in hopes of pushing that thought down, at least for the moment.

"William, what happened? How did she find out?"

"Long story short, my alibis blew up in my face. She found out I was not with my cousin last Sunday because he was out with Aujanae's girlfriend. She then went to call me at work on Monday to speak to me concerning what she learned regarding Sunday, and she discovered I was not at work. She figured out it was you by woman's intuition and your Sunday seating arrangements. She asked me questions to fill in the blanks. She now knows everything."

"Oh, wow. That is terrible, William. Had you planned on telling her, or were you just going to walk away from me and resume life as normal with her?" April's question was sincere.

"My plan was to handle things without having to say a word. I guess my plans meant nothing because God had other plans." William's response was regretful.

The sorrow in the pit of April's stomach came crawling back with a vengeance. William was not the first married man she had been involved with. He was also not the first one who had been caught by his wife. This was the first time, however, that she ever experienced any disappointment over the wife's hurt feelings. She attributed it to this being the first time she had ever had any real feelings for the woman's husband. Or maybe it was because God had truly started to deal with her since she had been going to church on a regular basis.

"So what are your plans now, William?" April asked evenly. There was no hope or disappointment in her tone. She was simply curious.

"Do you mean immediately, like right now? Or are you talking about my plans for the future of my life? My answer to the latter question is I have no real idea, but for an answer to the first question, I would like to see you. Right now."

Under normal circumstances, April would have been thrilled to see him and thrilled that he wanted to see her, but right now she held so much guilt. She did not know if she would be comfortable being with him and dealing with all the guilt. There was guilt over what they did to Aujanae, guilt over what she still had to share with William about her STD, and guilt over how that would again cause Aujanae more hurt.

"I don't know if that's a good idea, William. I'm not sure if I'm ready for that. I am dealing with a lot of my own stuff right now, part of it being the pain of our breakup. I don't know if I can handle having a wound that is still so raw reopened again when you walk out and leave me tonight." April was proud of herself for her resistance.

"What if I don't leave you tonight, April? What if I stay all night? It's not as if I have to rush home to my wife or anything. I can spend the entire evening holding you. I can get up in the morning, have breakfast with you, and we can leave for work together."

In the fourteen months they had been together, the two of them had never spent the entire night together. April could not resist the thought of laying her head on William's chest, with his strong arms protectively cradling her as they slept. She felt a twinge of jealousy as she realized he only wanted to stay with her all night because his wife had rejected him, but it only lasted a second. All of the guilt and shame seemed to melt away instantly as well.

"I will see you when you get off work," April replied softly, longingly.

David had talked with Toriyana at least four times in the past seven days, but had yet to tell her about the time he spent with Katrina. Each time, after hanging up from their conversation, he vowed to himself that he would be honest with her the next time. Each time he began the next conversation, he was sure he would tell her before they were done talking. Each time, the phone calls ended without a confession.

As he activated the Bluetooth in his car on his drive home from work, he determined that he would tell Toriyana the truth this time.

David had had lunch with his cousin William that day. William told him all about his marriage being over because he cheated on his wife. He even expressed how the other woman had been devastated when he would not leave Aujanae to be with her. William told him how the guilt of what he had done to both women was eating at his soul.

David still did not consider his budding friendship and growing attraction to Katrina to be as bad as what William did, because he and Toriyana were not married, but he had to admit to himself that there was definitely some guilt on his part. If there were not, he would not be having such a hard time being honest with Toriyana about spending time with Katrina.

David and Katrina had seen each other twice in the last seven days, with plans to hook up again for a quick bite to eat before choir rehearsal this week. David thoroughly enjoyed Katrina's company. Each time they were together, his attraction to her grew. Yet his growing attraction to Katrina did not in any way diminish the love stored in his heart for Toriyana.

"Call Tori," David said to his voice-activated service in his car.

After three rings she answered. "Hey, David."

"Hi, baby. I pray all is well with you."

"Other than me missing you, all is well," Toriyana said through her yawn.

David still had a hard time always remembering the time difference between Arizona and Detroit, for the most part. When he wanted to avoid talking to her, he usually had no problem using the time difference as an excuse. As he looked at the clock on his dash, he realized it had to be nearly 9:00 P.M. in Toriyana's world.

"I'm sorry, baby. I forgot about the time difference again. You are probably on your way to bed."

"It's no problem, sweetie. I was actually catching up on some reading. I was just finishing up a great book I have been trying to complete titled, *The List,* by Dr. Sherri Lewis."

"Dr. Lewis? Is it fiction or non-fiction?" David knew that Toriyana usually only read for pleasure.

"It's fiction. Dr. Lewis is a licensed medical doctor. Now she writes great novels. This is one of her older ones, but I haven't had a chance to finish it until now."

"Oh. Cool. How was your day at work?" David asked.

Their conversation was on its very familiar path of simple small talk, keeping each other abreast of the minute details of each other's lives. David kept it this way intentionally, hoping not to alarm Toriyana with the unsettled nature of his spirit about what he really needed to talk to her about.

"Work was interesting, as always." Toriyana said with the same exuberance about her job that she always had.

Toriyana worked as a paralegal in the district attorney's office. She was so great at her job that she was actually assigned to the D.A. himself. Her job always held so much excitement and gave her an opportunity to get an up close and personal look at some of the most interesting crimes and accused criminals in Detroit. Toriyana knew she could probably make a lot more money doing what she did for an attorney in a high-powered law firm, but the thrill of doing what she did kept her right where she was. The only thing that would make her walk away from her current position would be a proposal of marriage from the man she loved, which would mean an automatic move to Phoenix, Arizona, to be with her husband.

"And how was your day?" Toriyana asked as they continued their habitual banter.

Toriyana's question brought to David's mind the conversation he had with William at lunch, which immediately brought to mind what he knew he had to do. He would not share the personal business of his cousin with Toriyana, but he used it as motivation to propel him forward in his task.

"My day was interesting as well, love," David said dejectedly as he blew out a strained breath.

"Interesting how? You sound as if it was about as interesting as a prostate exam." Toriyana chuckled at her humor.

As strange as it felt thinking this way, David almost hated to hear the mirth in her voice. It made it that much harder to have to tell her something that he knew she would not find funny at all.

"Listen, Tori, there is something I need to tell you, something I know you are not going to be pleased to hear. Toriyana . . ."

Toriyana immediately tensed up. The only time she could remember David calling her by her full name was when he took her to dinner to tell her about his decision to move to Phoenix for work. The only thing he could possibly tell her at this point that would be so serious was that he was breaking up with her. She sat up straight in her bed where she had been leisurely reading and relaxing, and braced herself for the information.

"Tori, the last thing in this world I ever want to do is hurt you. I love you. I love you very much." David's heart actualized the depth of that truth as he said it, making it even harder to go through with his confession.

Toriyana surely appreciated hearing that right now, because she too loved David very much, but she knew there had to be some heart-shattering news that accompanied the endearment. She silently waited for it. Tears had actually begun to fall from her eyes as she anticipated hearing David end their relationship.

"It is because of my love for you that I have to be completely honest with you." David released another choppy breath then continued. "Tori, I have . . . um . . . gone on . . . um . . . a couple of . . . of dates with a female here in Phoenix." He rushed through the final part of his statement and ended it there.

Oh my gosh! It's worse than I believed. Not only was he breaking up with her, he had already found her replacement, Toriyana thought.

David pulled his car into the driveway of his house and hit the button for the garage door to open. He then pulled the car in, but did not get out. He sat in the car with the car running and left the garage door open, because he did not know when he would actually have the strength to get out of the car. He did not want to inadvertently die of carbon monoxide poisoning.

After several seconds of silence, David eventually heard Toriyana crying. At that moment, the thought of carbon monoxide poisoning did not sound like such a bad idea after all. He had no clue what he was supposed to say to her right then.

"So let me make sure I understand this, David. You . . . you started seeing another woman and you called me, sounding all normal in the beginning, only to set me up and tell me you want to break up with me. Is that about right?" Toriyana forced her words out past her pain. She then blew her nose loudly into her phone receiver.

"No. No, Tori. I was not calling to break up with you. I don't want to break up with you," David said eagerly. "I . . . I just wanted to tell you the truth. I . . . I did not want to be dating someone else behind your back."

Toriyana snatched the phone away from her ear so quickly it nearly flew from her hand and across her bedroom. She righted her fumble and instead stared at the phone like it had turned into some foreign object.

"What do you mean, David? How can you not want to break up? You are already seeing another woman, going on dates and shi—stuff." Toriyana was normally not a curser, but that *little* obscenity nearly got away from her. "Why are you telling me this if you are not breaking up with me?" Toriyana's sadness had not dissipated, but she spoke from the anger that had now joined it.

David struggled to find the right words to explain what he wanted to say to Toriyana. He decided to just start talking, and hopefully it would all just make some sort of sense when he was done.

"Tori, when we talked last week and you told me you were not going to be able to come for our planned visit, I was upset. I had been missing you so very much. I still do. After we hung up, I started to doubt whether or not our relationship could survive the distance between us." David got stuck there for a moment and became quiet.

"So because you *missed* me so much, you decided to go out and find yourself a temporary replacement for me right there in Phoenix. Distance problem solved, right?" Toriyana asked mockingly.

David actually had to admit to himself that there was a little truth in Toriyana's sarcastic statement, but he did not want to put it quite so crudely.

"No. I was not trying to replace you, baby, but I was lonely and frustrated, so I convinced myself that it was not such a bad idea to hang out with someone here." David was not sure if what he said was any better after he said it.

"And how did you convince yourself of that?" Toriyana had raised her voice a bit. Anger seemed to be the prevailing emotion now.

David tried thinking of a clever way to tell her without bringing up the fact that they were not married. He knew that if Toriyana had her way, they would be married, or at the very least engaged. Nothing at all came to mind, however.

"Tori, I just thought . . . I thought . . . I mean, technically we are both two single people. So . . . so there is no harm in a single person dating more than one person." David again rushed the final part of his statement. For him it was like snatching a Band-Aid off quickly to help lessen the pain.

For Toriyana, it did lessen the pain, but it fueled her fury. "What! Single? What do you mean we are both single? David, I thought we were in a committed, monogamous relationship. Last time I checked, which was earlier today, both of our Facebook pages said *In a Relationship*. When did you change our status to single?"

Even with the air conditioning in his car going at full blast, David had begun to sweat. He knew Toriyana would be upset, angry even, but he still believed in what he was saying, at least halfheartedly. David then thought of an ally to help foster his cause.

"Tori, Facebook is not the Bible. God does not recognize our relationship as monogamous. There are no instances in the Bible of exclusive relationships, other than those of married or engaged couples." Oops. He had slipped and said what he was trying to avoid saying.

Toriyana could not believe what she was hearing on her cell phone. She was so stunned she was not even sure if it was David Mathis, the man she loved, that she was talking to.

"So let me get this *all* straight, Mr. Mathis. You are now seeing another woman because *you* decided to move to Phoenix and, for lack of a better phrase, disrupt our relationship so much so that you obviously don't even consider it a relationship anymore. And because you are *single,* it gives you the prerogative to relieve your loneliness with some hoochie in the same area code, even though you know good and darn well that I wanted to get married and would have happily joined you in Phoenix as your wife, but only as your wife. Do I have it all correct, *single man?*"

Toriyana's tears were a mixture of pain and rage, confusion and resentment, sorrow and regret. She regretted that she hated and loved him at the same time. She wanted to scream, but she was afraid that once she started she would not be able to stop.

David sat on the other end of the phone with his heart in his throat. He felt terrible for making Toriyana feel like this and helpless to do anything about it right now.

"I don't know what you want me to say, Tori. Your statement was completely true. The only thing you left out was the fact that I love you. I really love you. I know that probably makes no sense to you at this moment, but the way I feel about you has not changed."

"Really? Really? Who is she, David? While you are being so honest, tell me the whole truth. Who is she?"

Toriyana's question caught David completely by surprise. David had introduced Toriyana to Katrina on her last visit. He was sure she would remember her. Even with all the hurt and trauma he had caused, he still felt a little gratification in the fact that he had been completely honest with Toriyana thus far. He had no idea what he was supposed to do now.

"Tori, baby, that is really not important," he said unstably.

"It is to me. I want to know the name of the woman who you have deemed my competition, since you seem to think that you can have both of us, *single man*."

David hated his new nickname.

"Really, I don't see the point—"

"Tell me, David. You owe me the whole truth," Tori said doggedly.

David hated the way his own words came back to bite him in the butt.

"Her name is Katrina." David tried to sound nonchalant.

Toriyana paused for a moment, thinking real hard, so hard David could hear the wheels turning in her head through the phone. He tried to divert.

"Toriyana, listen. This thing that I started out here is really nothing at all. We are really just friends. I mean, nothing has—"

"Katrina! That's that woman who works at the church, isn't it? I knew that name sounded familiar." Toriyana snapped her fingers as her thoughts finally came together.

David hated that Toriyana had a memory like an elephant.

"Did you sleep with her, David?" Toriyana hated the whining tone in her voice.

David hated it too. "No. No. As I tried to explain, we are really just friends. We have never even kissed."

Toriyana was surprised by the flood of relief that washed over her. That flood washed away a tremendous amount of anger, which allowed room for the love she felt for David to resurface. She was now confused. Part of her wanted to slam the phone down and never speak to David again. Another part wanted to fly out to

Phoenix and snatch Katrina's hair out of her head. And
the final part of her wanted get to Phoenix and convince David that he did not need anyone but her—after
she beat the crap out of Katrina.

Toriyana felt weak in her confusion. This did not sit
too well with her. She wanted to stay angry with David.
The anger was easier to deal with than the hurt.

"So at the end of the day, I guess this means it is
okay for me to go out with other men since we are both
single. Am I right?" She knew David would not be prepared to handle that thought, let alone the reality of it.

Toriyana was right. David was so furious that his
vision became blurry. In all of his rationalizing and
spiritualizing about dating other people, he never vi-
sualized that Toriyana would even consider doing the
same. He tried his best to be reasonable and look at
things from a sense of fairness, but his mind would not
wrap around the concept. He opened his mouth several
times to utter the word *yes*, but each time he slammed
it shut so hard his teeth rattled.

"I take it from your silence that you don't like the
idea, David. Well, guess what? That's just too darned
bad. You see, I'm just as unmarried as you are, sir.
And by the way, I am changing my Facebook status to
single. I suggest you do the same, *player*." With that,
Toriyana hung up the phone, ending the conversation.

Chapter Fifteen

The moment William walked into April's apartment the two of them were all over each other with animal-like lust and passion. All conversations became unimportant. All rational thought went flying out the window. They only wanted to be with each other in the most intimate way possible.

William lay in bed, cuddling with April. His head was spinning with the wild array of emotions running through it. He tried convincing himself that the swelling in his heart was a result of their wild sex. He tried telling himself that he loved his wife even though he lay in bed with this beautiful woman, sated and content. He rationalized that the unrest he felt, even though April slept peacefully in his arms, was a consequence of his dubious behavior. He attempted in every way possible to make sense of this seemingly senseless affair in order to calm the confusion in his heart and in his brain. But it all kept coming back to the straight fact that he truly cared deeply for April and that she satisfied something in him that Aujanae could not, something that went beyond even the physical.

At the same time, he loved his wife, who satisfied something in him that April could not duplicate. And for the life of him, he could not put words to what either had that the other was missing. He just knew he needed them both, but both women were of the mindset of all or nothing. Or at least one woman was.

The other had outwardly given up on him completely, which should have actually given him nothing more to think about. That should have made things easy, but they were not. He wanted them both.

He wasted no time trying to figure out how he could possibly have it all, though. He truly believed Aujanae was finished with him, so being with and staying with April seemed to make sense.

April stirred in William's arms. She burrowed deeper into his embrace. He instinctively nuzzled closer to her as well, and the two were as close as they could be without being physically joined. Though her eyes remained closed, a smile of contentment crossed April's face, making William realize she was no longer sleeping.

"Hey, beautiful. How long are you going to play possum?"

"I'm not playing possum. I'm just lying blissfully in the arms of the man I love. I'm experiencing a peace that rivals that of joyful sleep."

William reached down and lovingly placed his forefinger under April's chin to raise her eyes to his. "That was beautiful, what you said. It sounded almost poetic."

A smile the size of the Grand Canyon spread across April's face. At that very moment, Aujanae's features replaced those of the actual woman in his arms. William's body jerked suddenly, causing an immediate separation between him and April. The fear in his eyes was clearly visible to April.

"William, what's wrong? Are you in pain? Do you have a Charlie horse?" April moved near the foot of the bed and immediately began aggressively massaging William's right calf. "Is it this one, baby?"

William was glad for the distance April put between them. He took the out she offered and nodded affirmatively as she rubbed his calf. He felt tremendous relief at the fact that she did not correctly read the blatant fear that crossed his features as his wife's image popped into his head.

William had never been this confused about anything in his life. When he was with Aujanae, he missed and craved April. When he was with April, visions of his life with Aujanae crept into his mind.

April gently kneaded the imaginary ache in William's calf, while William lay wishing she could so easily rub away the very real ache in his heart. William knew the discomfort he felt was a result of the guilt in his conscience weighing on him, crushing any lasting effects of pleasure he may experience with April. He wondered, if he had ended his affair with April and Aujanae was none the wiser about their fling, would he be experiencing discomfort of a different type? It might not necessarily be that of guilt, but regret. What he felt when he was with April was like nothing he had ever felt with any other woman, not even his wife.

William lay back, eyes closed, wracked with turmoil, wanting to know how long the uncertainty would last.

April gently, lovingly, woefully rubbed William's calf. William had assumed she was sleeping contently in his arms before his little episode with the leg cramp. Honestly, he was not entirely incorrect. She started out feeling incredibly gratified to have William back in her life, hopefully forever this time; however, just before his attack, she had begun having an attack of her own. The cramp that gripped his leg had, at nearly the same time, begun gripping her conscience. Would he want to stay forever after finding out that she could have possibly infected him, thusly his wife, with a cancer-causing sexually transmitted disease?

April still had the option of waiting until she had the cryosurgery in a few days before she said anything to William. She could simply just enjoy their reunion for now and postpone the inevitable for a while longer.

"April, did you hear me, sweetie?"

"Huh? No, William. I'm sorry. I was just so engrossed in what I was doing."

"Well, I would believe that if you had not stopped doing what you were doing a few seconds ago. That's what I was saying. I was telling you that you could stop. The cramp was gone. So what were you actually concentrating on so hard?"

April crawled back up to the head of the bed and lay her head on William's chest, trying to find the serenity and joy she found there earlier. After lying for several quiet seconds, she realized that as long as she harbored her secret, that peace was gone. She then pulled herself up into a sitting position and crossed her legs Indian-style in the center of the bed.

"William, we need to talk. It's very important," April said solemnly.

William slowly pulled himself up against the headboard of April's bed. He did not like the look on her face or the sound of her voice. A million scenarios ran through his head in the quick span of ten seconds. The two he kept coming back to were either April had decided she did not want to continue further in a relationship with him for whatever reason, or she was going to press him about when the two of them could get married.

"Okay, April. Tell me what's on your mind," he said apprehensively.

The pensiveness in William's voice made April quickly reconsider telling him right now. She had no idea what he had conjured up in his own mind, but he actually looked terrified.

Keep the secret, lose the peace, her conscience echoed.

"William, there is a good chance that I may have cervical cancer."

The frightened look on William's face frightened April. His eyes bulged from their sockets, and his forehead crinkled in such an extreme way she was sure she would have to heat the iron if she ever hoped to see it smoothed out again. He immediately reached for her, causing her body to unfold in an awkward and painful way as he crushed her to his chest.

"Oh my goodness, April. Are you sure? How long have you known?" he asked as he continued to squeeze her like a boa constrictor.

"William, please. I can't breathe and my legs are all balled up," April murmured as best she could.

"I'm so sorry, baby," William stated as he quickly released April, who clumsily fell back on the bed.

April righted herself and left the bed to put on her robe. Under better circumstances she could spend all day in the nude with William. Now it just seemed uncomfortable. She also tossed William the matching robe he kept at her apartment. Once she folded her body into the outer garment, she sat in the arm chair near the window instead of getting back into bed with William.

William got out of bed and put on his robe as well. He then went toward the chair where April sat.

"No, William. Please, stay on the bed. I need this distance between us right now."

William again put on the fright face, but he slowly consented to April's request.

"William, cervical cancer is one hundred percent curable, so there is no need for you to look so terrified. According to my gynecologist, if I do have the cancer, it is in its very early stages, so that is a very good thing."

William visibly relaxed and sat up a bit straighter on the edge of April's bed.

April immediately began wondering how short lived that new look would be once she told him everything. She was now the one to visibly recoil as she folded her legs under her in the chair and pulled her bathrobe closer to her skin. She closed her eyes, but she could still feel William as he got up to again try to comfort her as he noticed her distress. She threw up one hand, silently stopping his steps. He slowly retreated, but made himself as comfortable as possible on the floor at the foot of the bed with his back against it.

April opened her mouth several times to begin telling William about the HPV, but closed it just as many times as she realized the words she was about to utter sounded corny, dramatic, rehearsed, insincere.

As William watched April sit there and mutter wordlessly, another thought popped into his head about what she was having such difficulty telling him.

"April, you're not pregnant, are you?"

April lifted her bowed head to find the frightened look had once again returned. *If only it were that simple,* she thought as she sighed audibly.

"No, William. I am not pregnant." She watched the look instantly disappear as William, too, released a loud breath.

April continued. "I was carrying something a little more menacing than a two-year-old child. William, I found out that I had an STD, a sexually transmitted disease, when I went to the doctor a few days ago."

April sat silently as she watched William's face morph from one expression to another as each phase of recognition hit him. His appearance went from confused to compassionate to angry to full-on terror as complete acknowledgement of what she told him resonated within him.

April's expressions changed too each time William's did. Hers went from remorseful to hopeful to fearful and matched his as it hit the terrified stage; however, she was certain their reasons for being terrified were quite different. William became terrified as he realized her admission could affect his wife, Aujanae. April was terrified because she began envisioning William walking out of her life again, this time for good, shattering her heart into tiny slivers too small to ever piece back together.

William came to stand in front of the chair where April sat, watching her silently for several seconds. He then bent his body to where he was eye level with April. He touched her face, not gently, but not too roughly either, to get her to open her eyes. When he could see her beautiful irises, he began his questioning.

"Which disease do you have, April?" The question came out very curt and barely above a whisper.

April heard him clearly, though. She straightened her spin and sat up a bit in the chair, keeping her legs tucked beneath her. She would not allow William to see her cower, especially not in her own home, in her own bedroom.

"I have HPV." She left the clipped reply hanging in the air, well aware that he was probably not very knowledgeable about the disease. She did not count on his next response.

"What the—How in the world can you sit there so calmly and tell me you have HIV?"

The question exploded from William's belly. He grabbed the front of April's robe, but he released her quickly. He had never before touched a woman violently, and even in his enraged state of mind, as delusional as it may have been, he would not start now. Next he began stomping around the small apartment-sized master bedroom, not getting too far before he began hitting his flailing arms and stubbing his protruding toes on April's bedroom furniture.

April jumped from the chair, trying to catch hold of a swiftly moving arm so she could get William calm enough to hear her more clearly. In her attempt to bob her way into slowing him down, she forgot to weave her way out of his swinging limb. She inadvertently caught a strong right forearm to her mouth, knocking her to the floor on the left side of her bed, just missing hitting her head on her solid wood nightstand. April instinctively put her hand to her mouth to check for missing or loose teeth. Though all of her choppers were intact, she did come away with a hand covered in blood from the split and rapidly swelling lip that began protruding from her face.

William stood stunned for a few moments as he stared down at April squirming on the floor. When he went to reach for her, she snatched away from his attempted grasp. She quickly brushed past him and ran to the bathroom to survey the damage to her mouth.

April wanted to scream as she saw the deep cut to her upper lip. The only thing that kept her from doing so was the fact her entire mouth had swelled to twice its normal size. She was afraid the sound would get stuck in her throat, unable to move past the grotesque disfiguration on her face.

William stood in the bathroom doorway, filled with regret as he stared at April's injury. He was definitely not trying to hit her or hurt her in any way. Despite the anger and fear that still clogged his soul, he knew he needed to help her now. While April stood gawking at her temporarily disfigured face, bleeding all over her fluffy pink bathrobe, William moved into action. He pulled a dark-colored bath towel from the cabinet in the bathroom and wet it with warm water. He moved the hands that April held to her mouth and gently applied pressure to her wounded lips to attempt to stop the heavy bleeding.

"April, this cut looks like it is going to need stitches. We need to get dressed and get you to an emergency room."

William's tone was flat and even. Even though he was deeply sorry for April's injury, he was still too upset to voice an apology. As he pressed the towel to April's face, he heard her muffled voice trying to say something. He moved the towel slightly to allow her to speak, not sure he really wanted to hear anything she had to say.

"Willum, I did not slay I had HIV. I slaid I had HPV." April's words were slurred as a result of the swelling to her mouth, so William could hardly understand what she was trying to say.

"What?" he asked, annoyed.

"I slaid, I . . . do . . . not . . . have . . . HIV." April slowed her words, speaking them one at a time, hoping William would better understand her.

"What!" William stated again. This time he understood April, but he was now shocked.

"What do you mean, you don't have HIV? April, this is not something to joke about. If you don't have it, why would you tell me that?" William asked as he held the towel to April's mouth and moved her back into her bedroom so they could get dressed.

"I slaid . . . HPV. Not HIV. It's a slexually transmlitted virus that can slead to clervical cancer."

William had to piece together what April was attempting to tell him, which was really irritating his already frayed nerves. "Look, let's just get dressed and get you to the emergency room. We can talk about this more when you make more sense verbally."

April was just fine with his proposal. She had talked enough as far as she was concerned. *What I have said thus far has already cost me greatly,* she thought.

The cut in April's top lip needed three stitches to repair. There were two on the inside and one on the outside. Since there were no bandages she could effectively put on her mouth, she would have to walk around for the next few days with the visible evidence of her and William's current state of affairs.

Neither William nor April talked about April's earlier revelation, neither in the car on the way to the hospital or while they sat in the waiting room. They actually did not talk much at all. William kept his head down, staring at the floor most of the time. April kept her face shielded by the bloody towel that seemed permanently glued between her hand and her face. Each of them, however, had conversations going on in their head.

The voice in William's head kept repeating itself over and over again saying, *"Will, man, I know the game of adultery is new for you, man. This is your first time on this playing field, but even the rankest amateur knows the number one rule of the game, and that is to always, always wrap it up. You never roll bareback with the other woman, especially a woman who has admitted to you she is highly experienced in this game."*

April's little voice gave a similar speech. *"How in the world did you allow yourself to get so caught up in this man, fall in love with this man, and permit this man to violate your number one rule? There is no love without the glove. Now you are sitting here with your lip busted, your heart busted, and your hope of ever legitimately having him to yourself busted."*

Each of them stayed stuck listening to the seemingly imaginary but hauntingly real people inside of their minds, until the nurse called for April to be seen by the doctor.

While the emergency room physician and his nurse tended to April's lip, they both kept staring at William from the corner of their eyes as he sat in the corner of the little room. April had explained to the doctor that he did not need to call the police and report the incident as domestic violence. She thought she had convinced him that her lip was a genuine accident, but by the time she was discharged, she was not so sure. His nurse had even whispered in her ear, in a not so hushed voice, "Girl, I don't care how fine he is. No man is worth getting my lip busted just to keep him."

Both William and April were certain that every staff person they encountered at the hospital believed April was lying about William *accidently* hitting April in the mouth by the time they left the hospital that afternoon.

The ride back to April's apartment was the first time the two revisited April's startling revelation.

"William, we have to talk about what I told you today," April said as she spoke from the side of her mouth.

William was not sure he was ready to go back into the discussion that landed them in the hospital emergency room in the late evening and her with a busted mouth.

"You are really in no position to talk right now, April. You need to just keep the ice-pack on your mouth and concentrate on bringing down the swelling. We can talk at another time. I'm just going to drop you off at your apartment and head on back to my hotel room. I think you should take the day off tomorrow, giving your lip time to heal, but I have to go to work."

April could feel him pulling away from her. Though they were relatively close in the front seat of his car, there was a chasm building between them the size of an ocean with each word he had just spoken to her. In spite of everything that had transpired in the past several hours, she was not ready to let him go.

"William, you promised me that we would spend the night together in each other's arms. Now you are telling me that you are dropping me off. I'm not accepting that. We need to discuss this. We need to work through this and we need to get past this." When April was done, she realized her mouth ached and she was drooling a bit, but that pain and the embarrassment were miniscule in comparison to what she was feeling in her heart. She wiped her mouth with the towel she still had and waited for William's response, which was slow in coming.

The last thing William wanted to do was to spend the night with April. His blood still boiled from her admission about having an STD. How could she sit there and attempt to hold a promise that he made while the skies were all sunny over his head, after the very dark cloud that she had cast? How dare she speak to him about working through this as if they were a married couple whose marriage was in jeopardy?

William was not silly enough to put all the blame on April for the predicament they were in right now. He begrudgingly recognized that he could have, should have, prevented all of this from the very beginning. He was sure this STD was a consequence of his infidelity to his marriage. But at the end of the day, he was one hundred percent certain that it was April who carried the STD and not the other way around. In his mind, this was more her fault than his.

April hung up her hopes on the deafening silence coming from William. She knew for certain that he was gone for good. It hurt. It hurt more than anything had ever hurt her before in her life. The tremendous pain was a result of the tremendous love she felt for him. It was that love that made her give him the details of what he needed to know about HPV, whether he wanted to hear them or not. After today, she would probably never see him again, so it was now or never.

April moved the towel a bit from her mouth and began. "William, I have HPV, human papillomavirus. It is nothing like HIV. This is an STD that cures itself naturally in most people within two years of contracting it in most cases; however, there are more serious cases, such as mine, where cervical cancer can occur. My doctor is not certain that I have it, but she is certain that if I do, it is curable. I go in for a procedure called a colposcopy in a few days. After that, the doctor will do another procedure called cryosurgery, which freezes the area of my cervix. Hopefully and most likely, that will be the extent of my treatment."

April took a breath as she watched William's expression soften just a bit, but when he still did not speak after several seconds, she continued.

"What this all means for you, William, is probably nothing. Like I said, even if you did contract the disease from me, it has probably cleared itself, which would also mean that if you passed it along to your wife, it has cleared in her as well."

April watched as the hardness quickly return to William's face. She shook her head to clear the fog that began to manifest in her head, telling her to give up this conversation now, and kept talking.

"But to be on the safe side, I think you should both be checked by your doctors."

   April pressed the towel back to her aching mouth, wishing there was something she could press against her aching heart. She and William rode the rest of the short distance to her apartment complex in silence.

   When they got to her building, William pulled into the first visitor's spot he saw. He quickly jumped out of the car and opened April's car door for her. Because of the lateness of the hour, he walked her to her apartment. He waited while she opened the door with her key, and the moment she crossed the threshold of her home, he turned and headed back to his car.

   April did not close her apartment door for several moments. She stood staring into the blackness of the night, recognizing its dark, symbolic meaning. When she finally did shut out the night, she turned and walked to her bedroom and allowed the levee to break on the dam of tears.

Chapter Sixteen

Maleeka loved Darrin today as much as she had during the course of their relationship and their subsequent engagement. She really did, but living with him, even for only the past six days, had proved to be more than a notion. The conviction she felt from their first night sharing the same bed was unrelenting. As of result of this constant nagging, her nerves were incessantly frayed, and she knowingly, though unintentionally, was a pestering nuisance to Darrin.

Now, as she got prepared to go to church, she felt as if everyone there would know all about her new living arrangement. She did not know how she was going to get through Pastor Abraham's sermon, believing in her heart that he would be staring at her the entire time, condemning her for shacking up with Darrin.

She considered for the millionth time since getting out of bed this morning not going to church, like Darrin. She was smart enough, however, to know that would only make her feel worse later in the day. She would feel no less guilty after going all day Sunday without her fellowship, worship time, and the awesome word she would be sure to miss from Pastor Abraham.

Darrin, the grown-up chicken, was purposely staying home from church this morning in an effort to dodge his parents. He had not actually spoken with them since the day before he moved in with Maleeka. His mom had called him twice this week. He returned her calls dur-

ing times when he knew she would be unable to answer
the phone, and he left voice mail messages just so she
would not worry about him. In the last voice mail she
left for him, she said that since she had not heard from
him all week, she was looking forward to seeing him in
church. He hated disappointing his mother, but he was
not yet ready to face Deacon Osborne. The moment his
mother looked at him, she would know something was
not kosher. When she asked him what was going on,
there would be no way he could lie to her and get away
with it. Lying in bed away from his mother's eyes was
the best place for him, Darrin rationalized.

Living with Maleeka for the past six days had been
bittersweet for Darrin. He loved coming home from
work, finding she had prepared dinner for him, but
he hated the way she would nag him about rinsing the
dishes before he put them in the dishwasher. He loved
cuddling with her at night watching television knowing
he did not have to get up and leave when the program
went off, but he hated how she would fuss about him
leaving his shoes in the living room in the middle of the
floor. He loved crawling into bed with her each night,
sleeping with her in his arms, but he hated how she
would cry after each time they made love, to express
her guilt and shame at them continuing to fornicate.
The thing he loved the most was that she had not once
tried to force his hand at setting a wedding date. The
thing that scared him the most was, perhaps after living with him for just a few short days, she had decided
she actually did not want to be married to him.

"Darrin, you know you are wrong for not getting up
and going to church with me this morning," Maleeka
whined as she sat on the edge of the bed and slipped
on her shoes. "I know you have been slacking in your
church attendance these last few weeks, but I thought

you would want to go with me this morning. We both need to be at that altar together, praying for forgiveness for living in sin."

Darrin hated waking up to the nagging, whining, complaining, and manipulating in the morning.

"Maleeka, you know I am not ready to face my parents yet about our moving in together. I will tell them in my own way in my own time. I just don't want to be cornered and admonished by them, especially at church."

"Am I engaged to a thirty-three-year-old man or a fourteen-year-old boy?" Maleeka asked sarcastically as she got up from her spot on the bed and stood over Darrin's prone body that still lay across it.

Darrin pulled the covers over his head and mumbled from underneath, "Drop it, Mal. I'm not going. You can call me all the names you want. I will deal with my parents when I feel like it."

Maleeka started to say something else, but instead decided to do as Darrin asked and drop it. It just was not worth fighting about this morning. Besides, she was already taking enough stress with her to church this morning.

"Fine, Darrin. I'm leaving. I'll pray for you while I'm at church, asking God to help you find your maturity." Maleeka just could not resist.

"Tell Jesus I said *hey.*"

"Don't worry. I will. I'm sure that will be the only way He will hear from you anytime soon." Maleeka left the apartment with that departing shot.

On the drive to church, Maleeka wanted to take her mind off the mess she left at home in her bed. She popped her favorite gospel mix CD in and turned up the volume, hoping to drown out her stress and nervousness about what she would face at church today.

As she listened to the music, her own troubles began to drift from her mind. Soon she was grooving to the wonderful up-tempo beats of great praise and worship music.

As the song "Shake Yourself Loose" by Vickie Winans began to play, she immediately began to think about her friend Aujanae. Maleeka called Aujanae last night to check on her, and she was singing this song as she answered the phone. Aujanae said this was her new theme song, because she was shaking herself loose from William and their marriage.

Maleeka had convinced Aujanae to come to church with her today during their conversation. She just hoped Aujanae was still planning on coming. She told her she needed to be running to the House of the Lord during her trials, where she would hopefully find some peace and some joy, and some wisdom from Pastor Abraham's message to help her get through what she was going through with her trifling husband.

Perhaps she, Aujanae, and Katrina could go out to grab a bite to eat together after church. That, too, would help Aujanae take her mind off her troubles for a little while. It would also give Maleeka an excuse not to rush back home after church, because Lord knows she was in no hurry to get back there.

Aujanae was also listening to gospel music as she headed to church this morning. She had her radio set to Gospel 860 AM, the only gospel music station in Phoenix. She tried to concentrate on the lyrics of the songs as they came through the speakers, but as with any other action she tried to become involved in, her mind kept drifting to the charred ruin that was now her marriage. Since William's last visit, she did not even trust herself to care for her child properly; however, instead of simply sending her son to her mother's, she too went there and allowed her mom to take care of them both for a little while.

This past Tuesday, the last day she saw William, turned out to be the worst day of her life thus far. He had come by to pick up B.J. to spend some time with him. While he was there, he had decided to share some news he deemed as important.

"Hey, Aujanae. You look great. But you have always been beautiful to me," William had said as Aujanae opened the door to let him in the house. He no longer had a key since she had all the locks changed.

Aujanae uttered a barely audible thank you as she walked back to the great room to retrieve their son from his playpen, leaving William to follow behind her, gawking at one of her best assets.

Aujanae had taken extra care to be sure she looked fabulous when William came by to pick up B.J. She wanted to throw in his face just what he had given up to be with his trampy mistress. Aujanae had to admit that April was quite a stunning woman, but in her opinion, April paled in comparison to her simply by virtue of the fact she was classless enough to stoop so low as to steal another woman's husband. In Aujanae's estimation, April's inner whore caused her outer beauty to be diminished to that of the warthog, like Pumba from the movie *The Lion King*.

When they reached the great room, B.J. was sleeping. "You can wake him while I get his bag. He's been down for a little while now, so it's time for him to get up from his nap," Aujanae told William.

"We can let him sleep for a bit longer. I really need to talk to you about something important."

Aujanae stopped and turned to find William shuf-
fling his feet anxiously. The look on his face said he
would rather be anywhere other than in this room
about to have the conversation he just mentioned. This
in turn made her nervous. She rationalized that what
William needed to talk about had to be bad news. If
he simply wanted to talk about the two of them getting
back together, he would appear, at least, to be much
more confident.

Aujanae sank slowly to the sofa closest to her, not uttering another word. She just waited for William to spit
out what he had to say.

"Can we please go into the bedroom? I would rather
not disturb the baby."

Aujanae looked at William as if her eyes were going
to pop out of her head and roll under her son's playpen.
What in the world was this all about? she wondered
wordlessly.

William headed upstairs to the bedroom they used
to share together without saying another word either,
leaving Aujanae to follow him this time, staring at the
back of his bowed head. It was a view not as nice as the
one he had when he followed her.

William moved aside as they approached the bedroom door, allowing Aujanae to enter first. She went
to the night stand by the bed to make sure the baby
monitor was on in case B.J. awakened. William began
talking before she had a chance to sit down.

"Aujanae, yesterday April told me she was in the process of having some test done to determine whether or
not she has cervical cancer."

Aujanae still had the monitoring device in her hand
when William completed his sentence. It took every
ounce of will power she possessed to not hurl it across
the room, aiming right for the center of his forehead.

She knew good and darn well this fool did not come to her all stressed out, stressing her out in turn, to tell her about his mistress's health challenges. Aujanae initially cradled the monitoring device in the palm of her hand. She then began bouncing it up and down in her hand.

"William, there had better be more to this conversation than the fate of your whore's cervix," she said menacingly.

William watched the movement of his wife's hand. Never before in the entire time he had he known this woman had he ever felt the least bit frightened or threatened by her. Even in their very recent past since she found out about the affair and attempted to pummel him that day, had he ever thought she really wanted to physically hurt him. Now, however, he feared for his safety, and he had yet to tell her the worst of the news.

"Aujanae, please sit down, baby." William attempted to take a few steps in her direction, but when she stopped bouncing the monitor and instead held on to it with a death grip, he halted in his tracks.

"I'm fine standing. I'm sure this conversation won't take too long, because I am sick of it already, so you need to hurry and finish what you have to say," Aujanae said impatiently.

William gulped at air and attempted to swallow the fear in his throat. He seriously considering just grabbing his son and leaving, letting the rest of his confession go unstated. But he knew he owed Aujanae the truth—full disclosure.

"The cervical cancer, if she has it, is the result of a sexually transmitted disease called HPV. I'm sure you've probably heard of it, or have maybe been warned about it by your gynecologist." William paused, allowing Aujanae an opportunity to grasp his statement.

It did not take Aujanae long to put together what he was trying to say. Before she knew it, she had attempted to sit on the bed, but missed and slid to the floor.

William's first instinct was to go to her to make sure she was okay. He quickly changed his mind when he realized that the floor was carpeted and her descent happened rather slowly. He knew she had not hurt herself. His palpable fear kept him rooted to his spot.

William heard the crash before he realized what had happened. Aujanae had actually thrown the baby monitor at him, but missed by a mile. It smashed into the wall over his head. She quickly rebounded, though. She stood up and grabbed the small reading lamp on her night stand and launched it at him, this time connecting with a loud thud in his chest.

William doubled over from the pain, while Aujanae looked for something else heavy enough to throw at him. The only thing she saw in her immediate vicinity was a calf-length boot she was trying on earlier in the day, but instead of tossing it, she picked it up and started swinging it at his head.

After she connected once, William grabbed the weapon and wrestled it from her hand. He then wrapped his wife in a bear hug and pushed her to the bed, landing on top of her. In her rage, Aujanae was a lot stronger than William was prepared for her to be. It took an awful lot of strength and force to keep her pinned as she attempted to wiggle and grapple from his grasp. He managed to hold on, though.

"Get off of me! Get off of me!" she screamed. "Get off of me so I can kill you, William! Then I'm going to kill your slut-whore girlfriend!"

William did not dare budge. He knew in her current state she was capable of doing just as she threatened.

Aujanae continued to struggle, until all the strength drained from her body. William could feel her yielding to her fatigue. She was so tired that she could no longer even scream. When he was certain she had nothing left to fight him with, he moved himself slightly off of her body, taking off some of the pressure of his body weight, but he did not say a word to her.

Their silence gave way to them hearing B.J. crying loudly downstairs in the great room. All of the thumping and bumping above his head had probably scared the poor baby senseless, Aujanae mused.

"Let me go. I'm going to get my son," Aujanae said angrily but honestly.

William was still unsure of what she might do, so he hesitated a bit, which only served to make Aujanae more infuriated.

"Get off of me!" she barked loudly. "My son needs me. I no longer have time to deal with you."

William released her completely, believing and hoping that her maternal instincts were stronger than her wifely need for murderous revenge.

Aujanae jumped up and ran toward the door, then stopped. "I suggest you take this opportunity to leave quickly." She then resumed her journey to get to her crying baby.

William considered asking her if he was still taking B.J. with him, but thought better of it. He did as he was told and got the heck out of Dodge.

The following morning, Aujanae had called her doctor and asked for an emergency appointment, explaining very transparently the reason why she needed to be seen as soon as possible. The doctor's receptionist had probably never heard such brutal honesty. The receptionist put Aujanae on hold and returned a short time later, instructing her that Dr. Avery would see her at three o'clock that afternoon.

Aujanae then called her mother and asked if she would watch B.J. while she went to the appointment, giving her all the gory details as well. Her mother suggested that both her and the baby come stay with her for a little while, so she could help Aujanae deal with her pain and her child.

Aujanae made one last phone call before she packed a few bags to take to her mother's. She called Maleeka and asked if she would go to the appointment with her for moral support, also giving her a complete blow by blow of everything that had happened the night before.

At the appointment, Aujanae's doctor had explained, after completing a full pap smear and blood work-up, that there was more than likely nothing to worry about. Aujanae had been seen by her gynecologist twice since B.J. was born for complete well-woman check-ups, and both of those pelvic exams and pap smears had come back negative. He assured her he would pay special attention to this one and give her a call as soon as all the results were back from the lab.

That Friday, Dr. Avery called and gave her a clean bill of health.

She was now headed to church for the first time since she found out for sure that William was having an affair. She prayed God would work a miracle while she was there and instantly wash away all the pain she had suffered for the past several weeks.

On Friday, April had the colposcopy and the cryosurgery. Dr. Palmer felt that she may as well go ahead and kill the two birds since she already had April open. The cryosurgery at this stage was more of a preventative, precautionary measure that would not hurt anything, even if the cells scraped during the colposcopy were not cancerous.

When Dr. Palmer asked April about the obvious injury to her mouth, she lied and said she got caught accidently by a door that someone was trying to exit at the same time she was trying to enter while at work. Dr. Palmer gave no indication one way or the other as to whether she believed April.

April then went home with the intention of spending the next two days relaxing, ready to return to work on Monday; however, peace would not come to her because she missed William too much. She decided to call him to tell him things went relatively well with her procedure. Considering it had cost her his love, her mind interjected as an afterthought.

"Hello, William," she said solemnly when he answered the phone at his desk.

"Hello, April." He intentionally removed all emotion from his voice as he returned the greeting. Unbeknownst to April, though, William had a horrible pain in his chest both from the hole in his heart this whole affair had caused him and everyone involved, and from the bruise left by the lamp Aujanae threw at him.

"I have not heard from you since you left the apartment the other night. How are you?"

"To be honest with you, April, not so great, but I guess that is to be expected with everything I have done and gone through these past few weeks. But I really don't want to go into all of that right now. I'm at work and I am swamped. I have no time to deal with it. But how are you? How is your lip healing?" William's tone remained flat and even.

"As well as can be expected, I guess. I also had my procedure done today. Dr. Palmer said everything looks good so far. I will have the full and final results in about a week. I'm pretty optimistic about everything turning out okay. I am honestly no longer worried about it." April also tried to keep the emotion out of her voice, but she was not as successful as William.

"That is good news, April."

"William, I would really love to see you, today if possible. I miss you so much." April's voice cracked as she fought to hold back the tears.

William heard the pain, and his heart broke just a bit more.

"April, I can't. I just can't. Things have been so crazy for these past few weeks. I'm not blaming you in any way. I was angry the other day when you told me about the STD, but I realize this is actually all on me. I had the power to stop all of this from happening over fourteen months ago and I didn't. I let it go, let it grow into this horrible mess that it has now become.

"You have no idea how horrific it was the other night when I had to tell my wife that I could have possibly infected her with a sexually transmitted disease because of my selfishness. Aujanae has done nothing, absolutely nothing to deserve what I have done to her, what I have done to our family. She will probably never forgive me, and I don't blame her. I honestly don't even know if I want her to, but I know I will never get over the pain I so unnecessarily caused her. In spite of all that, however, I am going to do all I can to win her back and repair our marriage."

William paused, realizing he was doing exactly what he told April he did not want to do. He was discussing this drama at work. He then realized he may as well go ahead and get it all out, since he had already started.

"Then there is what I have done to you. I allowed myself to love you and allowed you to love me, all while I was still loving my wife. April, you knew I was married even before I told you I was, but this is still all my bad. I was the one who was married. I was the one who should have allowed you, your beauty, and your charm to get up from that table that day and never seek you out again. Then in the end, I not only hurt you emotionally, but I physically injured you as well. Yes, it was unintentional, but if I think about it, all of this was unintentional. I never meant for any of this to happen. I was the only one in a position to have prevented it all.

"So I'm saying to you now, April, I am sorry for hurting you. I am even sorry for the day I allowed you to sit at my table. Sorry for not saying that yes, you are beautiful, but my wife and my son are more beautiful to me. I'm sorry for everything, April, but I can't see you today. I can't and won't see you ever again."

William abruptly ended the conversation there and hung up the phone.

William severed the phone call. William severed their relationship. William slaughtered her heart. William had changed her life. When she finally hit the end button on her phone, William was long gone tangibly, emotionally, forever.

April sat in her apartment for hours after the phone call, alternating between entertaining herself as the lone guest at her pity party, crying uncontrollably, and stomping around her apartment, attempting to convince herself she was better off without him, declaring and chanting the mantra from the old school Gloria Gaynor song, "I Will Survive." She started this all in the early afternoon, and it was past dark when she had finally exhausted herself from her confusion.

Then, in her final resolution to herself as she folded herself into bed that evening, April decided that on the following day, that Saturday, she would begin the healing by doing some retail therapy. She would go out and shop for herself, buying herself a new wardrobe for church, because on Sunday, the real healing would begin.

So today, Sunday, she was going to get her strength to survive, as Gloria Gaynor sang, from God. What better way to start walking in that strength than to go to the church where William and his wife attended, showing them both that she would not allow them to defeat her? She would walk into King David's Christian Tabernacle determined that the end of her relationship with William would be the beginning of a new and better relationship with God.

April's resolution did not completely eliminate the butterflies that rode in the car with her on her drive to church. She was as nervous as the proverbial whore in the church house, but she was going anyhow. She would face whatever demons she encountered with her back straight and her head held high. She was going in search of Jesus' forgiveness, not that of those lowly saints who judgmentally deemed themselves better than her.

April pulled her car into the first available spot she saw as she entered the parking lot. She checked her hair and makeup in the lighted vanity mirror she kept in her glove compartment and found nothing askew. She stepped out of the car, tugged at the skirt that hung, uncharacteristically, below her knee to be sure that the hem was straight, and began her stride toward the sanctuary.

Maleeka and Aujanae arrived at church at virtually at the same time. Maleeka was exiting her car just as Aujanae pulled into the lot a few spaces over from her. The two ladies joined up and began their trot to the sanctuary together.

"You look pretty today, Aujanae. I'm so glad you decided to come."

"I'm not so sure yet. I mean, as long as William doesn't show up, I think I will be able to enjoy service today, but if he is here, I don't know how comfortable I will be," Aujanae replied nervously and honestly.

Maleeka intertwined her arms with Aujanae's as they walked. "Don't worry about it. Me and God have got your back. We will all get through this together."

Aujanae smiled for what was probably the first time in at least a week. She was truly glad Maleeka was her friend.

When the pair entered the narthex, the doors to enter the sanctuary were closed. There were three or four other congregants standing there waiting to enter as well. Maleeka assumed someone must be praying before praise and worship got started, so the ushers did not want anyone walking in. Maleeka, still locked in the arm embrace with Aujanae, was looking behind her, preparing to greet someone as they entered the narthex when she felt a death grip so strong on her arm she was certain that all circulation to that part of her body had instantly stopped. When she turned to find out what was going on, she looked to see that Aujanae's face had turned as white as a sheet. Her friend was standing motionless, staring at the back of a woman's perfectly coifed head.

"Aujanae, what's wrong? You are putting a serious hurting on me," Maleeka stated as she attempted to pry her arm loose.

"She's here! April! She's right there," Aujanae stated without discretion.

Maleeka looked up and realized that at the mention of her name, April had turned around and spied her. Maleeka was staring at her with pure contempt in her eyes.

Maleeka shook Aujanae loose and advanced toward April and got right in her face.

"I can't believe you have the dirty nerve to show your face here. You must be crazy or suicidal or both," Maleeka spat.

"Excuse me. Do I know you?" April replied haughtily.

"Probably not, but I believe you know my friend here, Aujanae. And I know for certain that you know her husband, William," Maleeka responded loudly. Aujanae was now standing right by her side.

"I don't have anything to say to either of you. I am here to praise and worship God. I suggest you walk away and leave me alone," April said evenly as she lowered her voice to barely above a whisper.

"Walk away from you?" Maleeka asked loudly. She actually took a step closer to April. "Perhaps you should have taken your own advice and walked away from my friend's husband, tramp!"

Deacon Jonathan Ealy, who was amongst the small crowd still waiting in the narthex, approached the antagonistic group of women and stepped between Maleeka and April. "Ladies, I would like to remind you all that you are in the House of the Lord. Please conduct yourselves accordingly," the middle-aged gentleman said sternly.

Aujanae did not know which emotion was more prevalent in her right then, anger or embarrassment. Seeing April standing only a few feet from her was causing her to see so much red that she was instantly developing a headache. Maleeka practically broadcasting that April was her husband's mistress made her want the floor to open up and swallow all three of them whole. On their way down to wherever they would land, Aujanae was sure she would punch April straight in her face.

Maleeka was still out of control. "Why don't we just step outside to the parking lot, heffa? That way we will no longer be in God's House."

"Maleeka, let it go. This trashy hag is not worth it," Aujanae stated while staring directly at April.

"William certainly did not find anything trashy about me in the past fifteen months. And believe me, he looked in every nook and cranny of me," April replied nastily, sarcastically, and confidently.

Maleeka attempted to step around Deacon Ealy and lunge for April, but was stopped by both him and Aujanae.

"Young lady, I want you to stop this nonsense right now. I know your mother and your fiancé's parents would not be pleased with this behavior," Deacon Ealy reprimanded as he held on to one of Maleeka's arms.

"That's right, Maleeka. Besides, I don't know if you have ever had the HPV vaccination. Remember I told you this slut gave William a sexually transmitted disease. I don't want you to inadvertently catch anything from her nasty behind while you're beating her down. If one drop of her blood gets on you, you could get infected with who knows what." Aujanae's return jab was the knockout punch. Everyone in the narthex either gasped or laughed.

April, obviously mortified, did her best to act unaffected, but she turned and walked from the church, straining to keep her head up. Anyone with even one good eye could tell she was high-tailing it out of there with the quickness because she was humiliated.

Just then the ushers opened the doors for those waiting in the narthex to enter the sanctuary. Deacon Ealy had parting words for Aujanae and April before he went in.

"Ladies, I would love to stand here and say I don't know what that was all about, but you all made it quite obvious. I will for certain say this: that was not God-like behavior. You should never behave like that in the House of the Lord, or even in His parking lot." The last remark was aimed directly at Maleeka. With *his* parting shot, Deacon Ealy headed into the sanctuary.

Aujanae dragged Maleeka, who she could tell was still fuming, into the bathroom before they went in for praise and worship. They both sat down on the lounge sofa to catch their breath and calm themselves.

"Thanks for having my back, girl. I can't believe you were willing to fight her right here in the church."

"The Lord is going to have to forgive me for this one. I just got so mad when I realized who had you so unnerved, standing there like all was right in her universe. Please! That skanky troll better be darn glad you and Deacon Ealy stopped me from whipping her tail. I can't believe you were holding me back instead of it being the other way around. But that last insult was worth a thousand punches to the gut." Both ladies were stoic at first, and then burst into a fit of giggles.

Just then the last person Maleeka wanted to see at that moment came marching into the ladies room. The laughter stopped instantly.

"Maleeka Davis! Is it true? Did Deacon Ealy have to stop you from having a street brawl right here in the church?"

Maleeka took one look at her future mother-in-law and wanted to laugh out loud again. The ugly hat she had on looked like something she borrowed from Miss Piggy from the Muppets. It was so shocking to see her looking like that. Deacon Osborne was normally impeccably dressed at church.

Out of respect, Maleeka stood up before she answered. "Yes, ma'am," she answered apologetically as she looked the deacon directly in her eye. She did her best to avoid looking at that hideous hat again for fear of falling on the floor in laughter.

"Is that all you have to say for yourself?" Deacon Osborne chastised.

"I answered your question honestly, Mrs. Osborne. What else do you want me to say?" Maleeka's reply was laced with a *you are not my mother, so don't you dare try to check me* tone.

"I want you to apologize, Maleeka."

"To who?"

Now it was Aujanae's turn to stifle her giggles. She could tell Maleeka was purposely trying to irritate Mrs. Osborne. Mrs. Osborne turned and stared coldly at Aujanae as a snort slipped through her nostrils. She then directed her admonishment back to Maleeka.

"Well, first of all, to the Lord. And by the way, what happened out here that would send you into such an uproar you could not control yourself in church?"

"Let me first address your first statement. I will ask the Lord's forgiveness when I feel like it. I don't need you barging in here telling me I need to repent and treating me as if I have no home training, Mrs. Osborne. Secondly, I know Deacon Ealy has probably given you a complete rundown on what happened in the narthex, so don't come in here trying to see if you can get any more juicy details. And if he didn't tell you the full story, it is really not anything I want to discuss. It's a private matter that I should have never brought up in the first place. I won't make the same mistake by doing it again for your sake." Maleeka returned to her seat on the lounge sofa, raw attitude radiating like radium from her pores.

Both Aujanae and Deacon Osborne stared at Maleeka, mouths opened and eyes bucked.

"You know what, Maleeka? I'm going to be the bigger person here and leave before this gets to a place of no return, but please know that this conversation is unfinished. We will talk again when you are in a more calm and rational state of mind."

"Whenever, Mrs. Osborne!" Maleeka stated with as much calm as she could muster.

Deacon Osborne left the ladies room in a huff, nearly slamming into another congregant as she entered.

"What in the world was that all about, Maleeka? Why did you attack the woman who is going to be your mother-in-law like that?" Aujanae asked in hushed shock. She was trying not to give the woman who just walked in an earful.

Maleeka replied as if no one else was in the whole church, let alone the restroom. "Girl, please. She attacked me first, and had the nerve to do it with that ugly hat on her head. She is not my mama. Who did she think she was, barging in here and demanding that I apologize to the Lord like she was one of his cherubs?" Maleeka said hotly.

"No, you *did not* just say cherubs!" Aujanae's statement was filled with mirth.

The anger immediately drained from Maleeka, and the two women laughed like middle school pre-teens, barely able to keep themselves upright on the sofa.

"Oh my goodness, I needed that laugh," Maleeka said as they finally calmed down. "Girl, there is more to the story, but I will tell it to you after church. We can go and get something to eat and I will give you the full low-down. Right now let us go in this sanctuary and get some Word up in us."

The ladies washed their hands, left the restroom, and found themselves a seat in the sanctuary right as the choir was finishing their song. They got in just in time for Pastor Abraham's sermon, which was titled "Your Mouth Says You Love Him, but Your Life Says Otherwise." The scriptural text was John, 14:15, "If you love me, obey my commandments"; John 14:21, "Whoever has my commands and obeys them, he is the one who loves me. He who loves me will be loved by my Father, and I too will love him and show myself to him.": and John 15:10, "If you obey my commands, you will remain in my love, just as I have obeyed my Father's commands and remain in his love."

By the time Pastor Abraham had finished his sermon, all of the laughter and the last vestige of anger that was still lingering was gone. All she could feel now was convicted.

Aujanae was so caught up in the truth of Pastor's Abraham's words that she did not notice how glum her friend had become throughout the message. All she could focus on was how her trifling, cheating, no good husband and his skanky mistress should have been there to hear the sermon.

At the end of service as they were leaving their seats, Mrs. Osborne and her husband stopped at the end of the pew as Maleeka and Aujanae were exiting.

"I will talk to you a little later, missy, and if you talk to my son before I do, tell him I need to see him soon as well." Mrs. Osborne starting walking away quickly, not giving Maleeka a chance to retort with any more saucy replies.

Little did Mrs. Osborne know, all the fight had been drained from Maleeka as she felt so punished by Pastor Abraham's message. How could she really say she loved the Lord and yet be living in sin and fornicating with Darrin?

When Maleeka did not respond to Mrs. Osborne's quickly retreating back, Aujanae took a good look at her for the first time since Pastor started preaching.

"Maleeka, what's wrong? You look so sad," Aujanae asked.

"You certainly do. What's wrong? Your live-in boyfriend stressing you out?" Gerald Miller whispered discreetly, but not so much so that Aujanae, who was unaware of Maleeka and Darrin's living situation, did not hear. He appeared at the end of their pew as if he had popped up through the floor.

"Where is your man, by the way?" Gerald was being a little sly. Both he and Maleeka knew it.

"As you can see, he's not here, but I'm sure you knew that, because I would be willing to bet my next paycheck you have been watching me since I walked in the sanctuary."

Gerald chuckled at the very sharp but honest reply.

"Touché, my fair lady. I will reiterate what I told you when I first met you: If you were my woman, you would never have to attend church without me." Gerald left too, much in the manner that Mrs. Osborne had, leaving Maleeka with that thought to ponder.

"Okay, Maleeka, what was that all about? And why do you look so sad?" Aujanae asked, totally confused.

"What Gerald Miller said about me and Darrin living together is true. That is also the reason I look so sad. This is what I said I would explain to you after church over a good meal. I had no idea Pastor Abraham was going to put me and my situation on blast like this, though. Girl, I feel about as embarrassed as April the Whore did when she walked out of here. Pastor Abraham went straight for the gut shots."

The ladies started moving out of the pew once again, toward the door, and were out of the sanctuary before either of them spoke again.

"How long have you two been living together? And does Darrin's mother know? Is that why she was acting all crazy earlier today?"

"Darrin and I have been living at my apartment since this past Monday, and no, Mrs. Osborne doesn't know. That's one of the reasons Darrin did not come to church today. He has not told his parents, and he was not ready to face them yet. The only people who know are Katrina, my mom, David Mathis, and Gerald Miller."

The ladies continue their trek to their cars. Maleeka's explanation cleared a few of the cobwebs from Aujanae's head, but there were still a few unanswered questions.

"Okay, Maleeka, if Darrin's parents don't know, what prompted you to go off on her the way you did?"

"To be honest, Mrs. Osborne was kind of caught in the crossfire. I was still angry with April the Whore when she came at me the way she did. Then when I looked at her, all I could think of was her son and how upset I am with him right now. So I kind of took both sets of emotions out on her—not that she did not deserve it, though."

All right, a little clearer still, Aujanae thought.

"Gotcha. But tell me, why are you living with Darrin all of a sudden? And what is Gerald Miller's role in all of this?" Aujanae asked as they reached their cars.

"I'll tell you the rest when we get to the restaurant. Is the IHOP on Camelback cool with you?"

"I'll follow you there."

Chapter Seventeen

Katrina did not want her phone to be ringing right now. All she wanted to do was continue to mindlessly watch the Lifetime movie that was blaring on her forty-two-inch television screen in peace and complete quiet. Even so, she was none too surprised that the cute little jingle she used as a ring-tone was sounding. She was certain it was someone from church, probably Maleeka, wanting to know why she was not in service this morning.

When Katrina looked at the clock on her cable box, she realized church could only have let out a few moments ago. Dang! Maleeka could have at least waited until she got home to bug her.

Most people did not understand that when your full-time job is also the place where you worship, it can be a little overwhelming, stressful, and hard to separate the two. Add to that the stress of falling completely in love with David Mathis, whom she had not spoken to in several days. Since she was not ready to face him and find out why, Katrina figured she just needed a break today, so she skipped church.

When she picked up her ringing cell phone to confirm and ignore the caller, she was surprised by the face that displayed on her smart phone screen.

"Hello," Katrina answered awkwardly.

"Hey, Kat. I didn't see you in church today. I just wanted to give you a call and make sure you weren't sick or anything like that," David replied smoothly. His tone did not convey his truth, however. He was actually quite nervous talking to Katrina right now. Her absence from church gave him the perfect excuse to just pick up the phone seemingly out of the blue and give her a call.

"David. How thoughtful of you. I'm okay, actually. I'm just taking a much-needed day to relax away from my place of business, which also just happens to be my place of worship. Sometimes the lines get blurred, and in order to break away from one, I have to leave them both behind."

"I understand. It's good to hear you are not under the weather," David responded shyly.

Then there were no words between the two for several seconds. Katrina was caught up in how excited she was that David had finally called. David, after hearing Katrina's voice, was unsure of what was going on in his head; therefore, he was unsure of what he should say next.

David had spent the past several days flip-flopping back and forth between missing and loving Toriyana and wanting to continue to see Katrina. He'd had only a little contact with Toriyana, and other than a quick passing in the halls of King David's Christian Tabernacle, he had no contact with Katrina.

Toriyana had been so upset on that initial day she posted very negative things all day on both her and David's Facebook pages, calling him a cheater, a liar, and a womanizer. It had gotten so bad that he decided he needed to delete her as a friend from his page. David called Toriyana a few days after their fight to apologize, hoping she had calmed down. She told him then that she would only forgive him if he married her and either moved her to Arizona or he moved back to Detroit to begin a real life together. Since he was of the new mindset that the only real commitment was marriage, then she wanted a real commitment from him or nothing at all from him. David was completely taken aback by her ultimatum, but he told her he would think about it and get back to her in seven days. They were now on day four.

Now, here he sat on the phone with Katrina, missing her as if she too lived nearly two thousand miles away instead of only a few short ones. He was so torn between these two women. Yes, he was in love with Toriyana and his feelings for Katrina were just starting to sprout, but Katrina was a great woman who was here, accessible, and more than likely willing to continue to see him on his terms. Toriyana, on the other hand, was in Michigan demanding that he marry her. He was still not sure he was ready to make that move.

"David, are you still there?" Katrina asked.

"Uh, yes. I'm sorry. I zoned out for a minute thinking about some things."

Katrina was sure he was probably thinking about his girlfriend back in Detroit. She was unaware of their fight. She decided to steer the conversation in a different direction to hopefully erase the miles from his mind.

"So how was church today?" she asked nonchalantly.

"Well, from what I hear, it was way more interesting than just what happened *in* the sanctuary. In fact, your girl Maleeka's name was front and center in the drama."

"What! What drama? What happened, David?" Maleeka asked. She was shocked, a little frightened even.

"To be honest, I only heard lingering bits of gossip, but people were saying that she almost got into a fight in the narthex before service began. I didn't get the full lowdown on who she was going to beat down, but folks were saying it took a few people to hold her back from kicking some tail."

"Wow!"

Katrina was in complete shock. She had no idea who Maleeka would have that kind of beef with, especially not at the church. She surely hoped this had nothing to do with Darrin and her moving him into her apartment. Darrin had been known to cheat on Maleeka before, even though she did not see it that way. She prayed it was not about some other female. Katrina knew she had to call Maleeka quick to get the whole story, if there was even a story. Everyone knows that gossip and lies were spread in church quicker than the Gospel ever was.

"Katrina, do you have any specific plans for your day off? I would really like to see you," David said sweetly.

Katrina nearly came unglued on her sofa. All traces of Maleeka and her alleged drama vanished. She could not get her affirmation out quick enough.

"David, I have no plans whatsoever. I was just going to lie around and kick it here at home, but I'm open to seeing you as well," Katrina said excitedly. When she was done speaking, she sat hoping she did not sound desperate and non-discriminate where David was concerned, which was pretty much the truth. She just did not want him to realize it—at least not yet.

"Well, I have an idea. Why don't I just come to your place and we can kick back and relax together, just two friends hanging out. If we feel like getting up to go out to get something to eat later, we will. Otherwise we will just order something to be delivered. I'll bring a couple of my favorite DVDs. I'm sure you have a few of your own you could recommend. Wait. You do have a DVD player, don't you?"

Katrina giggled. "I actually have a Blu-ray player, but it will play your old school DVDs as well." They both had a good chuckle. "Your idea sounds like a great plan. What time should I expect you?"

"How about I see you in an hour?"

"Sounds like the plan is in motion. See you when you get here," Katrina replied as she hung up the phone, turned off the television, got up from the sofa, and began getting ready to receive her soon-to-arrive favorite guest.

After she had primped and prettied herself, Katrina sat back on the sofa waiting for David to get there. Instead of turning the television back on, she picked up her phone to call Maleeka. She needed to get the 411 on what really happened at church today.

"Hey, Kat," Maleeka said as she answered her phone.

"Hey, girl," Katrina sung in reply. "How was church today?" she continued, feigning innocence.

"Mm-hmm. Don't try to play slick with me, Kat. I see you have heard about the drama."

"Oh my gosh! So it's true? You were about to fight in church today? Girl, tell me what happened. And make it quick, because David is on his way over here."

"Ugh. Don't be rushing me for no man, especially one with a big mouth, because I now know who told you what happened at church today."

"Don't be talking negatively about my boo. Just tell give me the details so—" Katrina's doorbell rang before she could finish her sentence and get the low down.

"Shoot. I'm going to have to hear about it later. David's here. I'll call you later. Bye." She rushed off the phone and to the door.

Katrina opened the door and found David standing on the other side of it looking as scrumptious as ever. His beauty was so captivating that she nearly forgot to invite the man into the apartment.

"Hey, David. It's good to see you. Come on in." Katrina stepped aside to allow him to enter. She then leaned in for their customary church hug, facial cheeks and upper bodies touching, lower bodies intentionally separated by six inches or more.

David surprised Katrina, however, when he pulled her closer and embraced her just a bit more intimately. She tried not to let the shock register on her face, but she was sure she was beet red when they broke from the short cuddle.

She knew David noticed her surprise and blush, but being the sweet man that he was, he decided not to bring any attention to it.

"Look what I've got. *Rush Hour One, Two,* and *Three* for a little comic relief. Or if you're feeling more dramatic, I've got an old school classic, *The Color Purple.*" David smiled as if he was extremely pleased with his selections.

Once again, Katrina was embarrassed and tried to hide her inner blush. She was obviously thinking a little more along the lines of romance, because she had chosen *The Notebook, Meet the Browns,* and an old school but rarely recognized classic, *Love Field*, with Dennis Haysbert and Michelle Pfeiffer. Katrina had laid her selections on top of the television stand, but they were so casually sitting there, one really would not notice they were put there for the express purpose of watching any of them today.

"Oh. Let's see what you chose," David stated as he went right to the three movies.

So much for casual and inconspicuous, Katrina thought.

David raised an eyebrow as he looked over the titles. He looked at Katrina, back at the titles, and again at Katrina. He smiled a sly smile and placed the movies in her hand. He then picked up the four he brought over and asked, "So where do we start?" His question was laced with humor he tried his best to conceal.

Katrina was so embarrassed that her blush in her cheeks ran through her entire body and scorched the bottoms of her feet, but she did her best to conceal it.

"You're the guest. You choose," she said as she exhaled some of her shame.

"I was hoping you said that. I think I want to watch *Love Field*. I've never seen this one, and I have to confess, I have had a crush on Michelle Pfeiffer since *Scarface*."

Katrina appreciated David trying to make his selection seem matter-of-fact to help minimize Katrina's humiliation. She did not realize that in truth he really did want to see the movie. Michelle was his girl.

Katrina took the movie and loaded it into the Blu-ray player. She and David then sat down together on the sofa.

"I'm sorry. I forgot to ask. Do you want me to make some popcorn, or do you want something to drink?" Katrina asked.

"Umm, sure. I would love some popcorn. What do you have to drink?"

Katrina got up and placed a bag of popcorn in the microwave. She rattled off the list of beverages she had available. David made his selection, and when the corn was done popping, the two truly got comfortable and settled in to watch the movie.

***

Love Field was a sort of forbidden love type of story, but David would not necessarily classify it as a chick flick. He found himself actually enjoying it a great deal, now very pleased with his selection.

During the course of the movie, David subconsciously found himself scooting in closer and closer to Katrina. By the end of the movie, he was comfortably wrapped with her in a semi-embrace on the sofa. David had pulled Katrina's back against his chest, with his arm draped across the back of the sofa and his hand on her shoulder.

Katrina may have appeared comfortable on the outside. On the inside, her emotions were all over the map. There was an intimacy between them, in her mind, that ran far beyond the physical. Sure, they were close, touching even, but for Katrina the cocoon of pleasure engulfing them was what played on her heartstrings. The normalcy of their shared contentment was what made her feel everything but normal.

She stole a glance at David as the credits began to roll for the movie. The smile of satisfaction told her he was pleased with more than just the film they watched together.

Katrina knew she had a tendency to read more into situations than what was actually present. Considering how she felt about David, and that she wanted so desperately for him to feel something akin for her, she knew allowing her fantasies to run amok at a time like this would be easy.

The credits had completed and the television had returned the DVD back to its original cover photo. The pair continued to remain in position, sitting in silence, enjoying the peace of their connection.

David was the first to move. He pulled away from Katrina, and she felt his absence immediately, but only momentarily. David slightly switched his position and placed himself directly next to Katrina. He shifted his head, then, using his forefinger, he shifted hers as well so that the two of them were facing each other.

"I have wanted to do this since the moment I walked in your door and hugged you."

Katrina opened her mouth slightly to ask "what," putting her lips in the perfect position for David to cover them with a warm, wet kiss. The kiss was short and sweet, yet it left a long-lasting impact on both parties. When they separated, Katrina laid her head on David's shoulder and sighed audibly. The sweet rush of wind carried with it unspoken desire, unanswered questions, and unfamiliar territory for both of them.

"Katrina, we have to talk," David said wistfully.

The tone of his voice made talking the last thing Katrina wanted to do. His tone said the conversation would be none too pleasant, but she wordlessly lifted her head and shifted her body, putting a little space between them. David grabbed her hand and began speaking.

"I talked to Toriyana a few nights ago. I told her about us going out, and it turned into a really big ordeal, a fight even. She felt like I betrayed her and cheated on her. She initially broke up with me, but when we talked the other day, she gave me an ultimatum. She wants me to either marry her and move her here, or I go back to Detroit, or I leave her alone for good."

Katrina's heart sank to her feet. The mere mention of him and Toriyana getting married or even contemplating marriage made her sick to the pit of her stomach. She had fallen in love with David and wanted him completely to herself. She tolerated his relationship with his girlfriend back in Detroit *because* she was in Detroit, but the truth of it was that it drove her crazy to think about the two of them as a couple.

This is what I get for going out with someone else's boyfriend, she thought silently as her heart melted in her chest and dripped burning remnants into her belly. Now she had kissed him, shared an intimacy with him that for her escalated her love for him, only to have him tell her he was going to marry Toriyana.

David tightened his grip on the hand she had forgotten he still held and continued speaking. "Katrina, I would be lying to you if I pretended I didn't know how you feel about me. It would be so cliché for me to say I never meant to hurt you, because I know hearing this does bother you. It is written all over your beautiful face. But I would also be lying if I said I have not seriously been considering Toriyana's proposition."

Well, since he had admitted he would not pretend with her, Katrina would then not pretend with him. She removed her hand from his and used it to cover the pain on the face he thought to be beautiful. She thought that she would cry, but the tears did not come. She held on to the anguish in her heart and sat silently as he kept talking.

"I really do like you, Katrina. I have enjoyed every second of every moment we have spent together. I honestly look forward to spending even more time with you . . ."

Katrina looked up at him through the fingers that covered her face. She hoped her hand masked the contempt she instantly felt. How dare he say he wanted to continue to spend time with her after telling her he was going to marry his girlfriend? Did he think he was just going to use her to fill the gap in time between now and the day he marched down the aisle with Toriyana?

David was oblivious to the boo-boo face Katrina was giving him, because he kept on talking. "Katrina, I'm so confused. I care deeply for Toriyana. We have been together for over two years, and I must admit I love her . . ."

The boo-boo face quickly turned back into the hand-covered sad face.

"But I'm not sure I am ready to get married to her. I'm not as confident as I feel I need to be that she is the woman I am meant to spend the rest of my life with. I mean, as I thought about this just last night, I realized that if we were in that place, I would have never left Detroit without her."

It took a moment for David's words to seep past Katrina's skin and penetrate her pain-filled heart, but eventually they did get through. The hand slowly came down from her face, the boo-boo face transformed into one of expectation. The pain in her heart was quickly displaced and replaced with a great hope. Katrina did not want to assume anything, so she kept the smile that was threatening to split her face on the inside of her soul.

"David, look. I really care about you. I don't want to play any word games with you. I'm not trying to hold on to any pride here or save face, hoping you say what I want to hear, or hoping against hope that you don't say something I don't want to hear. I appreciate your honesty and you telling me about your conversation with Toriyana. But plain and simple, I need to know what this means for you and me. What exactly are you saying to me here? And please, don't worry about sparing my feelings. Give it to me honestly. I would rather know the absolute truth than to spend any more time unsure, guessing, assuming, hoping, speculating, or even fantasizing."

David looked Katrina directly in her eyes, suddenly proud of the decision he had made to ask her out that very first time. He saw a woman of integrity, a woman

he believed he could count on to tell him the truth and
be willing to hear the truth and openly deal with it. This
was a woman who would give as good as she got and
perhaps even go a step above for those she truly cared
for.

"Katrina, like I said before, I am not ready to make
the kind of commitment Toriyana is requesting. In
fact, being completely honest, I'm not ready to make
that kind of commitment to anyone . . ." David softened
his voice. "Including you."

Katrina believed David was expecting some sort of
painful reaction from her, but the truth of the matter
was she totally understood him. As crazy as she was
about David, she knew she was not ready to accept a
proposal from him, even if he offered her one at that
moment. She kept quiet and continued to simply listen
to him speak.

"Katrina, I want to continue seeing you. I think what
Toriyana and I had has run its course and it's time to
call it quits. Her ultimatum actually gives me no other
choice, but I do believe in my stance that until I am
ready to at least get engaged, I am a single man. You
can trust that I will always be honest with you, and
right now there is no one other than you I am interested in hanging out with like this. But I will not com-
mit myself to anyone other than the woman I plan to
spend the rest of my life with someday. I hope you can
accept me on those terms and still want to spend time
with me."

Katrina finally allowed the smile that teased the
back of her mouth to fully present itself to the front
of her face. She felt relief and a bit of a challenge in
what David said. She was extremely happy he wanted
to continue to spend time with her. She felt a bit sorry
for Toriyana and their demise, but she refused to take
blame in any way for that demise.

She was now on a mission to be a great friend to David, since *girlfriend* seemed to no longer be a part of his vocabulary. She would pray, asking God to give her wisdom, clarity of her mind and her steps as far as David was concerned, and the patience to wait for him to decide if she was the woman who would become his wife. She believed in her heart that David was exactly the kind of man she wanted to marry, but the Bible said in proverbs 18:22, "The man who finds a wife finds a treasure, and he receives favor from the LORD." So she would wait on God to give him to her, if it was His will for their lives.

"Of course I want to continue to spend time with you. Like I said, I'm crazy about you. Your stance on commitment is cool with me, as long as you keep your promise to be honest with me. And I promise you the same thing. I will always keep it real with you about any decision to see others."

Katrina threw that last part in for good measure. She could not imagine any man more interesting, intelligent, or irresistible than David Mathis.

For some reason David did not like the idea of Katrina hanging out with other guys any more than he did when Toriyana expressed it during their initial conversation about his level of commitment. David decided he would not worry about it, though. He would just be sure to keep Ms. Hartfield very busy.

Chapter Eighteen

Maleeka and Aujanae were trying to enjoy their meal at Applebee's while going over their very eventful day at church. Maleeka purposely steered the conversation in this direction in hopes of avoiding having to truly explain her living situation with Darrin as she had promised at the church.

"What was April thinking, showing up at church like that today? You would think the homewrecker would find another church to attend. I could have squeezed the life right out of her with my bare hands," Maleeka said as she demonstrated her words.

"Girl, I could not believe that skank had the nerve to get all funky, talking about William didn't find anything trashy about her. How dare she?" Aujanae fumed.

"Yes, child. That was just way too much for me right there. She better go to bed tonight thanking God for you and Deacon Ealy. I was about to punch her straight in the mouth for that comment."

Aujanae chuckled. "Yes, you were. Girl, you surprised me. I did not know you were this feisty, Maleeka."

"You know what? I'm normally not that crazy. I have not actually had a fist fight since fifth grade, but seeing her all bold and brazen, standing there like the Queen of Sheba just set something off in me. That cow probably doesn't think she did anything wrong either. She probably thinks that she had every right to date William because he allowed it. You know what I mean?

She probably also blames you. You know how they do and what they say: 'His wife wasn't keeping him happy. He was so unsatisfied in his marriage,' like she was doing him some sort of favor. Women like that make me sick."

Maleeka had worked herself up into another semi rage just talking about April and her audacity. She was so angry that she almost neglected to notice the pained look on Aujanae's face.

"Oh, Aujanae. I'm so sorry. I was just rambling on, being all insensitive. This is all still pretty raw for you." Maleeka reached across the table and rubbed Aujanae's hand.

"Maybe she would be right. Maybe I was a bad wife. Maybe I didn't satisfy William," Aujanae said somberly.

"Don't you dare! Don't you dare blame yourself for this. Did William ever complain to you about being a bad wife or not satisfying him?" Aujanae remained quiet and sullen. "Answer me, Aujanae!"

"No! William has never said that he was unhappy in our marriage. I mean, we were not perfect. We had issues like every other married couple. I had no clue that he was dissatisfied."

"Then there you have it. I don't care if you were the worst wife on the face of the planet. It would have been his job to alert you that he was not happy and then try to work through things with you, not go out and get himself a hooker." Maleeka slapped the table to emphasize her point.

Aujanae tried to smile and allow Maleeka's wisdom to seep into her psyche. Maleeka was right, she thought. William's affair was in no way her fault, and she would not allow herself to take any blame.

The pair sat at the table, chowing on more of their meal for a few moments before speaking again. Maleeka was the first to call it quits with her Asian chicken salad. She looked at Aujanae carefully, measuring her next words before she blurted them out like she had done earlier without considering Aujanae's feelings. Aujanae looked up to find her friend staring at her intently.

"What is it, Maleeka? Why are you looking at me like that?" Aujanae asked, puzzled.

"I know what William did was jacked up, Aujanae, but no one will be mad at you if you decided to forgive him and try to work on your marriage." Maleeka's voice was the softest and most compassionate it had been all day.

Aujanae's eyes filled with tears at the heartfelt statement of her friend. Many women colleagues would be singing every woman-done-wrong, girl-leave-him-alone song ever created, but even in the midst of nearly coming to blows with her husband's mistress, her good friend Maleeka was telling her it was okay to take him back and forgive him. Aujanae viewed that as true godly friendship—a friendship she would be sure to cherish.

"Thank you for saying that, Maleeka, but I don't think there is anything left for me and William. Like you said, if he was unhappy with me he could have at least told me, warned me even, but he was too selfish to say anything. He did not just have an affair, a thirty-day fling with a beautiful woman he ran into in the mall and just could not resist. He had a long-term relationship. Heck, he even went as far as to fall in love with another woman."

That statement made one of the tears that rested in her eyes fall, but Aujanae choked back the sentiment and continued to share with her friend what she felt in her heart.

"I don't think I could ever trust him enough to let him back into my life after that. Not to mention the fact that he thought so little of me, so much of her, that he did not even think to protect me from what could have been a life-threatening disease. No. That is not a man I want to share the rest of my life with any longer." Aujanae's pain was tangible, but her strength was admirable.

"I'm not trying to be an advocate for William or his behavior, girl. I support you whether you stay or leave the marriage, but you two have a son together. Have you thought about how this will affect him?"

"Of course I have. B.J. has been my number-one priority in this whole sordid mess, but William and I don't have to be together to properly raise our son. William is a great father. I don't think that will change. I won't play games with him or anything of the sort when it comes to him spending time and contributing to raising our child. Even if he and April stay together. I know William won't allow any harm to come to my baby, so we will just work through parenting our child together."

Maleeka was very proud of Aujanae. Not many women—including herself, if she was honest—would be so amiable under the same circumstances. Aujanae was truly letting her Jesus light shine in this situation. Maleeka realized she was actually glowing with it as she spoke so confidently and sincerely.

"You know, you sound like you know what you're doing, Aujanae. Good for you. Now me, even though I was trying to be Christ-like when I said what I said about it being okay to take him back, I don't know if I could in reality be so calm and rational if I had to actually wear your shoes. Me, I would be burning up some clothes, setting BMWs on fire, having a true *Waiting to Exhale* moment before I let go and let God." Both women cracked up laughing.

When the laughter quieted down, Aujanae had some questions of her own to ask.

"Speaking of relationships and marriages and what-not, when did you and your fiancé Darrin start living together? What prompted you all to move in together instead of waiting until you were married?" Aujanae asked, surprised.

Maleeka rolled her eyes, thoroughly through even with herself for her harebrained scheme at this point. She initially started to give Aujanae some made-up story that would possibly make sense of her decision, but she could not even think of one. In light of all Aujanae had endured today and these last few weeks, she felt she owed her the truth. She told her of her reasoning, from the beginning of her plan all the way to how she felt it was the most foolish decision she had ever made as she woke up this morning.

"Girl, the sight of Darrin makes me sick right now, and it has only been one week. The truth of the matter is it's not really him specifically. I think it's my own guilt and conviction that makes me so sensitive to every little thing he does wrong. I know I have been cranky, irritable, and virtually impossible to live with, but I can't help myself. Pastor Abraham's sermon today did and did not help matters. I mean, it helped amp up my guilt, but it made me realize I messed up big time, girl."

In light of how helpful and insightful Maleeka had been to her in her crisis, Aujanae wanted to be just as supportive to her friend and offer her godly advice in return.

"Mal, the fact that your decision is tearing you up the way it is, is a good thing. It shows you do love the Lord. You have just got to love him more than you love Darrin. I don't know the details of your living arrangement or what Darrin's options are, but you all need to put an end to this. Let him get his own place or go back to his old place or whatever, but the last thing you want to do is get comfortable in the situation you are in. You need to rectify this while you can and wait until you two are properly wed before living together, no matter how close your wedding date is. By the way, have you two set your date yet?" Aujanae asked curiously.

Maleeka rolled her eyes and groaned loudly. "No. I have been engaged to this fool for four years. I have foolishly moved him into my place, hoping to prompt him into hurrying up and marrying me, and I have turned into this mean woman, filled with guilt that I don't even recognize anymore, only to be no closer to being a proper wife than I was on Valentine's Day, four years ago."

Maleeka dramatically plopped her head down on their table loudly. The noise prompted a few people nearby to look in their direction. Aujanae smiled an embarrassed smile at the other patrons then got up from her side of the table to check on Maleeka.

"Girl, are you okay? Look up. Let me see if you have a knot on your head," Aujanae asked, concerned.

"I'm fine," Maleeka stated as she raised her head. No bruising or bumps were visible. "I think I just knocked some sense into myself. I have decided when I get home I am going to tell Darrin that he needs to move back into his house with David. The transition will be annoying, but it will be less painful than continuing to live in the cocoon of guilt and misery."

"Good for you. If you need me to, I will even help."

"Thanks, Aujanae. I truly appreciate your ear and your advice."

"Right back at you, girlfriend. But I have one last question. How in the heck did Gerald Miller find out about you and Darrin living together? What is going on between you two? There were sparks flying like crazy between you two."

"That's like three or four questions, Aujanae." Maleeka chuckled goodheartedly. "But to answer your question, Gerald Miller has been flirting incessantly with me since the first day we met. I have told him I am engaged, but he keeps insisting, none too subtly, that Darrin is not good enough for me. He thinks he's better. He knows about our living arrangement because he was at David's house the day we moved Darrin out of there."

"Hmmm. I see," Aujanae said subjectively.

"Girl, there is a whole lot being said in that *hmmm*. I know what you are thinking: the same thing my cousin Tammy has been saying and thinking for quite some time as well. You both think Gerald is better for me too," Maleeka said dismissively.

"Don't sleep on that man, Maleeka. He seems like a catch to me. He is good looking. He is in church every Sunday. He is one of the leaders in the Men's Ministry. He seems very interested in you. He is obviously single. He is always dressed so nice. He drives a nice car. And did I say he was good looking? Honey, if you don't want him, pass him my way."

Maleeka gave her patented eye roll and said nothing else on that subject. If she were to say something honestly, she would probably tell Aujanae to keep her still-married paws to herself.

"Let's get out of here. I have got to get home and kick a certain man I'm engaged to out of my apartment. No use putting it off. The sooner it's done, the sooner I can get this shame out of my spirit."

Aujanae paid the check for both meals, and the ladies got ready to leave the restaurant. Just as they approached the door, none other than the man of the last five minutes' conversation appeared as if he were a conjured-up apparition coming through the same door.

"Gerald!" both ladies exclaimed simultaneously.

Gerald's eyes bucked at the urgent tone in the women's voices.

"Hello, ladies," he said inquisitively.

"Funny you should show up here, at this moment, today," Aujanae said comically. Maleeka shot her a contemptuous look.

"Are you stalking me, Mr. Miller?" Maleeka asked in mocked suspicion.

"Stalking you? A man brings his favorite niece out for their ritual biweekly dining experience, trying to do a good deed, and he gets accused of criminal behavior. Wow. Only in America, and by a Christian woman no less," Gerald mocked in return.

"Your niece?" Aujanae asked.

"Yes. She ran in ahead of me. She had to make it to the restroom in a hurry."

Gerald's answer was for Aujanae, but he never took his eyes off Maleeka. She was so riveted by his stare that she was unable to pull her own eyes away.

"Ahem." Aujanae simulated clearing her throat to break the trance. "I think that is very sweet of you, Gerald, to purposely spend that kind of time with your niece. I would love to meet this blessed young lady."

"But we really don't have time. We must get going," Maleeka said, feigning disappointment.

"Oh no, Maleeka, we have a few minutes. I'm sure Gerald's niece won't be too long."

Maleeka wanted to choke Aujanae. To continue to protest, however, would make her look silly and too eager to get away from Gerald.

Gerald laughed at the look of aloofness on Maleeka's face.

"My niece is the only child of my only brother. He's a couple of years younger than me. He became a dad when he was barely out of his teens, but he's had custody of his daughter since her mother ran off and left when Deidre was just a few months old. I spend as much time with her as possible. She's thirteen. I believe in young ladies having positive male role models in their lives before they start dealing with these knuckle-headed young boys out here."

Aujanae none too subtly nudged Maleeka with her elbow. Just then Gerald's niece appeared.

"I'm sorry, Uncle G, but I really had to go," the pretty young teenager announced.

"It's okay, sweetie. Deidre, these two beautiful ladies attend church with me. This is Ms. Aujanae," he stated, pointing in her direction, "and this is Ms. Maleeka." When he said Maleeka's name, he reached out and actually touched her shoulder.

Maleeka was surprised by the surge of comforting heat that penetrated her skin at his touch. She wanted to jerk away for fear of truly leaning into its appeal, but she did not want to embarrass any of the others standing with them; so she just stood there like a statue, willing herself not to move.

"Both of you have very pretty names," Deidre stated politely.

"Thank you. And you are a very pretty young lady," Aujanae responded.

Maleeka was barely able to eke out a "Thank you." She was so thankful when Gerald finally removed his hand.

"Well, we won't hold you two any longer. It was truly a pleasure running into you again today." Gerald was addressing both ladies, but again his eyes were on Maleeka.

Then, to the ladies' surprise, Gerald stated, "Maleeka, you need to give me a call. I think we should talk."

"I don't have a number for you, Gerald." Maleeka's response surprised all the adults in the circle, including herself.

Gerald reached into his jacket pocket and removed a gold case, holding his business cards. He handed one to Maleeka. As an afterthought he gave one to Aujanae as well.

Maleeka took the card silently and read it. Aujanae took hers and stuck it in her purse without so much as a quick glance.

"Thank you, Gerald. Nice to meet you, Deidre," Aujanae said.

"Looking forward to hearing from you." Gerald did not address his comment to either lady specifically, but everyone knew who he was talking to.

Chapter Nineteen

On the drive home, Maleeka could not keep her thoughts focused on where they needed to be. She needed to be thinking of the best way to tell Darrin he had to move out and hopefully not have it turn into a big scene. Instead she kept focusing on the still-lingering touch of Gerald Miller. Aujanae's list of Gerald's good qualities kept popping into her head. Couple those with his declaration and desire to spend time with his only niece in an effort to shield her from the bull of the boys her age, and future bull of the ones Darrin's age, and she had to admit Gerald Miller was suddenly, overwhelmingly interesting to her.

The card he gave her stated he was a financial analyst for Merrill Lynch. Maleeka was not the least bit materialistic, so the money he made in his career was not very important to her, but she assumed a job title like that had to require substantial intellect. Darn her for thinking it, but the man did just happen to be good looking. Goodness gracious.

Maleeka forced her thoughts to return to the issue at hand and at home. Darrin. Her fiancé of four long years. The man she could barely get to attend his own church, the church where he grew up. The man who was still afraid to stand up to his parents. The man who was probably sitting in front of the television waiting for her to return home to feed him and pick up his wet bath towels and funky socks. Maleeka thought about

Gerald's list and Darrin's list and realized why she was having such a hard time keeping her mind off Gerald and on Darrin.

When she walked into the house, Maleeka found Darrin exactly where she thought he would be, glued to the television with a stack of DVDs that he had either already watched and/or planned to watch throughout the rest of the day. She walked in and gave him a curt hello, then headed back to her bedroom to exchange her church shoes for her house slippers. She needed to be comfortable for the conversation she was getting ready to have.

While in the room, she found a shoe on top of her antique vanity table and a wet towel strewn over the back of its chair.

"Lord, help me," Maleeka said aloud, speaking directly to God.

As she marched down the short hallway, she tried her best to keep her mind focused and her thoughts clear. It would not do her any good to conjure up images of Gerald as she prepared to confront Darrin. The last thing she wanted was the impression of a perfect man, which in basic reality did not exist, clouding her thoughts, allowing that to be the reason she asked Darrin to leave. She needed to stay on task, remembering that it was the only perfect man, Jesus, whom she was trying to please.

The moment she crossed the threshold into the living room, before she even had a chance to make herself comfortable in a chair, Darrin began speaking first.

"Hey, baby. I'm glad you're home. How was church? Did you see my parents? Mom has been blowing up my phone since what I'm assuming was right after church let out. Did she say anything to you?" he asked curiously.

More fuel for the fire, Maleeka thought. Here she was engaged to and living with a grown man who was hiding from his mama.

"Darrin, I did see your mother at church, and she wanted me to tell you to give her a call, so I think you should do that as soon as possible," Maleeka stated with more calm than she felt. Suddenly she was nervous about her proclamation to make Darrin leave.

"Mal, look. I have told you I'm not ready to tell my mother about us living together yet. I know you want me to make this announcement to my parents and have it somehow validate us to them, but I will tell them when I'm more comfortable—maybe once we have at least set a wedding date. That way this shacking up thing may look a little less sordid and a little more practical. So baby, let's not argue about this, okay? What's for dinner?"

Maleeka stared at Darrin without saying anything for several moments. She was really at a loss for words. She did not know whether to concentrate on being excited that he at least mentioned setting a wedding date, or perturbed about him asking her what's for dinner. Maleeka made her way to her favorite chair, suddenly exhausted from merely being in her own skin. Her seesaw emotions were wearing her out. Finally she found her voice.

"Darrin, are you ready to set our wedding date?" she asked simply.

Darrin looked away swiftly from his movie and gave his full attention to Maleeka.

"Aw, man, Maleeka. See, I should have known you were going to take this conversation way out of context. I was just trying to help you understand why I am not ready to tell my parents about us living together. I should have known the only thing you would hear would be *wedding date*." He shook his head and refocused on the television just that quickly.

Maleeka lowered her head and closed her eyes. She sat in her chair, in her apartment, with her now ex-fiancé and started praying aloud.

"Father, I come to you at this very moment, asking You, Lord, to forgive me. Forgive me, Father, for my sin of fornication. Forgive me, Father, for allowing my heart to take control and not staying close to You through the Holy Spirit. Forgive me, Lord, for allowing my fleshly desire to be married to choose for me who I thought would be my husband. Lord, I ask You to give me the strength to turn this situation around and to lean on You to get me through the grieving process as I let this relationship die. Father, give me the strength and the wisdom to depend on You and to wait on You to send me the man You have prepared for me as my husband. Lord, I am depending on You to comfort me, to show me that You are all I need until or unless You move me in that direction. This is my prayer in Jesus' name. Amen."

When Maleeka lifted her head, she found Darrin staring at her in complete and utter shock. She chose not to concern herself with his look, however. She needed to stay focused.

"Darrin, you got to go. This past week we have lived together has been more stressful for me than any other time in my life. I'm not saying you have done anything particularly foul or anything like that. I'm just saying that the guilt and shame I have been feeling has been unbearable. You can hide our living arrangement from your parents, but you can't hide it from God, and neither can I; therefore, you have got to leave. I pray David lets you come back to the house with him. I'm sorry for the inconvenience of the move. Heck, I am sorry for the inconvenience of the past six years."

Maleeka got up from her seat and walked toward Darrin as she removed her engagement ring. "But I refuse to continue to be your long-term fiancée, translation: strung-along girlfriend, for another moment."

She dropped the ring in Darrin's lap as she walked past him into her bedroom. She returned a few seconds later with the other three rings and gently placed them in the opened palm that matched his wide open mouth. Maleeka ignored his crazy look and resumed her speech, pacing back and forth in the living room.

"It's still kind of early in the evening. It's only four thirty. We can start packing your stuff now. I will take tomorrow off work and move you back to your place while you are off. Aujanae has already agreed to help me. Do you need me to call David and make sure it's okay that you return? If he has a problem with it, I will give you the money to stay in a Days Inn or Motel 6 for up to a week while you find a new spot. As a matter of fact, I will pay for you to stay there tonight, too, because we will not spend another night under the same roof."

Maleeka sounded and moved in the living room as if she had overdosed on caffeinated energy drinks. The truth of the matter was that she was actually very controlled and steadfast. When she finally stopped moving and talking, she leaned against a wall and waited for Darrin to say something, or even better, say nothing and just get up and start packing. Suddenly the song "When a Woman's Fed Up" by R. Kelly started playing in her head.

Darrin sat on the sofa, stunned, unable to find the words to reply to anything Maleeka said. He was literally shocked speechless.

After about sixty seconds of listening to Darrin say nothing, Maleeka again took up the charge.

"Okay, Darrin. Since you don't have any ideas about how to start facilitating this move, I'll go ahead and get you started. I've got about seventy-five dollars cash in my purse. I will pack you a few things for tonight, making sure you have what you need for tonight and to get you to work tomorrow. You can take the money and find yourself a room."

Maleeka walked to the bedroom and returned with the money and her cell phone. Darrin was still sitting glued to the same spot.

"You know what? I'm going to give David a call. He's probably still at Katrina's. I'm going to ask him if you can move back in with him, or at the very least see if you can stay there tonight. No use wasting money if I don't have to."

When Maleeka began looking through her cell phone contacts to find David's number, Darrin finally got up from his seat. He rushed over to Maleeka in a fury, grabbed her cell phone, and threw it against the wall, smashing it into seemingly a million tiny pieces. Maleeka recoiled at the noise as the phone smashed into the wall. She had never seen Darrin react so violently. She wanted to move from the spot where she stood, face to face, noses nearly touching, in front of Darrin, but because the wall was against her back and her ex-fiancé was right in her face, she really had no place to go. Maleeka began praying in her head that Darrin would not try to hurt her.

"I don't need you to do anything or call anybody for me. I don't need your money and I don't need you," Darrin yelled before turning on his heels and heading to Maleeka's bedroom.

Maleeka moved slowly from the wall and returned to her chair. Darrin remained in the bedroom for about twenty minutes. Maleeka stayed glued to the chair. She was very curious as to what he was doing back there, but the violent act he committed on her cell phone made her stay put.

Darrin emerged with a huge duffle bag stuffed to capacity on one arm. In the other he held a bag that more than likely housed his computer. Darrin put those bags down by the front door. He then began walking toward Maleeka, which immediately made her stiffen in her seat. He stopped short of reaching her chair, opting instead to only go as far as the sofa. He reached down and grabbed what Maleeka now realized were her engagement rings. Up until that point, she had paid the jewelry sitting on her sofa no attention. Darrin stuffed the rings in his pants pocket. He glared at Maleeka for a few brief seconds. He suddenly opened his mouth to say something, but just as quickly clamped it shut so hard she heard his teeth click. He moved back to the front door, grabbed his bags, and left the apartment wordlessly.

Maleeka did not realize she was holding her breath until she actually exhaled after Darrin left. The first thought that came to mind after he left was that he still had a key to her apartment. She got up on very shaky legs and walked to the bedroom to see if he had left the key there, but came up empty handed. She wanted to change the locks, but had no idea how to go about doing it other than calling a locksmith. She had seen enough TV shows depicting the difficulty and expense of hiring a locksmith to come in an emergency on the weekend to know she did not want to go that route.

Since Darrin had turned her cell phone into a thousand-piece jigsaw puzzle, she had to opt for using her home phone to make contact with the outside world. She was probably the only person she knew who still had a land line phone in her apartment. She went to the phone to call Katrina, to let her know what happened and for her to help calm her down in the aftermath of her breakup. She then realized she did not have a clue what her best friend's phone number was. As a matter of fact, she could not think of a single phone number by heart. With the convenience of simply pushing a button or two on her cell phone and reaching those who were closest to her, she never took the time to actually memorize their phone numbers. She could not even call Darrin if she wanted to, which she absolutely did not want to do. She knew she was officially and forever through with him.

Maleeka found her way back to her chair to try to come up with a solution to having her locks changed without having to take out a loan to do it.

"God, what am I going to do?" she pleaded aloud.

Then it hit her. She remembered that Gerald Miller had given her his business card earlier in the day, stating he would be looking forward to her phone call. Maleeka jumped up from her chair and ran to the bedroom to retrieve Gerald's card from her purse. She sat on the bed and decided to call him from the phone in there.

After dialing the number, Maleeka's stomach turned into a butterflies' nest. When the phone started ringing, her mouth went dry. When his velvety smooth voice came on the line, all fears were calmed.

"Hello," he answered

"Hi, Gerald. It's me, Maleeka."

The need to tell him everything and even ask for his help overwhelmed her. Rather than allowing her pride to overrule her senses at that moment, Maleeka gave in to her desire and poured her heart out to Gerald.

"Wow. You have been through a lot today, haven't you? Look, why don't you give me your address. I will stop by Home Depot and grab a standard lock and head over there to change your lock, hopefully giving you at least a little peace of mind for the night. What do you say?"

"I say thank you so much. I don't know why, after the way I have treated you in the past, but I knew you, the only person actually available to me right now, would have no problem coming to my rescue."

"I must admit, I am very happy to be the only person you could turn to at a time like this. I could say a lot more, but I won't. You have had a pretty rough day. Give me your address and I will be on my way."

Maleeka recited her address then said aloud, "Thank you so much, Gerald. And thank You, God."

Chapter Twenty

Two weeks ago, April had put in her notice at the firm, letting them know she was resigning and moving back to Chicago. She had actually decided a month prior to that to make the move, which was right after she received the news from her doctor that she was completely cancer free. Life in Phoenix held absolutely no appeal for her any longer.

In the time since the humiliating fallout with William's wife and her ghetto girlfriend at the church, April had been doing some serious soul-searching, hoping to find answers that would cure the savage pain she felt behind losing William for good.

After the last time he told her he would not see her again, William held steady to his resolve. He stopped taking her phone calls, would not respond to her emails, and even had her escorted out of the building by security when she showed up on his job one morning insisting that she needed to see him. Standing on the sidewalk outside of his office building, staring at her reflection in the windows, wearing her broken heart all over her face, was the final straw for her. She knew at that moment she had hit her rock bottom.

In her quest for healing, she decided to try to remember the last time there was happiness in her life, the life before she knew William. The answer came to her with the jolt that held as much power as a lightning bolt. April remembered she was happiest when she was not in love with anyone but herself, so it only made sense to return to the life she once knew—a simpler place and time for her. That meant going back home. She needed to put William Rucker and everything that reminded her of him out of her life for good.

Well, almost everything. The one thing she would hold on to was her desire to continue to attend church. She made a promise to herself and to God that she would begin visiting various churches in Chicago when she arrived and would eventually find one to pledge her membership to.

So here she sat at Sky Harbor International Airport, waiting to board the plane and get comfortable in her first class seat back to the place before life included relationship, love, and heartache.

April decided to check her emails on her phone while she waiting to board. As she fished through her cute new Prada handbag for her phone, the area around her seemed to lose its sunlight. April looked up to see what had caused the sudden eclipse. Standing before her was a beautiful six feet four inch, two hundred and fifty pound specimen of a man who had seemingly dropped straight down from heaven.

He eventually took the seat right next to her, not paying her any particular attention. April knew better, however. There were several unoccupied seats near where she was sitting, so his sitting smack dab next to her, practically in her lap, considering his size, was by no means a coincidence. Somebody needed to tell this man that he was dealing with a woman who had once upon a time been an expert in the game.

April decided to play along. She pulled out her phone and continued with the task she had begun.

"Excuse me, miss. Do you happen to have a pen I can borrow in that beautiful bag of yours?" Heaven Sent asked.

April was impressed that he recognized and was impressed by the quality and splendor of her bag. This was a man with an eye for detail and the finer things in life.

"I believe I do, sir."

April reached into her bag, removed her Mont Blanc writing pen from the slot in the purse, and handed it to him

Heaven Sent gently removed the pen from her fingers and studied it ceremoniously.

"Nice. Very nice. I'd be willing to bet my first class see that you are flying first class as well," he said in a voice that oozed both sensuality and style.

This man was obviously familiar with quality, but he was definitely a novice in the game of subtlety. She decided she would not hold it against him, though.

April smiled. "You, sir, would be able to keep your seat," April replied smoothly.

Heaven Sent smiled as well, revealing a very expensive set of well cared for, natural teeth. He held on to the pen April had given him, making no moves whatsoever to utilize it.

"May I ask why you asked for my pen? You look as if you are about to hijack it," April said suspiciously.

Heaven Sent placed the pen between his large fingers on his ring-less left hand and eyed it curiously, as if he were looking at it for the first time. He then snapped the fingers on his right hand, indicating he had suddenly remembered something.

"Oh, yes. I was going to use it to write down your number," he responded cleverly.

Cute, April thought, but she was not prepared to give in to his charm just yet.

"Write down my phone number? That's a bit old fashioned, isn't it? I thought things like that were done electronically now."

"I'm an old fashioned guy, beautiful. Besides, I plan on presenting the piece of paper back to you on our wedding day, reminding you of the day we first met."

Wow! Now, that was smooth, April thought.

Just then the airline announcer came on the microphone announcing that all first class passengers could begin boarding now.

"What is your name?" Heaven Sent asked.

"Why don't we discuss all of our particulars while we are in flight?" April responded flirtatiously.

Heaven Sent stood, again blocking out the sun, and offered April his hand.

God was just going to have to be patient with her, she thought as she placed her small hand in his palm and allowed him to glide her back to very familiar territory.

David was filled with trepidation as he approached the door cautiously. He honestly could not understand the incessant need he had to see her, to talk to her, especially under the circumstances. He had not spoken to Toriyana since he told her he was not ready to marry her and therefore could not give in to her ultimatum.

David had been in Detroit for three days now. Each day he talked himself out of going by her house to see her.

"She does not want to talk to you. She wants nothing else to do with you," he would convince himself. Yesterday, however, he had given up arguing with himself and decided to just given in and go see her. He at least persuaded himself to wait until the following day, as it was Thanksgiving Day when he made his decision. He did not want to ruin her holiday.

David was certain Toriyana knew he was in town for the holidays. They had talked about it often when they were still a couple; yet she did not once try to reach out to him. His urge to see her in spite of that was still baffling to him as he rang her doorbell.

Toriyana sat on her sofa in her living room snugly wrapped in her favorite blanket after finishing off a plate of leftover Thanksgiving Day food for lunch. She was hunkered in for a day of catching up on her favorite television programs. There were so many shows on her DVR that she had to pray she would get through them all before she had to return to work on Monday.

Yesterday had been a great day for her. She enjoyed spending time with her family, eating a great meal, and introducing her mother to her new friend, Treyvon. She met Treyvon about two weeks ago in the city county building while running an errand for her boss. He stood in the middle of the floor, looking as lost as a displaced puppy. She could not help going to see if he needed assistance, especially since he was such a cutie-pie.

"Hello. Is there someplace I can help you find?" Toriyana asked sincerely.

"Yes. Oh my goodness. Thank you. I'm here to file for a business license," Treyvon said gratefully.

"Well, let's come over here to the big board which will direct you to exactly where you need to go."

Toriyana led the way to the directory in the main lobby of the building. She stood with Treyvon as he looked at the menu. She watched has his eyes brightened and his lips curl into a smile when he found what he was looking for. His excitement made her smile.

"Wow. I never paid any attention to this board. Thank you so much for taking pity on a lost soul," he said genuinely. Toriyana noticed he had a Southern accent for the first time.

"No problem at all. You are not from Detroit, are you?" she asked.

"No, ma'am. I moved here from Florida three months ago. My name is Treyvon," he said as he offered Toriyana his hand.

"Hello. My name is Toriyana Kent. Welcome to Detroit. It's nice to meet you," she replied and placed her hand in his.

"Please call me Treyvon. Toriyana. That is an unusually pretty name." Again he gifted Toriyana with his smile.

Toriyana could not help but return the gesture.

"Thank you," she said shyly.

The two new acquaintances stood silently staring at each other until it became a little obvious and uncomfortable to them both, although they both seemed to like what they saw.

"Well, I need to get back to the courthouse before my boss sends out a search party for these files," Toriyana said finally to break the trance. "Again, it was nice to meet you, Treyvon."

Toriyana slowly put her feet in motion, heading for the revolving doors.

"Wait a minute, Toriyana. I would really like to repay you for your kindness and generosity," Treyvon jogged the couple paces to reach her. He then reached in his back pocket to retrieve his wallet.

Toriyana was taken aback by his action. Perhaps that was how they did things in the South, she thought.

"No, no, Treyvon. That won't be necessary. It was my pleasure," she said quickly. When he pulled out a business card instead of a monetary bill, she felt quite silly.

"No. I insist you let me take you to dinner sometime soon. You can show me around your great city," he said enthusiastically.

Toriyana could not help but to laugh out loud at herself.

Treyvon cocked his head to one side as he watched the woman laughing in front of him. "What's so funny, Toriyana?" he asked, confused and perhaps even a bit insulted, Toriyana assumed.

"I'm so sorry, Treyvon. I was laughing at my own silly self. I thought you were about to offer me money for my help." Toriyana again started laughing and was struggling to stop herself.

Treyvon found her laughter infectious and joined her in the amusement. They both stood there cracking up for several moments.

"Okay, now I have to insist that you allow me to take you out after that blatant offense," Treyvon joked.

The two had seen each other a few times since then, including yesterday at dinner. Treyvon happily accepted Toriyana's invitation to Thanksgiving dinner, since he had no family in town.

Toriyana smiled as she thought about Treyvon. She actually realized she would miss hanging out with him while he was away in Florida visiting his family for the next few days. He said it was a whole lot cheaper to fly out the day after Thanksgiving, so he opted to leave to go home today.

Toriyana purposefully checked her giddiness as she thought pf Treyvon. She did not want to get caught up with this man too quickly. Her relationship and subsequent breakup with Darrin had taught her a thing or two. She decided she would heed his example of dubbing herself completely single until she met the man who asked her to marry him, but she did have to admit that Treyvon was proving himself to be a good candidate so far.

Toriyana was taken from her revelry by the ringing of her doorbell. Realizing she had not invited anyone over, she was very curious as to who could be on the other side of the door. She got up from the sofa and checked the peephole. Though she had not invited him, she was not all that surprised to see David standing on her porch. She considered leaving him out in the cold for a little while before opening the door, but she then realized that would not be very Christ-like.

She opened the door, unhooked the screen, and offered him access to her home. She returned to the sofa and attempted to resume the comfy position she had vacated, all without saying a word to David.

Toriyana was not really angry with David. She actually felt more discomfort and annoyance than fury. As Thanksgiving approached, she had wondered if he would try to contact her, since she knew he would be in town. She resolved in herself not to allow it to bother her one way or the other.

David was not surprised by the chilly reception he received from his ex-girlfriend. He was just grateful that she let him in at all. It was mighty cold in Detroit in November.

"Hi, Tori. How are you?" he asked as he stood in the middle of the living room.

"I'm well, David," she replied evenly.

"Do you mind if I have a seat?" He tried to keep his voice as level as hers, but he was in fact pretty nervous.

"Certainly not, David. Have a seat," she said, still cool.

"Thank you." David sat on the chair. "It's good to see you, Tori. You look good. Very relaxed today." David tried to relax himself. He knew Toriyana well, and he knew that if she were truly angry with him, she would not have let him in her home. He took a deep breath and prepared to state the reason for his visit.

"Tori, I wanted to come by and see you, face to face, so I could apologize to you for hurting you this past summer. I'm very sorry for how things ended between us," he said sincerely.

Toriyana just looked at him for several seconds in silence. David was unsure how to interpret her quiet.

Toriyana stared at David wordlessly, trying to figure out how she felt about his apology. His words and his attitude were so typically David Mathis. Everything about him was completely the same as it was since the last time she had seen him several months earlier. Everything, that is, except his feelings for her. She could feel that the love the two of them once shared had diminished, if not completely disappeared. Now he was sitting in her living room as if he was never any more than a platonic friend, casually apologizing for a menial offense.

Toriyana knew not to expect much more from David, but she did think she would feel more of something. She always suspected that the next time she saw David, she would be bubbling over with something—anger, unrequited love, remorse for the wasted years. Something. Yet she felt nothing. Not anything more than okay for how things turned out between them.

"David, thank you very much for coming by to see me and offering me your apology. You are right. I was very hurt when we broke up this past summer, but truthfully, and I really mean this, I am good. I am really okay."

David looked at Toriyana and tried to decipher the truth of her statement. He only thought about it for a moment before he allowed a small smile to crease his mouth. He knew she was being completely honest with him.

"Tori, as you can probably tell by the goofy grin on my face, I am very happy to hear that."

Toriyana smiled in return. "Then I guess we are both cool then."

Toriyana rose from the sofa and approached David. She held out her arms for a hug, and he quickly got up to oblige. When they broke the familial embrace, Toriyana spoke.

"David, like I said, I'm glad you stopped by, but I actually have plans for my evening. Since you came by without calling, you have actually rudely interrupted them. So if you don't mind, I would like to return to the solitude of my sofa and spend the rest of my post-Thanksgiving Friday relaxing alone and enjoying the television programs on my DVR."

David laughed lightly. "Please forgive me, Tori. I have never been kicked out of anyplace so politely before."

The pair laughed as they walked to the front door.

"You be well, you hear, Toriyana Kent. God bless you," David said sincerely.

"I hope and pray the same for you, David Mathis. Have a great trip back to Phoenix and a great life."

One final hug and David was on his way out the door and Toriyana on her way to the mindless entertainment of her television.

Chapter Twenty-one

One year later, after the breakups and the startup in Phoenix.

"I know the best man is supposed to give a special toast at the wedding, but is it okay for a good friend to offer a toast during the engagement party? I have something I would really like to say to the soon-to-be-newlyweds."

"I don't think that will be off-handed at all. In fact, I would love to hear what you have to say about my fiancé and me."

"Thank you, beautiful bride-to-be. As Christian people, we are called out by God to be set apart, a peculiar people, living by a different standard than that of the rest of the world. For in 1 Peter 2:9, Peter says, 'But you are not like that, for you are a chosen people. You are royal priests, a holy nation, God's very own possession. As a result, you can show others the goodness of God, for He called you out of the darkness into His wonderful light.' You two people personify this scripture for me. I watched you two for this past year grow in love and respect for each other. I watched you two represent God in your courtship. You did not allow the values and ideology of the world to corrupt your purposes. In doing so, you brought sanctity back to the institution of marriage.

"There were a couple of times, man, when we would be together, I would ask you about your lady or her whereabouts. You would simply say, 'I'm not sure where she is, but until I make the commitment to make her my wife, she belongs solely to God in that manner, which means I know she is in good hands.'"

The speaker stopped for a moment to look at the beaming couple, who smiled broadly at each other, happy to hear their example had been a testimony and an inspiration to others.

He resumed. "I have been dating the same woman for the past nine months. I have tried to celebrate little monumental anniversaries with her, like thirty days from the time she allowed me to kiss her for the first time, or six months from the time of our first official date. And me, being a silly, sentimental person, stereotyped her by thinking that as a woman, she would find these things sweet and romantic. But she would say each time, 'The only anniversaries I want to celebrate are the date you ask me to marry you, the day you marry me, and the dates of the birth of our children.' I say that to say you have impacted us both in such a great way.

"So the two of us, as I am sure everyone else here rejoicing in your engagement do too, salute you two for being Matthew 6:33 made manifest. 'But seek first the kingdom of God and His righteousness, and all these things will be added to you.' Congratulations, David and Katrina, soon-to-be Mr. and Mrs. Mathis."

Gerald lifted his glass of champagne, and everyone else in the cute little reception hall did the same with their glasses filled with either cider or champagne. They drank in unison to acknowledge the happy couple. Maleeka beamed at the best man from her seat in the chair of the maid of honor, so proud of him, hoping

to one day soon be saluted at their very own engagement party.

David and Katrina shared a light kiss and then stood
in appreciation of their friends. The joy flowed unani-
mously between almost everyone in attendance at the
party. One lone attendee could just not bring himself
to be excited for the couple. He, too, sat at the head
table as a groomsman, trying his best not to sulk in
plain view of all the other guests, including the date he
brought along in hopes of making his ex-fiancée jealous.

Darrin did not see the need to applaud a speech
given by the man who stole his fiancée about the mile-
stones in their new relationship. Darrin was also plenty
salty that David had not chosen him as the best man
for the upcoming wedding ceremony. Just as he had
known Maleeka longer and better than Gerald, Darrin
had also known David longer and better than Gerald.

He apparently did not know Maleeka as well as he
thought he did. He was quite certain she saw him enter
with the beautiful woman on his arm as his date. Darrin wanted to get under Maleeka's skin by bringing
another woman to the engagement party. In an effort
to make the jab more painful, he went out of his way to
track down Trisha, the woman he was sneaking around
seeing behind Maleeka's back before they got engaged.

After four years, Trisha, who had moved on to another department with the company they both worked
for, had completely forgiven him. She just happened to
be single and not dating anyone seriously, and she was
anxious for the opportunity to hang out with Darrin
now that he was also completely unattached.

However, his plan seemed to be all for naught.
Maleeka paid absolutely no attention to Darrin and/
or his date. She walked around the party seemingly

happy, content, and completely unfazed by Darrin and convincingly not giving two shakes of a lamb's tail who he brought to the party with him.

When Maleeka broke off their engagement and asked him to leave her apartment a year ago, he was angrier at her than he had ever been before. At the time, he felt that Maleeka should have counted herself lucky he only destroyed her cell phone and not put his hands on her directly.

The day after their fight, Darrin returned while he assumed Maleeka had gone to work, to retrieve the rest of his things from her apartment. His intention was to get his stuff and leave her key on the countertop in plain sight. As far as he was concerned, he never had to see her face again. He wanted nothing in his possession that reminded him of her. When he attempted to use his key, it did not work. He checked his key ring several times to be sure he was using the right one, but it would not turn the lock. Soon after he arrived, the door opened suddenly, and there stood Maleeka with her hands on her hips.

"I know you did not think I was going to allow you access to my home after the way you behaved yesterday," she stated with royal sista-girl attitude.

The sight of her at that moment instantly made his temper flare, but he kept it in check this time. He only wanted to get his things and get back to his former, now current home again, with David.

"Maleeka, I thought you would be at work. I came by just to get my stuff. I was going to leave your key on your countertop. I promise. It's all a moot point, though, now since I see you have apparently paid somebody to change the locks. It must have cost you a pretty penny being that it was the weekend. But whatever. It's your dime, not mine. Can I get my things?"

Maleeka, too, was angry and hurt even further by Darrin's demeanor. She knew she could get back at him, though, by telling him the truth about her "locksmith." She opened her mouth to spill the beans, but quickly snapped it shut. She was not about to let Darrin drag her into any more ungodliness. She also did not want to drag Gerald into the middle of this ugliness with Darrin. Instead, she stepped aside and allowed him to enter the apartment.

Darrin was amazed to find all his stuff was neatly packed and stacked in the living room. He was not amazed it was there, but amazed that she had not destroyed anything after what he did to her cell phone. Not a thing seemed to be out of place. His clothes did not smell of smoke, nor were they discolored after being soaked in bleach. Everything was completely intact. Even though he was still simmering in his anger, he actually gained a new modicum of respect for his fiancée—or former fiancée—at that moment.

As Darrin began to grab his things, he expected Maleeka to start nagging or fussing, but she did not say a thing. He made three trips between her living room and his car, and not one word was exchanged between them. Maleeka did not even look like she wanted to say anything to him. She just looked like she wanted him gone.

In the months following their breakup, Darrin had begun to realize he had made a big mistake stringing Maleeka along for years with the promise of marriage, but never making good on the promise. Maleeka loved him, supported him, and believed in him in ways not even his own parents had. His mother coddled him and his father tolerated him. Maleeka encouraged him and made him feel like a man capable of anything he chose to do. He foolishly, probably even unwittingly, took

advantage of her, and now he had to suffer the ulti-
mate humiliation of watching her interact with another
man—a man who treated her better than he had.

    Katrina could not have been happier even if this was
her wedding day instead of just her engagement party.
There were not a lot of people at the gathering, just her
and David's closest friends and family. They wanted
to keep this celebration small, choosing to have an
intimate dinner party as their celebration, but she was
planning a real big affair for her wedding in six months.
    David looked at Katrina from across the room,
where he stood talking to Pastor Abraham. He was so
enthralled with her beauty that he was scarcely paying
any attention to what the pastor was saying.
    "David, son, did you hear me? I said be sure to sign
up for the premarital counseling with Dr. Madison.
Love is a many splendored thing, as the saying goes,
but it is not enough to sustain you through the sometimes very harsh realities of marriage."
    "I heard you, Pastor Abraham. I will mention that
song to the choir at our next rehearsal." David was responding to the pastor, but his eyes were glued on his
fiancée.
    "What are you talking about, son? I didn't say noth-
ing about no song for the—" Pastor Abraham stopped
himself short as he realized his words were falling on
deaf ears. He saw that David was anxious to get back to
Katrina's side.
    "Go on back over there to your woman, David. We
will talk about the technical stuff later."
    David took off walking seemingly before Pastor
Abraham could finish speaking his last word. David approached Katrina's side and slid his hand into the hand

that held her engagement ring as she talked to Gerald and Maleeka. He gently pulled the hand to his lips and kissed the finger with the ring on it.

"You two are a mess," Maleeka stated with a laugh.

"We are not a mess. We are just very happy together, that's all," Katrina replied in their defense as she snuggled closer to David's side.

"Well, I hope your deliriously happy man will allow me to steal you away for a moment. I want you to go over here with me to talk to Aujanae. We have some ideas about the wedding that we need to discuss quickly. I know it's your engagement party and all, but six months is not a lot of time to plan the spectacular wedding I have in mind." Maleeka started steering Katrina away before either she or David had a chance to protest.

"Man, if she is planning on making our wedding spectacular, you can only imagine what she will be expecting when you two get ready to get married," David joked with Gerald.

"I'm not making any firm commitments, declarations, or anything like that. I will just say I look forward to the time," Gerald said as the two men took to their seats.

"Hey, Aujanae. I'm so glad you could make it," Katrina said as she hugged Aujanae. Maleeka followed suit.

"Hello, ladies. I'm so sorry I'm late. I did not plan my morning well, knowing full well I was going to have to drop B.J. off at his dad's before I got here. William couldn't pick him up because his car is being serviced today."

"Aujanae, I hope I am not being insensitive by asking you to be one of my bridesmaids, considering your divorce just became final a little while ago," Katrina pouted.

"Oh, Katrina! Not at all. I am so honored you asked me to be in your wedding. Trust me. I am fine. The divorce was painful, but not ugly. William was very amicable throughout the entire process, which made it that much easier," Aujanae replied honestly.

William and Aujanae had been officially divorced for one month. For the first three months after permanently breaking things off with April, who eventually packed up and moved back to Chicago, William tried relentlessly to win Aujanae back. He promised her he would never, ever cheat on her again, and he would do everything in his power to make her happy and give her and their son the best life possible.

Aujanae never even considered giving him another chance. She knew deep in her own heart that she would never again own William's heart completely, if she ever owned it completely to begin with. Though he said he would be faithful, and she believed him, she did not believe that he would be undeniably satisfied with just her. Sure, he would make the sacrifice, but Aujanae did not want to be anybody's good enough, especially someone she once loved as much as she loved her husband.

So William finally gave up his pursuit of his marriage and agreed to the divorce, completely on Aujanae's terms. He refused to be bitter or fight with her over anything, considering what he had done to her and their family. Aujanae, who was not out for revenge, only asked that he pay the mortgage on the home that they formerly shared and that he pay a fair amount of child support to help take care of their son. She did not want to rake him over the coals as many women who were presented with the same set of circumstances as herself would have. The visitation schedule for B.J. was very liberal and open. They shared joint responsibility for their son, while Aujanae retained physical custody. William was allowed to see him on whatever schedule the two of them worked out together. Aujanae also returned to work as a high school English teacher.

"I can't believe you want to start planning the wedding right here at my engagement party, Maleeka," Katrina said, feigning exasperation as she completely changed the subject.

"That is what you get for giving me only six months to work with, Katrina. And don't you dare turn into a bridezilla on me. Quit all that whining."

"I do have a wedding coordinator, you know."

"I know. And she is going to do things just as I tell her to. You are my best friend, not hers." All three ladies cracked up laughing, even though they knew Maleeka was dead serious.

"Well, you want to know what I think? I think we will be planning another wedding ceremony as soon as yours is over, Katrina. I think that if Mr. Gerald Miller has his way, he and Ms. Maleeka Davis will be headed into wedded bliss too. And soon."

Maleeka made a very poor attempt at looking shocked. She bucked her eyes and threw her hand flimsily over her heart. "Why, whatever do you mean, Aujanae?" Maleeka asked in a poor Southern imitation.

"Girl, stop it," Katrina said. "You know it's true, and you know you want it." All the ladies laughed out loud again.

"What about you, Aujanae? Do you think you will ever marry again?" Katrina asked.

Aujanae pondered the question, realizing she had actually never given it much thought until Katrina just mentioned it.

"I don't know. I mean, I'm not opposed to or sour on marriage just because mine did not work out. I guess I would have to just simply leave it in God's hands. If He wants me married, He will let me know and send me my husband. But until then, I'm okay being single."

Just then, David, Gerald, and a man Katrina and Aujanae did not recognize approached the ladies. Maleeka knew the man well enough, though.

"You three are over here having way too much fun without us," David said jovially as he walked up behind Katrina and wrapped his arms around her waist.

"Don't be jealous, David," Maleeka joked in return as Gerald possessively put his arm around her shoulder.

Aujanae and the stranger were standing there unlinked, both feeling a little awkward.

"Gerald!" Maleeka said as she gently nudged him, trying to discreetly get his attention.

"Oh yeah. My bad. Katrina, Aujanae, this is my little brother, Christopher. He's Deidre's dad." Both ladies nodded their acknowledgement of Gerald's niece, whom they had met on previous occasions when she was with her uncle.

"Christopher, this is Katrina, the bride-to-be, and this is Aujanae."

"Who is newly single," Maleeka threw in.

Suddenly Aujanae felt as if this introduction was part of a setup on at least Maleeka's part. She looked at Christopher and could tell they shared the same thought.

"Nice to meet you, Katrina. Congratulations on your engagement," Christopher said.

"Thank you, Christopher. It is nice to meet you too."

"Nice to meet you too, Aujanae. I don't know if I should say congratulations to you on being newly single or not, but Maleeka here is grinning like that's a good thing." Everyone in the circle laughed.

"It is nice to meet you too, Christopher. You and your brother look a lot alike. Your daughter looks like the both of you. She is such a beautiful young princess."

"Thank you, Aujanae. Should I take that to mean I am a beautiful old king?" They all had another good laugh.

"You could probably get away with taking it that way," Aujanae said flirtatiously after the laughter waned a bit. "And by the way, there is no harm at all in you congratulating me on being newly single."

The four other adults sang a harmonious chorus of, "Ummmmmmmmm."

"You know, God is truly good," Maleeka said. "And He works quickly too."

The three men stood there looking very puzzled, but Katrina and Aujanae knew exactly what their sneaky little friend was talking about....

Readers' Questions

1. What is your true opinion of *The Book Store Rule* as stated in the preface of the book?

2. Which of the male characters did you like best? Why?

3. Do you think Aujanae should have forgiven William and tried to work on their marriage? Why or why not?

4. Here is an opportunity for you to be truly transparent. What do you think of April Colston? Have you ever walked in her shoes?

5. Do you think it is possible to be in love with two people at the same time, like William says that he was?

6. Were you upset with Katrina for dating David even though he had a girlfriend?

7. Do you feel Toriyana had a right to give David an ultimatum in Chapter 17?

8. What do you think of Darrin and Maleeka's long engagement? How long is too long to be in a relationship before getting engaged? How long is too long to be engaged before getting married?

9. Discuss your favorite part of the book. Now your least favorite.

10. Do you think Gerald and Maleeka will get married and live happily ever after? Is there really such a place?